The Night Visitor
and Other Stories

Books by B. Traven

THE JUNGLE NOVELS
Government
The Carreta
March to the Monteria
Trozas
The Rebellion of the Hanged
The General from the Jungle

The Death Ship
The Cotton Pickers
The Treasure of the Sierra Madre
The Bridge in the Jungle
The White Rose
Stories by the Man Nobody Knows
The Night Visitor and Other Stories
The Creation of the Sun and the Moon

B. Traven

The Night Visitor and Other Stories

ELEPHANT PAPERBACKS
Ivan R. Dee, Publisher, Chicago

First ELEPHANT PAPERBACK edition published 1993 by Ivan R. Dee,
Inc., 1332 North Halsted Street, Chicago 60622. Manufactured in the
United States of America and printed on acid-free paper.

Library of Congress Cataloging-in-Publication Data:
Traven, B.
     The night visitor and other stories / B. Traven. -- 1st Elephant
paperback ed.
         p.   cm.
         "Elephant paperbacks."
         ISBN 1-56663-039-8 (acid-free paper)
         I. Title.
     PT3919.T7A2   1993
     813'.52—dc20   93-11240

Contents

The Night Visitor
and Other Stories

The Night Visitor

A Mexican had sold me fifty acres of raw land located in dense tropical bush. I'd paid him twenty-five pesos down, the balance to be paid on receiving the titles.

I built myself a type of Indian hut and started cultivating the soil. It was no easy task, there in the midst of the jungle, but anyway I started.

Soon I learned that I wasn't the only white man in that region; a one hour's ride on my pony brought me to my nearest neighbor, a Doctor Cranwell.

The village, inhabited by Indian peasants, was twelve miles away, and the depot was eighteen. Close to the depot, two American families were trying their luck; besides farming, buying and shipping charcoal and firewood fuel produced by local Indians, each of these two American families ran a rather sickly looking general store.

Doc Cranwell's ranchito was situated on a hill in the midst of the bush, just as was my own place. He was all by himself in a three-room, crudely constructed bungalow. I didn't know why he buried himself in this jungle, and I never tried to find out. It was none of my business.

1

He did a little farming, or what he said was farming. He had a couple of cows, a couple of horses, three mules, and a score of beehives. Wild birds were after the bees all the time, catching them as they left or returned to the hives. That limited the bees' production to just enough for the doc to have some honey for breakfast now and then.

His closest neighbors were two Indian families who lived about half a mile from his ranch. The men were employed by him as farm hands, while their women attended to his little domestic affairs.

He spent most of the time reading. When he wasn't reading, he just sat on the porch of his bungalow, staring down at the thousand square miles of jungle spread out before his view in a cheerless color of dull, dusty green. It was a bright green only during four months of each year, after the end of the rainy season.

A score of Indian settlements, none consisting of more than three families, were scattered over that vast region, but the only way you could tell they were there was by the smoke which at certain hours of the day could be seen playing above those hidden jacalitos.

The average person could get tired, perhaps even go insane, if he had no other object to look at but such an immense space of gloomy jungle. The doctor, though, liked this view.

So did I. I could gaze over that jungle for hours on end without ever getting tired of it. It wasn't what I could actually see that interested me. It was being able to imagine the big and little episodes which were happening in those thorny thickets down there. There wasn't a minute's rest in the eternal battle for survival, for love. Creation and destruction. . . . I wasn't sure, but I guessed that the doctor felt the same way. Only he never said so.

My place was on the same mountain ridge as the doctor's, though slightly lower than his. I was farther away from any neighbors. Very rarely did I feel lonesome. But when it happened, I saddled my pony and called on the doctor, just to see a human face and hear a human voice.

A tropical jungle is so rich with life that you simply cannot become desolate if you feel the whole universe in every little insect, in every lizard, in every bird's chirp, in every rustle of leaves, in every shape and color of flower. But, once in a while, I did have sort of a spell of fright and a sinking in my heart. It was something like being on a solo flight, surrounded by clouds, with the motor idling and with no instruments to guide you. Or like sitting alone in a small boat, far off the coast, with no bird in sight, on a quiet sea, and dusk falling.

The doctor was not much of a talker. Living in the tropical bush all by yourself makes you silent, though very rich in thought. There is never one second of the day or night when the bush does not talk to you, whether with its never-dying voices, or by its permanent growing and decaying. Inevitably you reach the conclusion that life has but one meaning: "Enjoy it as long as it lasts and get the most out of it—for death is within you from the moment you are born."

The doctor and I would often sit in our rocking chairs for two or three hours without either of us saying a single word. Yet, somehow, we felt happy.

2

Now and then the doctor would say, "You know that little rain pool up there on the other side of the ridge, close to that patch of prairie? Well, there's a primitive palm hut near by. It's going to pieces now. I wonder who built it. I have all sorts of calculations about who might've set it up to live there all alone—maybe it was even somebody with a murder on his conscience. One afternoon I rode by there. I got off about thirty feet away and went the rest of the way on foot. I

looked inside the opening that's supposed to be a door, and I
saw—I saw—I——"

Here the doctor would slow his words until they faded into
a mumble. A few seconds later, this mumble, too, would
trickle off—and yet I could clearly see that he was still telling
his strange adventure, though he was telling it to himself alone.

I knew he thought I could hear his tale, and I refrained
from telling him that I could not distinguish one word of what
he was saying. One story, more or less, doesn't count, as long
as it isn't a story you have lived yourself.

Again, on other occasions, he would start off, ". . . and
. . . and . . . yes, as I was saying—there was the day when I
happened to be in a very dense part of the bush. It was dark
there in the thicket, but the bright sun was heavy upon the tops
of the trees. You have to stop and wait in silence for half an
hour or so before the bush will let you see or hear something
of interest. I observed a tarantula cautiously crawling on the
decaying trunk of an ebony tree.

"It was a dark-brown, very hairy little beast the size of my
hand. On the ground and close to that same tree, two huge
black scorpions moved more cautiously still, both apparently
not seeing the tarantula—any more than the tarantula was
aware of the two scorpions. I thought it strange for scorpions
to be walking about in the daytime. They rarely do, you
know. Now, the tarantula and the two scorpions moved in the
same direction, the three having their eyes fixed on a—on
a—a——"

At this point he fell into his customary mumble and soon his
voice faded out.

Sometimes, when watching the doctor, I was under the
impression that he was dead, that he had died many years ago
and was kept alive for no other reason than that he had
forgotten wholly that he was dead, since no one had noticed it
and told him so. In such occasions I thought that if I could

make a newspaper print a short note announcing his passing away, and showed him that note, he might actually fall dead at the same instant, and half an hour later wither away so rapidly that he would take on the appearance of a man buried fifty years ago.

I didn't have these ideas often—only when I saw him sitting in his chair, silently, without moving, gazing down upon the gray ocean of the jungle with eyes that hardly blinked and seemed dead and empty.

Then again, on other days, I would find him very lively and active, given to easy talk of ordinary daily happenings at his place, even of such common affairs as the beating one of the men who worked for him had given his woman, with the result that the woman couldn't see out of her blackened eyes.

Once, when he was in the mood for talking, I asked him if he'd ever written a book. It seemed to me that he had a way of telling things which would make him a great writer if he'd only take the pains.

"A book?" he said. "One book? One only? Fifteen, or—let me see—I think it must be eighteen. Yes . . . eighteen books. That's what I've written. Eighteen books."

"Published?"

"No. Never published. What for?"

"For people to read them!"

"Nonsense. For people to read them? There are thousands of books—great books—which they have never read. Why should I give them more if they don't read the ones they already have?"

"You might've published the books to become famous, or to make a lot of money."

"Money? Money for books I write? Don't make me laugh. Besides, I've got enough money to lead the life I do. Why should I want more? What for? And as to fame—don't be silly, Gales. Fame! What is fame, after all? It stinks to hell and heaven, fame does. Today I am famous. Today my name is printed on the front page of all the papers in the world. Tomorrow, perhaps fifty people can still spell my name correctly. Day after tomorrow I may starve to death and nobody cares. That's what you call fame. You shouldn't use such a word. Not you. Of course, there's another fame—the glorious one, the fame that reaches you after you're dead, and when nobody knows where your bones are bleaching. And what good does it do you to be famous after you've kicked off? It makes me sick even to speak about fame. It's the bunk."

"Okay, Doc. Let's can it. Forget it. Anyway, I think a good book—the kind I reckon you'd write—is always welcome to readers who appreciate good books."

"Provided the books reach the readers they're meant for. This happens now and then, maybe, but very rarely."

"Perhaps you're right, Doc. I've never given that problem any special thought. By all means, though, I'd like to read the books you wrote. Can I have them? At least one or two of them?"

"If I still had them, I guess I wouldn't want you to read them. But I don't have them. They've gone back to where they came from. Eternity, you know. I got full satisfaction out of my books in writing them. In fact, I think I got far more satisfaction than any writer who has had his work published will ever get."

"Sorry, Doc," I said. "But I don't see the point."

"Not so difficult," he answered. "It's like this. Once a book is published, the writer's satisfaction—if he is a true artist and not just a merchant—is marred by scores of things which have no connection with the pillars on which the universe rests. You see, I think of books as pillars of the universe. If a book is truly yours, it hurts your soul and heart to think of mailing it to a publisher. At least that's the way I felt, and still feel.

"Whenever I had finished a book, I read it, revised it, made changes which I thought essential to make it perfect—as nearly perfect as I could ever make it—and when this was done I felt happy and satisfied beyond measure. As soon as I had that satisfaction, I destroyed the book."

"You did what, Doc?" I blared out. "You don't mean——"

"Yep, I meant it. That's exactly what I did. Sometimes I think that the trouble with people today is that we don't destroy enough of the things and systems which we believe perfect . . . and by destroying them make room for absolutely new and different things and systems infinitely more perfect than the ones we destroyed. Have you ever destroyed something which you loved, or which you thought the finest and most perfect object under heaven? Have you?"

"No, Doc—at least not that I know of." I felt cold along my spine.

"If you haven't, try it some day. Try it once or more than once. If you're the right kind of man, one who can do it without remorse, you'll see for yourself how great a satisfaction you'll get out of it and how happy it will make you. You'll feel like you're newly born. Be like God, who destroys with His left hand what He created with His right."

"Who wants to be like God?" I said. "Not me."

"Depends. Frequently I think how different our art, our writings, our techniques, our architectures, our achievements would be if, let's say, at the year sixteen-hundred-fifty, everything which man had made so far would have been destroyed, destroyed so thoroughly that no human would have been able to remember what a cart wheel had looked like, and whether the Venus de Milo had been a painting or a poem or a ship's keel, and whether democracies and monarchies had meant something to eat or were church bells. As far as I'm concerned, I am convinced that the world would likely be a hundred times better place to live in today if mankind had a chance now and then to discard all tradition and history and start fresh with no worn-out ideas, platitudes, and opinions to hamper the birth of an entirely new world."

3

One morning when I went to see the doctor, he said, "Very good, Gales. I'm glad you came in. I was just going to send for you. I have to go back to the States today. Got to attend to a certain affair which has been pending for quite some time. Of course, I might skip it altogether. Fact is, I'm not much interested in the outcome, anyway. But there's a score of books, of very rare books, which I've been after for years. Seems that now, owing to a change in circumstances, I've got a good chance to get them at last. So, I can combine both matters on the same occasion. I'm positive I can be back inside of eight weeks. Still, I'm thinking about the place. It isn't that these Indians really steal—it's just that they think you've left everything to the jungle, or to them, or to whoever comes along and takes the trouble to pick it up. Well, how about it? Will you mind the place while I'm away?"

"All right by me, Doc," I said. "Guess I can put in eight weeks easily. What is time here, anyway? It goes as fast as it comes. Sure, I'll stay here and keep tigers and lions off the porch."

"It's the dry season," he said, "so there isn't much you can do at your place, except cleaning out two or three acres. And that can wait without hurting you much. I'll tell Ambrosio to take two mules and go with you, and bring your things up here. Nobody will steal your roof."

He chuckled. His farm hands must have told him that the roof I had made was safe from marauders. Any Indian would be ashamed to have such a roof on his jacal.

"Of course," he went on, "I ought to tell you that you'll be all alone here while I'm away. The two families working for me are going to visit their relatives, to celebrate a few weddings and a dozen baptizings as I understand. They won't be back for ten weeks. There isn't any important work to do around here on account of the season. So I let them have their vacation now. They would go anyway, permission or no permission. You won't have much trouble with the animals. They look out for themselves. Let them have some maize three or four mornings every week. Examine them occasionally for open wounds to see that no worms are growing in them. You'll find two gallons of creoline and some other things in that shed over there, if you need anything to cure them with."

"Don't worry, Doc, I'll feel just fine here. And I can do swell without any neighbors around here, anyhow. The animals will be okay. Don't I know what farm life is like? Don't you worry a bit. Leave everything to its own ways and leave all the rest to me."

When I returned with my tools, kettles, pans, blankets, mosquito bar, cot, and what I had on, the doctor was all set to leave.

"Make use of whatever you find in the house," he said. "Whenever you need something, just look in the boxes, cases, drawers and on the shelves. Help yourself to whatever you find. You'll have plenty of milk, and more eggs than you can eat."

He didn't have much baggage. Just two lean suitcases. He loaded them on a mule and then mounted his horse. The horse and mule were to be left with one of the American farmers by the depot.

"Well, hasta luego," he called, and rode off.

4

I sat on the porch for an hour or so, gazing down upon the jungle sea, following in my mind the doctor's ride to the depot. Late in the afternoon I would see a thin smoke ribbon creeping over the surface of the jungle close to the horizon, which would indicate the train in which the doctor was going home.

Home . . . ?

Aw, the hell with it. Forget it. Home is where I was, and nowhere else.

For the first time since I'd known the doctor, I went inside his house. We'd always had our coffee or tea on the porch, and I'd never gone beyond it.

He was well stocked with canned food. There were enough groceries to hold out for half a year if necessary. During the rainy season the nearest general store often could not be reached for a period of as long as two months. Neither man nor mule could pass the muddy and swampy stretches without sinking into them up to his knees, and sometimes even deeper.

The doc had told me to look around so that I'd know where to find things. I began with the table in the corner. I pulled out the drawer, hoping to find old magazines. There weren't any. Just some bills and other papers in which I had no interest.

I stepped out on the porch again and pushed the rocking chair close to the farthest corner. There I sat down and looked over that greenish-gray sea of jungle. I could think of nothing. My mind came to rest. A wonderful feeling of tranquillity took possession of my soul and body. I forgot earth, and heaven.

The eternal singing of the jungle, so soothing to the nerves once you have become used to it, lulled me into slumber, and I did not awaken until I heard the pitiful, harsh shriek of an animal caught by its enemy in the depths of the jungle.

5

It was during the next forenoon that I came upon the doctor's library.

The books were carefully kept in bookcases, which were

lined with tin sheets to protect them from tropical insects and from dampness and mildew during the rainy seasons. Apparently Doc had discovered the secret of how to keep books well preserved in the tropics. The books were in excellent condition.

The collection was a treasure. Most of the books were about ancient Indian civilizations which used to exist in Mexico, Central America, Peru, Ecuador, and Bolivia. They treated of Indian history, traditions, religion, language, arts, craftsmanship and architecture. Many were on the so-called archaic culture of the early inhabitants of the Americas.

Some of the books were richly illustrated with ancient Indian hieroglyphs and with old Indian paintings. There were books and manuscripts dating as far back as the first half of the sixteenth century.

As far as I could judge, practically all the books were first editions. Only a few of them might have been other than firsts, and perhaps there had been no more than fifty copies printed of some of them. In early times, certain books of a scientific or historic nature were printed by order of book lovers who paid for the entire limited edition in advance.

Some of the manuscripts, documents, and parchments might easily have been the only ones still in existence. The value of that library could never be estimated in money.

As I learned later from other persons, the doctor had built up this unique library by hunting books and documents all over the Republic—in monasteries, convents, old churches, in haciendas, and in out-of-the-way ranches. He had bought them from old families and from Indian peasants, from priests and from teachers in little country schools, and from soldiers and officers who had come into possession of books and manuscripts during the long revolution when convents, churches, and haciendas had been plundered.

He must have spent many, many years in collecting so many

rare books. It seemed that when he'd obtained all the books he wanted or ever hoped to get he'd buried himself in that jungle region to be alone with his treasure and enjoy it in peaceful surroundings.

That he had left me alone with that priceless treasure without even mentioning it proved how much confidence he had in me.

I had not seen a single book in more than a year. I had hungered for them as a man living in a great city may hunger for green woods, blue lakes, murmuring creeks and cloudless days. And now I was standing before the very books I'd so much desired to read ever since that day I first heard of the great, mysterious civilization which existed and flourished to the south long before Columbus ever thought of sailing to what he came to believe was a new world.

6

I was soon completely under the spell of the histories and mythologies. I forgot the present. I forgot to cook my meals. I felt no physical hunger. I milked the cows as if I were in a dream, and I drank the milk and swallowed the eggs right where I gathered them in order not to lose a single precious hour. I read from sunrise until midnight, day in and day out. The lamp I had was just an ordinary kitchen lamp which didn't give much light. I did not mind. I put the lamp as close to the pages as possible.

It was so hot that the days seemed to be wrapped in flames, and when at times I took notice of the tropics and heard the eternal singing of the bush I considered all this not as something real but rather as a part of the histories and narratives which I was reading. Everything that I read about had happened in the same country or nearby, under the same blazing sun, with the same insects and the same singing of the jungle.

Stories, time, tropical sun, the singing bush, the bites and stings of mosquitoes, the constant whirring of multitudes of moths around the lamp, an occasional glance over the dream-gray jungle ocean now and then—all that melted into a unit. Often I was not quite sure whether I had read a certain episode or description or had seen it or dreamed it. I didn't know whether the fiery tropical sun was actually shining upon the corrugated iron roof of the bungalow or whether I was only reading about it in connection with a battle which the Aztecs fought against the Chichimecs.

Sometimes it happened that I didn't realize when day had gone and night fallen. I had been reading by the light of the little lamp, yet I could not remember that I had lit the lamp. I could not recall when and how I had brought the lamp in, set it on the table before me, filled it up with kerosene and put a match to its wick. But there was the lamp right by my side and it had been there for a certain length of time.

I had done these things unconsciously, while my mind was fully concentrated on the great events of the Tarascans, the Otomis, the Toltecs, the Totonacas, or whatever the people were about whom I was reading.

My only fear was that the doctor might return before I had finished with the books. Although he had left the treasure with me without saying one word about it, I felt positive that he would not let me have one book once he was home again. I knew he would be jealous and nervous, and fear that he might lose a book if he lent it.

I was reading constantly, marveling that such various cultures and great civilizations had existed in the Americas at a time when the Romans were still semi-savages and the Britons ate the brains of the bravest of their enemies slain in battle.

It all read like a fairy tale, but then again it was so very sober and logical. Somehow, every book read easily—like excellent fiction. Some of the books were in English, a few in

French, and the majority in Spanish. Whatever the language, the writing was so vivid that the bungalow, the ranch, the patches of prairie, even the bush seemed to become populated with people I read about. Not for one single hour did I feel lonely. I was constantly under the impression that the people of the books were near me.

I began to look at the surrounding country, and at the natives, in a different way. So far I had seen them only as ordinary peasants. But now, when a peasant passed the ranch and asked for a drink of water, I searched his face for a likeness to the ancient kings and nobles whose pictures I saw in the old paintings and hieroglyphs.

But I was not satisfied with merely studying their faces; I studied their gestures, the manner in which they walked, the particular characteristics of their voices when they spoke to me.

This material for practical study was scarce. For three, four, or even six days at a time, not one single wanderer would come by the ranch. This was true because the main trail which communicated with the principal hamlets and settlements did not pass by the doctor's.

7

One morning, after having slept badly, I decided to give myself a rest from so much reading lest I should lose my connection with the real world. I ate a hearty breakfast and took a stroll through the bush for exercise.

After walking for two hours along a trail which as I could see had not been used for months, I suddenly realized that I was far in the depths of the bush where I had never been before, although I had thought I knew the region very well.

I stopped for a moment to get my bearings, wondering whether I ought to go on and learn where this new trail might eventually lead, when I was filled with a sense of the desolation of that dense jungle creeping around me like the horror of an ugly nightmare. What if I should be lost? What if I should have to spend the night here in the depths of the jungle?

Looking around to see from which direction I had come and hoping to see a mark familiar to me, I saw a thin ribbon of smoke curling above the trees hardly a quarter of a mile away. There had been no thunderstorms for months, so the smoke I saw could not have been the result of lightning.

I got to work with the machete I carried and began cutting my way through to the point where I had seen the smoke. Finally, I came upon an open space in the jungle.

An Indian charcoal-burner was squatting before his primitive kiln, a mound of chopped mahogany covered with earth. The Indian watched the play of smoke around the kiln as if he were meditating on where the smoke might go.

No move or gesture indicated that he had heard my approach. Still, I knew he must have heard my cutting through the underbrush. Somehow I was sure that he was perfectly conscious of somebody near him. Had he believed me to be an animal of the wilds, he would have taken an attitude of alertness.

I was still hidden from him by the dense foliage, but now I stepped out of hiding and went straight up to him.

He showed no surprise.

"Buenas tardes, señor," I greeted.

"Good afternoon to you, señor. Welcome. Be seated. Visitors are rare around here."

I offered him tobacco and corn leaves and we rolled our cigarettes. He had a strange way of rolling his, I noted, a way I'd never seen before anywhere. But I suppose there are a hundred and one ways a cigarette may be rolled.

His brown skin had a certain yellowish-copper tint which made it look like bronze mixed with gold. He was slim but wiry. The features of his face were fine-drawn, and they had a noble symmetry which indicated that he must be of high intelligence even though he might be ignorant of reading and writing.

There were two things about him which I thought strange.

One was that he had a beard. Beards among Indians are not frequent. The purer the blood, the rarer the beard. A white man, of course, would hardly call such thin silky hairs a beard. For an Indian, however, this flimsy chin web of his would entitle him to be named "The Bearded One." This beard, insignificant as it was, gave not only his face but his whole person a certain dignity which most Indians of that region lacked. It was a dignity which would stand out in a crowd of natives.

The second strange thing I noticed was his hands. Indians in general, both men and women, have smaller and finer hands and feet than the white man has. But in spite of the hard work this man had to do as a charcoal-burner, he had hands so conspicuously fine and nobly shaped that I could not remember ever having seen hands like them before. At least not belonging to a real person. In old paintings, perhaps, one might find such hands. No great artist would paint or model such hands, because he would deny that any human being could have hands like them and still be human.

These hands irritated me. They made me feel inferior to him. I could not believe it possible that a man, any man, might work as hard as did this charcoal-burner and still have hands like his.

"Yes, señor, you are right," he said in the course of our talk. "Yes, it is true that my ancestors have been princes of the people living in this region of land. On the same plain where today there is jungle, there used to be more than one hundred and twenty cities, towns and villages. There were sacred cities as well, temples and pyramids by the score, all of them covered now with earth—with a pitying earth to protect them from profanity. Cities and towns destroyed; their inhabitants, once so happy, murdered by the Spaniards when they conquered our lands. Our people wanted peace. A contract was celebrated with the conquistadores. But these men, with no true god to guide their hearts, broke the treaty and our people took to arms to throw off the yoke with its tortures, terrors and slavery. The first army sent against us was defeated by our men.

"Then the captain-general came with his special troops, and with him he brought twenty thousand hired Indian auxiliaries, traitors to their own blood. And he brought with him animals to ride upon, and cannons by which to spit fire on our warriors. Men, women, children were slaughtered without mercy. Our cities, villages and temples were burned to ashes.

"Within six days, five hundred princes, nobles and chiefs were hanged by the Spaniards. These were the princes captured while three times as many perished in battle. Had it not been for faithful servants to take the children of six or seven of our kings and hide them in the mountains until the region was quiet again, I most likely would not be here. I would never have been born a member of a princely family."

As he was telling his story he did not look at me but kept watching the curling smoke ribbons on their way up in the air.

Then he slowly turned his head and looked searchingly into my eyes.

I had not observed his eyes before. But now, forced to look at them at close range, I noted that he had deep-brown eyes of a warm, velvet tone. They were slightly dreamy, their lids covering about one-third of the iris. It might have been the back glare of the bright sun upon the sandy ground—but whatever the reason, he had in his eyes a very distinctive glimmering fog. I had the curious feeling that no mortal man could possess such eyes. With such eyes a man might enslave the whole world, should he decide on it.

"You know the history of your people astonishingly well, señor," I said. "Did you read it somewhere or learn it at a school?"

"No, señor, I never read it. It was told to me by my father and uncle, and it had been told to them by their fathers, and so on back to the times when it happened."

"Felling those iron-like trees and chopping them up and then making charcoal must be hard work," I said.

"It surely is hard work, señor," he said. "Nonetheless, I like it. What is more, it is honest work, work we have done for thousands of years—ever since our god gave us fire. I can work alone, all by myself, without a master ordering me . . . a thing I would not like. Here I can sit and think for days and months and years while watching those little snakes of smoke playing about like faraway music that comes and goes and comes again. Do you notice, señor, that each snake curling out of its little hole has its very own way of creeping out, playing about and disappearing in the air? Each has its own life, its own story to tell, just like a man. But each has its own personality, while many a man has none at all. Don't you think so, too, señor?"

"You are right," I said. "And I certainly believe that the work you do—while it may be hard—is honorable work."

"It makes me very happy, señor, to hear you say that. You asked me about your way back home, didn't you?"

The fact was that I had not asked him, though I had been thinking about it all the time I had been sitting on the ground beside him.

"You are well out of your way, señor," he said. "But you'll be all right in a minute. See that green shrub? Turn to your right there and count two hundred well-measured paces. You will then come upon a path, which you follow to your left. Good luck and many thanks for coming here and paying me such a delightful visit. Mil gracis, señor, adiós."

I followed the way he had showed me, and I came upon the trail he had mentioned. When I was sure of my way once more, I stopped and turned around to see whether I might remember that trail if I ever returned.

I could not make out the place where I had talked to the Indian. The more I looked around the more I became confused about even the direction from which I had come.

8

I arrived at the bungalow late in the afternoon. As soon as I finished dinner, I again buried myself in the books, more eager than ever to finish them before the doctor returned. I read as if I were in a fever. I always dropped on my cot at midnight as though all my limbs were filled with lead. Morning would not find me refreshed.

My sleep was no longer sound. My temples often hammered and the veins of my arms and legs seemed to swell larger every day. My head frequently got so hot at night that I thought it might burst.

All this, however, was only physical. Mentally, I felt happy and good. No longer did I live in the present; it seemed that I was living in the remote times of the books. Emotionally, I lived the lives of the people I was reading about. As I had no opportunity to speak to living people, save on those rare occasions when a peasant passed by, I spoke to the people living in the books.

Gradually it came to me that I thought I could speak as those people did—that I could think their thoughts, and that I had their ideas and their outlooks on life.

The feeling that I believed myself living in the past was particularly strong at night while reading by the weak light of that little kitchen lamp with all the doors open and with the eternal singing of the bush in my ears.

9

One night, while reading a book on the civilization and history of the people of Texcoco, I happened to raise my eyes from the pages. It was not entirely of my own will that I had done so, I realized; it was more as if I had somehow been forced to. I had the curious impression that somebody else was with me in the room, that someone had been watching me for a length of time.

How this amazing sensation had come to me became clear almost immediately.

My active mind had been fully occupied with the book, whereas my subconscious mind, during the time I was reading, had carefully marked everything that was going on in the room. It was as if my subconscious mind had been trying to protect me against some sort of danger.

During my travels in the tropical jungles, this new sense had slowly developed within me like a special instinct. Often that new sense had wakened me in my shack or in a tent—and when this happened I usually found something wrong inside or near the place. Once it was a rattler only five feet away; another time it was a tiger lured to the shack by the meat I had hung up to dry; once I found the tent just beginning to catch fire because an unexpected breeze had stirred up some nearly dead embers and thrown them on the canvas.

Now, while still reading, my subconscious mind had called upon me to be on my guard because something was not as it should be. Strange as it may appear, I very positively felt that no actual danger was threatening me. I felt calm and safe, though slightly irritated. This irritation had grown steadily stronger until I could no longer resist it. I had to look up to see what caused that annoyance.

I turned my head.

And there, in the middle of the room, stood an Indian. He gave me the impression that he had been standing there and watching me for some time. It might well have been ten minutes or so. And strange to say, at the very moment I looked at him I could tell exactly the page and line I had been reading when he entered, unseen by me.

He looked straight at my face.

With refined tact and patience he waited until I would speak to him. Quite obviously he had stepped up to the porch without making any noise. Seeing me busy with my book and paying no attention to him, he had finally entered, apparently hoping that I would notice him at once.

It is the custom of the land that before entering a house one asks, "With your permission." I was sure he had said so, and that I had, while reading, mumbled something which he had interpreted as, "Please come in."

Be that as it may, there he stood, motionless as a statue.

He obviously regarded my looking at him as questioning what he had come for, because at that instant he bent a knee, touched the floor with the palm of his right hand, lifted his hand up to his head with the palm toward me and rose at the same time, holding that gesture.

It was an odd sort of greeting; I couldn't remember ever seeing an Indian salute that way before.

"Good evening," I said to him in Spanish.

"Night is long and cold," he began without actually answering my greeting in the manner I had expected. "Hogs do bother me. Oh, it is horrible, ever so horrible to be on defense and have nothing to defend with. Built up with sacred care so as to be sure and safe for eternity. Yet now decaying and breaking into pieces. Long is the night, oh, señor, long, dark, and cold. Above all and everything, though, it is the hogs.

Hogs are the incarnation of all that means horror in this world and in the one beyond. Nothing on earth or anywhere else is more dreadful than hogs."

He raised one arm and pointed in a certain direction. Somehow his gesture did not agree with what he had just said. At least that was what I thought.

What was I supposed to answer?

I had not the vaguest idea of what he was talking about. It seemed confused. He was not drunk. His eyes were steady and there was no indication that he might be out of his mind or under the influence of a drug.

Not knowing what to answer, I bent over my book, stalling for time. I caught up with the line I had been reading when I had lifted my eyes—and then a terrible thought flashed through my mind. What if the strain of constant loneliness and the continuous reading about strange people and bygone days were driving me insane? Of course there was the possibility that it was merely a fever or some tropical sickness. I knew that certain fevers start by one's seeing things and hearing voices which are not real.

I found it difficult to define clearly where reality ended and imagination began.

Only to say something, and hear my own voice sounding in the room, I asked, "Excuse me, señor, but what do you mean? I've no idea what you're talking about. I'll listen to your story, but please tell it plain—just one thing after another."

I looked up again. But he was gone. He had left as silently as he had entered.

I rushed to the door. I wanted to make sure that I had in fact seen someone—or had had an hallucination. If it turned out to be a delusion, then I knew I'd better stop reading those heavy books.

Thank heaven, I was sane and my mind was still in good

shape. There he was, moving like a shadow, but clearly cut out against the lower part of the sky.

He was not very tall. From a distance, he appeared to be a slender youngster of seventeen, and even his walk showed the pure blood of his noble race. He moved with the beautiful grace of a deer going to the brook for its evening drink.

10

I returned to the table to resume my reading, but I found it difficult to concentrate. The visitor stayed in my mind.

Strange . . .

I couldn't recall with any accuracy the words and phrases he had used, but I knew for certain that he had not spoken Castellano or any other language familiar to me. And still I had clearly understood every word he said, even though some of the connections had failed to make sense.

I reviewed the episode in my mind. There had been his singular greeting. He had greeted me in the way which had been customary with some of the ancient peoples about whom I had been reading. Of course I realized immediately that this was sheer nonsense. I had begun to confuse the things I had read with the things I imagined having seen. Something was happening to my mind; otherwise such confusion would not be possible.

The fact that my visitor had been in rags meant nothing at all. Practically all Indian peasants wore nothing better.

And then I remembered that he had worn neither pants nor shirt—at least not a familiar kind. He had been bedecked with ragged fabrics which had the appearance of costly garments, except that they looked as though they were badly deteriorated by time and weather. They were so threadbare that one might expect to see them fall apart any minute. The texture of

the garb seemed fantastic, like the kind one may see in a
museum in the department of ancient clothes.

Perhaps I was altogether wrong about his clothes, but I was
quite positive about something else. His upper arms as well as
his ankles were adorned with armlets and anklets of heavy
gold, beautifully worked. And he wore a necklace which only
a highly skilled goldsmith could have made.

Again, on trying to recall more details, I discovered that I
had, in fact, seen nothing of what I believed I had seen. I had
equipped the man with the clothes and jewelry I had read
about during the last few days and which I had seen in the
illustrations found in the books.

The whole episode was ridiculous.

With that thought in mind, I closed my book and went to
bed.

11

While standing on the porch next morning, I noticed three
hogs roaming about the place. Two of them were black and
one was yellow. It occurred to me that I had seen these same
three hogs before, without taking any special interest in them.

But this time I actually stared at them—for all of a sudden
they reminded me of my visitor of the previous night.

Hadn't he said something about hogs and how horrible they
were? Somehow I couldn't see any connection between my
visitor and those hogs. Not at that moment, at least.

The hogs must be the property of an Indian family living
somewhere in the bush. Perhaps they were foraging for the
food which the jungle offered them in abundance. As a rule,
Indian peasants let their hogs go free to look out for themselves. Only during the last few weeks before they are sold or
butchered are hogs tied to a tree and given plenty of corn.

If those hogs were the property of the man who had visited

me last night, and if he didn't want them running away from
his place—well, it was his business, not mine. I thought it
rather peculiar that he should bother me so late at night for
such a trifle.

Still, I might do a little for him. I threw stones at the animals
to chase them off. It helped. After trotting a hundred yards or
so, they turned to their right and went into the bush, making
for a mound covered with weeds and underbrush.

It looked as if they had found food near the mound, because
I saw them moving about, digging their snouts here and there
in the shrubs, apparently plowing the ground for sweet roots.

I gathered the eggs in the chicken coop and cooked my
breakfast. I forgot all about the hogs.

12

Three days later, about eleven o'clock at night, I was once
again absorbed in my books. And once again I had the same
strange sensation which had overcome me the night the Indian
visitor had entered the bungalow, unseen and unheard.

Casting a look sidewise, away from the book, I felt an ice-
cold shiver running up and down my spine when I saw the
same Indian. He was watching me silently.

The shiver I had felt left me at once. It angered me to see
him there again without having asked for permission to come
in.

I yelled at him. "Just what do you mean by sneaking in here
in the middle of the night? This is no saloon and no cantina
either. This is a private home, strictly private. And I want you
to respect that privacy. What the devil do you want, anyway?
If you're looking for your hogs, get them away from this
place and tie them up. I don't like hogs around here. In fact, I
hate them. Do you understand? I despise hogs."

He looked at me, and his eyes had a pronounced emptiness,

as though he had to interpret carefully what I had said to him.
Then, in a heavy voice, he said, "So do I, sir. So do I, believe
me, I, too, despise hogs. More, I am afraid of hogs. Hogs are
the terror of the universe."

"That's none of my business," I said. "If you don't like
them, butcher them and have done with them. Or sell them.
What do I care? Only, for heaven's sake, leave me in peace."

I looked straight at his face. His eyes were so very sad that
all my violent outburst subsided into nothing. I began to feel
immense compassion for him. He seemed to be suffering.

He kept his eyes fixed on mine for long minutes. Then he
said, "Look here, señor. Please look at that." He pointed at the
calf of his left leg.

About six inches above the ankle there was a repulsive
wound.

"This," he explained, "has been done by the hogs."

There was a twang in his voice that nearly made me break
into tears. My overtired brain was beginning to tell on me.
This singular desire to weep, sure, was a warning of nature
that I'd better be more careful about my unceasing occupation
with the books. I would not go that soft unless there was
something wrong with my nerves.

He continued. "Oh, sir, it is ever so horrible. How can I
make you understand? To know that I am so utterly helpless
and without any means for defense against the gruesome
attacks of those ugly beasts. Pray, señor, pray to all the powers
of providence that never in all eternity may befall you so great
a misfortune as the one I am suffering. It will not be long now
before those loathsome monsters will gnaw at my heart. They
will suck my eyes out of my head. And then there will come
the day of all days of horror when they come to eat my brain.
Oh, sir, by all that is sacred to you, please do something for
me. Help me in my pains so bitter that I have no power in my

words to describe them to you. I suffer a thousand times more than any human can bear. What else, pray, can I say so that you may be convinced of how horribly I suffer?"

At last I knew what he had come for. He believed me to be the doctor. It was known in the whole region that the doctor did not practice medicine any longer, but as the next nearest doctor lived some seventy miles away, Doctor Cranwell helped out in urgent cases for the sake of kindness. For such emergency cases he kept a well-equipped medicine chest on hand.

I took out bandages, cotton, a disinfectant, and an ointment. When I approached the man to apply the disinfectant, he stepped back one pace and said, "This, señor, is useless. Quite useless in my case, I assure you. It is the hogs which make me suffer. I do not mind the wound. The wound is only a warning for me of what is going to happen in the future if I cannot be helped against the hogs."

I ignored his refusal to be treated, and grasped him firmly by the leg.

But I grasped empty space.

Looking up, I saw that he had stepped back another pace. How ridiculous, I thought, to be deceived that easily. I could have sworn that my grasping hand had been exactly at the very place where his leg had been at the very moment I reached out for it.

I rose and did nothing about the wound.

I put the medicaments on the table, and stood there a moment, wondering what else I might do. Then, as if by some impulse, I turned around and looked him over.

"Those are beautiful ornaments you're wearing," I said, pointing to his bracelets, his anklets and his rich necklace. "They're wonderful. Where did you get them?"

"My nephew gave them to me when I had to leave him and all the others."

"They seem to be very old. They look like Aztec or Toltec craftsmanship of ancient times."

He nodded slightly. "They are very old, indeed. They were part of the house treasure of my royal family."

I smiled indulgently.

He was too polite, though, to take notice of my grin.

However, in this silence, I realized that I was again confusing the present with the past of which I had been reading so much lately.

Strange, I thought to myself. Hadn't he said, "My nephew gave them to me"? Why, this was the custom with the ancient Aztecs, as it was with the Chichimecs and many other ancient Indian peoples. After the death of the king, not the son but the nephew of the king became the ruler of the people, a continuance which proved the Indians of old had a great knowledge of the natural laws of heredity of which we know so little. Even their calendar made more sense than ours of today. This man had a right to be proud of his ancestry.

"With your kind permission, I must go now," he said. "Only, sir, please do not forget my plight. It is the hogs that make my pains so horrible. Perhaps two or three big stones well fixed and cemented might do. I feel profoundly ashamed of myself because I have to beg for help, señor. But you see, I am unable to defend myself. I am so utterly helpless and powerless. I am very much in need of a friend alive. Oh, but that I could make you understand."

Tears were slowly rolling down his cheeks although he had obviously tried hard to keep them back.

As if in a solemn ceremony, he now raised his right arm, touched his lips with his open hand, and brought his hand slightly above his head. For a few seconds he kept the palm of his raised hand turned toward me.

I noted that his hand was of a very noble shape, and in the

same instant I thought that I had seen such a hand somewhere before, and not so very long ago, either. However, I could not clearly remember where and when it had been. It must have been in a dream, I decided. And now I noted that he had a beard, which was like a silken web. Never before had I seen such a thin, silky beard—at least not that I could recall at the moment. Yet that beard reminded me of stories of fights which Indians seemed to have been forced into by their oppressors a long time back. A mental picture appeared before me of hundreds of Indians hanging lifeless from trees and of Indian children running madly toward the huge mountains.

I tortured my memory, but I could not place precisely where I had heard or read such things. If only I could remember whether I had read about them in one of the books, and in which book, I would feel relieved.

I decided to ask him where he was living, a question which seemed to me, at this moment, the most important problem in the world.

I looked up.

To my surprise, I saw that he had left while I had been dreaming with my eyes open.

I leaped to the door.

He strides like a king, I thought, as I watched him walking along the path.

He must have sensed that I was watching him, because, after he had gone about a hundred yards, he stopped, turned around, and with his outstretched arm pointed toward that mound to which the hogs had waddled after I stoned them away from the house. Then he continued on his way.

After another few paces, he left the path, hesitated a moment, then moved along in the direction of the mound. He ascended the mound slowly, as if his feet had become very heavy. Then he was swallowed by the high brushwood, and I could see him no longer.

13

Right after sunrise next morning I took a machete and cut my way through to that mound. I carefully investigated the ground and the shrubs near it to find the trail by which the Indian had left the night before. My astonishment was great when I saw that there was no trace of any trail whatever. Not even a branch or twig was broken to show where he had gone after having passed the mound.

It was by no means as easy to follow him on his way as I had thought it would be. I wanted to find him because I wished to trade for some of his ornaments. I could offer, in exchange, things which might be of real use to him, such as leather for new huaraches, a pair of new pants, a shirt, or whatever he might prefer, money not excluded.

I looked more closely at the mound, and I made a curious discovery.

The mound was not, as I had imagined, a natural little hill or rock. It was, instead, a man-made mound, built of hewn stones perfectly joined together with some sort of mortar as hard as the best cement. Thorny shrubs and brushes had taken root in crevices and cracks, covering the little monument, or whatever it was, so densely that it could not be told from a natural elevation of the ground.

This strange find made me forget about following the Indian on his trail of last night.

After I cut down the weeds and shrubs, I made another discovery. Stone steps led up to the top of the mound, from west to east.

The height of the mound was twelve feet, more or less. Thirteen steps led to the top. This was of great interest to me, for with the Indians of old, thirteen meant a definite cycle of years. Four of these cycles, or fifty-two years, had the same significance to them as has a century to us, and served as the means by which they recorded their history.

After all the shrubs and weeds had been cleared away, the mound stood out like a sort of pyramid with a flat top, each side of which was about six feet long. Close to its base, one side of the mound had been broken in. From the appearance of mortar and pieces of stone strewn over weeds which were still green, I judged that this breaking-in must have occurred only a few days ago. I was positive that the hogs must have caused it the other day when I stoned them away and they had crossed over to the site.

On looking closer, I found that the hogs had managed to work through the construction so as to reach the interior of that little pyramid—a job which would not be difficult to accomplish, considering that the masonry at this part of the mound had begun to decay.

I had the idea that, right here, at least part of the solution to the two night visits I had been honored with lately might be found.

I hurried back to the house to get a pick-ax and a spade.

I broke off stone after stone, lump after lump of hard mortar from the broken side of the pyramid, which because of its state of deterioration was easiest to work on.

The job was tough. The concrete proved far more resistant than I had thought it might be. Whoever built the little monument had certainly known how to do a good, lasting job.

After more than two hours' work, I had opened a hole just large enough so that I could squeeze myself through it.

Once inside, I struck a match.

I had no sooner lighted it than I dropped it. I was out of that cave so quickly that my bare arms and shoulders, and my ears and neck, were covered with bleeding scratches caused by the glass-like edges of the broken mortar and rocks.

I sat on the ground, breathing heavily. Sitting there under the clear sun, I tried to catch my breath and I thought of how little a man can trust his eyes. I was certain that my eyes had played a trick on me.

My first intention was to leave the mound exactly as I had found it, save that I would close the hole I had broken in. Yet now, after having been inside and seeing its ghastly contents, I had no choice. No longer could I afford to leave everything inside as I had seen it. It would haunt me for the next twenty years. It might disturb the quiet of my mind forever. Most surely it would keep me awake for hundreds of nights and bring me to the verge of insanity. I would now be afraid to go into a dark room or sleep with all the lights out.

There was nothing else left for me to do but clear up the whole thing—if only to make absolutely certain whether I was already mad, or only on the road to madness, with a faint chance of being cured in time.

I decided to get at it immediately, lest I spend a terrible night.

14

Mindless of the blazing sun thundering down upon me, I started breaking through the thick concrete layer of the top which separated me from the interior. I had to have light—light, and still more light.

It was almost noon when I had laid the top open and the inside of the little edifice was fully exposed to the bright sunlight.

I was neither out of my mind nor dreaming. The painful bruises on my hands told me better than anything else that I was wholly awake.

In the now wide-open pit, built so strong and fine as if meant to keep its contents safe until the last day of the world, squatted that same man who had visited me at night on two occasions.

His elbows rested upon his knees. His head was bent down and his face was partly hidden in the palms of his hands. He sat as if in deep meditation or as if asleep.

He had been buried with utmost care, and in a way which told better than a tombstone in what high esteem he must have been kept by his people, and how much he must have been loved by his friends and kin.

Next to him there had been a few vessels made of clay which originally might have contained some food and drink to be used by him on his journey to the beyond. Unfortunately, these very fragile and richly painted dishes had been smashed by a lump of mortar which I could not prevent from dropping down when it came loose.

I knew that the tomb had been absolutely airtight until quite recently, when the hogs had succeeded in breaking through the masonry. They could not have done so had not vigorous tropical shrubs and parasitic vines, for long centuries, driven their roots deeper and deeper into the concrete, finally cracking it partly open, and thereby starting its decay. Once that decay had occurred, it was easy for the hogs to widen the cracks and push their snouts through. After a certain length of time—probably only three days ago—they had found it possible to crawl inside.

The appearance of the body was not that of an Egyptian mummy. It was not bandaged. The body looked exactly as though the man had died only the day before yesterday, if not last night when I had seen him go to this mound.

The rags in which the body was clothed looked far more costly in the bright light of the sun than they had at night. The fabric was of the finest texture, a silk-like goods such as the ancient Aztecs and Toltecs are known to have manufactured from the fibers of specially cultivated maguey and henequen plants. That texture was interwoven with strong threads of cotton to give the whole a very durable appearance. The colors had faded, but it could be clearly seen that at least six or seven different dyes had been used.

I saw that the calf of his left leg had been gnawed deeply at exactly the same spot which he had shown me last night. However, there was no blood, either fresh or dry, although the hogs had reached the bone.

It seemed strange that the hogs should have chewed off his calf, because I observed that the flesh of his breast, face, arms, legs, and yes, that of the whole body, was thoroughly hardened. I touched it. It felt like wood. In my opinion, the body could have no food value whatever. But then hogs, perhaps, think differently.

It was easy to explain how the body had kept its life-like appearance for such a long time. In the first place, it must have been embalmed. This was a custom with the ancient civilized Indians, and it was applied mainly to priests, kings, and nobles. Their embalmings were probably superior to those in vogue in ancient Egypt because, as in this case, they had proved more effective. In the second place, the tomb in which the body had been buried was thoroughly airtight, a fact which also helped to preserve the body in such excellent condition. And, perhaps, the soil which covered and surrounded the whole structure possessed certain chemicals which aided a great deal in protecting the structure and the body from disintegration.

The body was so strikingly life-like that I almost expected at any moment to see it move, raise its head from its hands, stand up, and talk to me.

15

The sun was right above my head, and its heat became more and more unbearable. It occurred to me that leaving the body exposed too long to the scorching sun might have a bad effect on it.

I ran to the house and returned with a wooden case, into which I meant to set the body and carry it to a shady place, either on the porch or right in the house.

Why I was so eager to get the body away from its pit instead of leaving it where I had found it and where it belonged, this I did not know. Here the man had rested for so many hundred years, and here he ought to remain.

However, I was not guided by any definite thought or idea at all—at least not by one that was my own, born in my mind. I acted in a purely mechanical way without giving the why a single thought. I acted as though there was no other way of doing what I did. Yet, at the same time, I knew perfectly well that I was under no suggestion from the outside.

With utmost care, I went about the job of putting the body into the wooden case I had brought. There was not room enough inside the pit to set the case right beside the body, so I left the case outside near the base of the structure.

I crept down into the cave with the intention of lifting the body up and getting it out of the cave. I grasped the body firmly, but I could not get a hold on it because my hands clapped together without anything between them save air.

Between my grasping hands the body had collapsed entirely and nothing was left but a thin layer of dust and ashes which, if carefully gathered, would not have amounted to more than what a man might hold in his two hands.

Hardly ten minutes had passed since I had positively convinced myself that the body was as hard as dry wood. All was gone now. The thick black hair, the dyed fingernails, the costly rags he had worn, had all changed to dust—a grayish powder, so fine that the slightest breeze would carry it away.

Still wondering how all this could have happened, and in so short a time, I noticed that the body dust had already mixed with the earth upon which it had fallen—so much so that I could no longer tell exactly which was the dust and which was the soil.

There was no use in standing there any longer in the excavation, with the broiling sun above my head and the steaming bush all around me, while I waited for something to happen.

Of course I was dreaming. Yes, that was it. And the tropical sun made things worse. I tried hard to wake up and shake off the drowsiness accumulating in my head.

I was near a grave sickness. The bush was like a huge monster whose fangs I could not escape. Where should I go for help? Wherever I might run there was only jungle and bush and that merciless sun above me making me feel as though my brain was slowly drying up to a spoonful of dust.

16

What was I to do with myself? I was sick, terribly sick. I had lost the faculty of distinguishing between what was real and what was imagination.

And then, right at my feet, glittering lustily in the bright sun, I saw the golden ornaments of my Indian. Those wonderful trinkets, which I had admired only last night, had not turned to dust. There they were in full sight. Since they were lying right at the bottom of the pit, in the dust, and since I could feel them distinctly with my fingers, take them into my hands, lift them out of the dust, they must be real—and no doubt about that.

If the jewels were still here, then the Indian or his dead body must have been here, too. So I had sufficient, satisfying proof that I was as sane as I had always been. I wasn't sick. There couldn't be any such things resting in my hands if all that which I had experienced had been only a dream.

I took them into the bungalow, sat down and examined them minutely with all the knowledge I had acquired from the books. What great artists were those men who had been able to create such beautiful ornaments—and with tools which we would consider very primitive.

I wrapped them in paper, made a little package of them and put that package into an empty can which I placed on top of a bookshelf.

Before sunset I returned to the mound and filled up the pit with stones and earth. I wanted to prevent stray horses or cows from breaking their legs. Even a wandering peasant might come this way by night, fall into the cave and do himself harm.

After I had filled up the pit, I realized that it would not have been necessary. Neither man nor animal would be likely to take his way across the mound instead of simply going around it. Yet, somehow, a certain call in my mind had urged me to close the cave the way I had done. And I felt that it was only to have an excuse for that extra and practically useless job that I had thought to protect people or animals from being harmed.

I spent the whole evening and half the night recalling to mind all the details of what I had experienced during the last few days. But when I tried to bring all these different happenings into a logical connection, I discovered so many contradictions, so many non-fittings, that I had to give up without having reached a single conclusion.

I turned in at midnight.

17

My sleep was anything but quiet. One wild dream was chased by another wilder still. But each dream had its climax and none broke before it reached that climax. As soon as a dream reached that point, I awoke—and then fell asleep again instantly when I realized that it had been only a dream.

I dreamed that I was strolling about the market places of ancient cities. It seemed impossible for me to find what I so badly needed. Whenever I thought I had found what I wanted, I discovered at the same moment that I had forgotten what it was.

So as not to appear ridiculous or draw suspicion upon myself, I bought just anything at a certain stand.

No sooner did I have it in my hands than I knew it was something different from the thing I had bought. I tried to put the bought object into my pocket, but found to my dismay that there was no pocket in any of my clothes. The clothes themselves were ragged, yet of very fine fabric.

Now the merchant asked me to pay, but I could not find the cocoa beans, which served as money.

Instead of the cocoa beans, I found my hand full of pepper corns, ants, painted fingernails, dust, and bits of black, wiry Indian hair.

Naked Indian policemen chased me for being a market cheat. I dashed off into the jungle, where I was entangled by thorny brushes, by weeds and vines, and by fantastic cactus plants which cried and shouted and tried to hold me and deliver me into the hands of the naked policemen.

My skin was torn almost to shreds by thorns and stings of all kinds. Wherever I set my foot down, there were gigantic scorpions, ugly tarantulas, hairy little monkeys. The monkeys had greenish eyes, and they tried to lure me into their caves. But the caves were too small and I could not squeeze myself through.

From the branches and around the trunks of trees, hundreds of snakes were curling—tiny ones, green and black and purple ones. Some were lashing out like whips. And there were snakes which were half lizards, and others which looked like a human leg with a chunk gnawed off at the calf.

While I was fighting off the snakes, tarantulas, and scorpions, I heard the policemen yelling after me. They were now setting police tigers on my trail to hunt me down more quickly.

There was no way of escape other than over a steep rock. I began to climb.

When I reached the top, I found a pack of mountain lions waiting for me on a cement platform. Huge birds were circling above my head, waiting to catch me and feed my carcass to their young. Just as one of those gigantic birds dashed straight down upon me and was so close I could distinctly feel the rush of air from its wings, I began to fall down into a deep ravine.

The fall lasted many hours.

While I was falling, I noticed many things, all of which were happening at the same time.

The Indian policemen were now clad in parrot feathers. They whistled at the police possums, which they used instead of police tigers, the tigers having mutinied because they had not been paid their wages in advance.

The whole police force marched home, led by a brass band. They went right back to the market place, arrested the merchant to whom I still owed three cocoa beans and a half, and sold him to his neighbor, into slavery. He did not mind because he shouted all over the place that it was just the very thing he liked best to be. He would no longer have to worry about the house rent and the taxes and the light bills going up and the ever growing demands of his greedy family. He said he knew very well that the Aztecs always treated their slaves as well as if they were members of the same family and all nephews.

Meanwhile, I had reached the bottom of a canyon. I bumped my head hard against a stone, so hard that I woke up, and found the canyon flooded with light. It was the moon which lighted my room.

Realizing that I was safe on my cot, and that there were no naked policemen after me, I immediately calmed down and at once fell asleep again.

18

This time I found myself fighting on the side of the conquistadores.

The Aztecs took me prisoner. I was carried to their main temple to be sacrificed to their war god. The priests threw me upon a great, well-polished stone. The high priest approached me, asking what I wanted to have for dinner. He said that he was going to tear my heart out while I was still alive and throw it at the feet of the war god. The war god himself was looking at me in a horrible way.

The war god grinned at me and winked with his glittering eyes. Although I knew perfectly well that he was only a stone god, I nevertheless saw him grin constantly and blink one eye, and I heard him say that he was highly pleased to have my throbbing heart thrown at his lips so that he could suck it with gusto, because he was tired of Indian hearts and would like a change in his diet once in awhile.

The high priest came closer to me. He tucked up the wide sleeves of his white robe, grasped me brutally by my chin, bent my head down in a cruel manner as if he had to slaughter an ox, and then thrust his obsidian knife into my chest.

Suddenly I awoke from the imaginary pain in my chest, and fell asleep again right away.

I saw myself fighting on the side of the Tabasco Indians.

They called Malinche a traitor and they fought to throw off the hard yoke of cannons and horses.

The Spaniards caught me and, nearly mad with joy, danced around me, yelling that they were glad to get another American for breakfast.

I was court-martialed and sentenced to the loss of both my hands. The hands were chopped off with a pocketknife which, as a special favor to me, they had made extremely dull.

After my hands were off, my arms felt very numb and I woke up because my arms were hanging sideways out over the edge of my cot, thus making the circulation of blood difficult. Immediately I fell asleep again. And now . . .

19

Now, being a licensed owner of a sweatshop in the ancient city of Tenochtitlan, I had received an order to make the coronation mantle for the new king who was to be crowned, and would then put the syllable *zin* at the end of his name.

The mantle was to be made from the beautiful feathers of tropical birds. Yet all the feathers came alive and flew off. I had to chase each single feather and get it back while only a quarter of an hour remained before the coronation was to begin.

The princess, chieftains, nobles and ambassadors were already assembled. A huge crowd hummed in front of the king's palace and on the streets leading to the great pyramid.

Hundreds of royal servants and high officials came running to get the mantle so urgently needed for the important affair.

But no sooner had I sewn on a feather than the one previously fixed on flew away again.

Then there were thousands of marshals, generals, and courtiers surrounding my art shop and yelling at the top of their voices. "The coronation necklace! The feather necklace!

Where are the armlets of gold? Quick, oh, ever so quick! We all have to die! We are all condemned to death! We are flown to death!"

In my great hurry to finish the mantle in spite of all obstacles, I became slightly careless while reaching for a needle, and there the mantle seized upon that opportunity, jumped to the open door, walked down the path of my bungalow, turned to where the mound was, and flew away.

It was still flying high up in the air when suddenly all the thousands and thousands of feathers, which, in so many sleepless nights, for thirteen weeks, I had sewn on with so much labor, fell off the mantle and winged away, chirping like birds and disappearing in all directions.

I woke up and heard the millions of crickets and grasshoppers fiddling, twittering, and whistling in the bush.

20

Once again I fell asleep, certain of the fact that I was well in my room and on my cot and that the coronation mantle of the emperor of Anáhuac might well take care of itself, leaving to a skilled Indian artist the task of making a gorgeous feather mantle, while King Netzahualcoyotl could write the poems for the great event.

And then the door of the room in which I slept suddenly swung open.

This surprised me, because I remembered very well that I had not only locked the door but had also bolted it firmly with a heavy bar. In spite of that care, the door opened, and in came my visitor, the same Indian I had seen falling to dust only twelve hours ago.

The room was lighted by a strange pale light, not unlike a thin, glimmering fog. I could not make out the source of the light. It was not the moon. The moon had gone down awhile ago. It was just a diffused silvery mist which filled the room and seemed, somehow, to move. The idea struck me that this might be the tail of a comet passing the Earth.

The Indian came close to my cot. He stood there very calmly, looking me full in the face.

I had my eyes wide open. I felt that I could not move should I want to. No longer did I seem to have any will of my own.

I was under the impression that if I wanted to move, I would first have to find my will again. It was as if my will had slipped away from me like the feathers of a coronation mantle carelessly sewn on.

I felt no fear, no fear of ghosts or of any danger threatening me. Quite the contrary. There was about me a rich and wonderful feeling of true friendship and of immaterial love such as I could not remember ever having felt before, not even in the presence of my mother. I thought that if a similar state of feeling should accompany me when I was about to die, I would believe that there was nothing more wonderful than death.

My visitor lifted the mosquito bar and laid the flap on top of the netting. This he did with a solemn gesture, as if it had been part of a ceremony.

In spite of the fact that we were no longer separated by this thin tissue, the floating diffused light filling the room did not change. I had thought that perhaps the strange light had been caused by my seeing the room through the white veil-like mosquito netting.

He greeted me in the same manner as he had on the two previous nights. Again he looked at me with profound earnestness and for a long while.

At last he spoke, spoke slowly so as to give each word its full meaning and weight.

"I ask you, my friend, do you believe it right to rob somebody who is defenseless and take away from him those little tokens which are his only companions on his long journey to the land of shadows? Who was it that gave me these little gifts? They were given to me by those who loved me, by those whom I loved dearly, by those who shed so many, many bitter tears when I had to leave them. I want so very much to make you understand that these tokens brighten my road through the long night.

"For love, and for nothing but love, is man born into this world. It is only for love that man lives. What else is the purpose of man on Earth? Man may win honors, man may win fame, man may win the high estimation of his fellow men, man may win riches, unheard-of riches. Yet all this, however great it may appear at first sight, as compared to love counts for nothing. Before the Great Gate, through which all of us have to go some day, even our most sincere prayers sent to heaven are valued no better than cheap bribes offered with the mean intention of winning special favors from the One who cannot be but just and Who is by far too great to consider prayers.

"Face to face with eternity, only love counts. Only the love we gave and only the love we received in return for our love will be taken into account. In the face of the Everlasting, we will be measured only according to the amount of our love. Therefore, my friend, pray return to me these little tokens which you took away from me, misunderstanding their meaning. Return them to me tonight, because, after my long journey to the Great Gate, I shall need them. When I shall be questioned then, 'Where are your credentials, newcomer?' I must have them with me so that I may answer, 'Behold here, oh, my Creator, here in my hands I carry my credentials. Few and small are these gifts, true, but that I was allowed to have them with me and wear them all along my way here—this is my evidence that I, too, was loved while on Earth, and so, my Lord and Maker, since I was loved, I cannot be entirely without worth.' "

The voice faded off into a deep silence.

It was not his eloquence; it was the profound silence, taking full possession of the whole room like a visible power commanding words, things, deeds, which influenced all my acts from then on.

I rose from the cot, dressed quickly, put on my boots and went to the bookshelf.

I opened the little package, hung the necklace about his neck, put the thick ring on his forefinger, shoved the golden armlets up his arms, and put the anklets around his legs.

Then he was gone.

The door was closed and bolted heavily as before.

I returned to my cot, lay down and fell asleep at once.

My sleep was as deep, as dreamless, as wholesome as is the first refreshing, sound sleep after a long illness. For weeks I had not slept so well as I did that night.

21

It was late when I woke up the next morning. I felt so fully re-animated, so rich with energy, that it seemed the whole world could be mine just for the taking.

In remembering the dream which I had had during the night, I thought that never before had I had a dream in which every detail had been so clear, so logical as this last one. It could not have been more clear and impressive if it had not been a dream at all but an episode of the day, a slightly strange episode, but nonetheless real and natural.

I looked for my boots.

Why, they were not stuffed with paper and neither were they placed on a chair. Experience had taught me, when living in the jungle, to stuff my boots with balls of crumpled paper or something else, and to put them on a chair or box or hang them up. Otherwise, when you started to pull them on in the

morning, you might find a scorpion or a small snake inside
them. It had happened to me once; I still remembered the
speed with which I got the boots off on that occasion, and since
then I know that one can get his boots off just as quickly as a
hat from one's head. To have a little red snake in the lowest
part of your boot while your foot is inside is not so very
pleasant, because the snake, as terrified as you are, wants to get
out, as do your feet. The worst thing about it is that you don't
know exactly what it is that's under the sole of your foot. It
drives you nearly crazy while your foot is still in, and makes
you feel aghast with horror after your foot is out and you see
what was, or still is, a tenant of your boot.

Anyway, my boots were not stuffed and they were not
standing on the chair.

All of a sudden I remembered that I had dropped the boots
rather carelessly last night, due to the fact that I was very tired
when I turned in again after the Indian had left. I remembered,
too, that while he had been in the room I had pulled out the
paper from my boots and had put them on to go to the room
where the bookshelves were. It is no sound practice, when
living in the jungle, to walk with bare feet by night. A native
can do so, but a white man avoids it. When I had come from
the other room I had lain down immediately on my cot, not
paying any attention to the boots or anything else, and had
fallen asleep as soon as I had touched the pillow.

Had I really dreamed that or had I not?

One long jump and I was at the bookshelf.

The can was not there. I looked around and found it thrown
on the table, open and empty. The paper in which I had
wrapped the jewelry lay torn and in scraps about the floor. No
sign of the ornaments anywhere, no indication where they
might be.

The door was still locked and bolted, exactly as I had fixed it
last night before turning in.

I hurried to the mound.

In feverish haste I cleared the pit of the stones, the earth, and the shrubs with which I had filled up the excavation last afternoon.

Nothing was on the bottom. No clue to where the ornaments might have been hidden.

Where, for all the foolish and silly dreams of mine, had I put those things while asleep? Or was I walking in my sleep? Impossible. It couldn't be.

No matter how hard I worked my mind and my memory, I had not the slightest hunch to follow up. I searched the whole house, in every nook and corner. I moved all boxes and cases about. Every loose board was inspected. I opened sacks and investigated every pot in the house and in the yard. Nothing. Nothing in the house nor about the house nor around the house nor on top of the house. Nothing anywhere.

Perhaps . . . perhaps the hogs.

It was silly to think of the hogs in relation to the ornaments. I might try, anyway.

22

Two weeks later, the doctor returned.

My first question after he had seated himself was, "Say, Doc, have you ever noticed three hogs around the place here? I refer to particular hogs, two black ones and one yellow, all three practically the same size, the Indian kind, sort of hairy."

"Three hogs, you say?" He looked at me, rather appraisingly, I thought. "Hogs?" Again he repeated his question in a queer tone, as if he had not heard right.

There was something in the tone of his voice and in the way he stared at me. It might have been a well-concealed, though firm, examination of my mental soundness.

"Hogs," he said again. "Is that it—hogs? With some people

it is mice. White ones. Sometimes green ones. With others it is
ants. With some, strange kinds of mosquitoes or bats. With
you, it is hogs. Something new in pathology. I am quite sure,
old man, you mean dogs. D, D, D, and not H, H, H. Understand, Gales, it is D, D, D, dogs, dogs, dogs. Three dogs. Two
black ones and one yellow, all nearly the same size, and hairy,
too. Just mongrels, the sort the Indians have. I am positive, old
chap, that you mean dogs. It is just the tongue sometimes
which mixes up one letter with another. We know this trick
of dropping words and taking one letter for another without
realizing it. Apart from that, you're right. I've seen about this
place here, and at various times too, three dogs, two black ones
and one yellow. I've even asked people to whom they might
belong.

"Nobody seems to know them. What is more, no native
around here seems ever to have seen them. Anyway, it's none
of my business to look out for stray dogs. To the devil with
them. Dogs, or hogs, or pox, what the hell do I care about
stray animals. Let's talk about something else. Dogs. I don't
wish to talk about these three dogs, do you hear? Why did
you have to bring them up right when I come home and wish
to feel easy and happy again with the sun and the jungle and
all the things I've missed during these last weeks. I'm happy to
be back here. Why, for heaven's sake, do you have to speak
about dogs?"

"Why? See here, Doc—listen to what has happened to me
and you will understand the why."

I told my story, leaving out no detail.

I had expected to see him go wild over it. Since I had seen
his library, I knew how much he would be interested in things
like the ones I was so anxious to get off my mind.

"Wait a minute, wait a minute," he said. "What is it you
mean to tell me? A dead Indian—that's what you're telling me
about? A dead Indian coming to visit you on two nights?" He

shrugged his shoulders in a way to indicate that such affairs happened to him thirty times every month.

After awhile, though, he again began searching every line of my face with the piercing eyes of a suspicious doctor.

"Ornaments? You mean ornaments and not something else? You are sure? Just ornaments? Ancient, too? Ancient Aztec craftsmanship? Ancient? And you, in person, have held them in your hands? Now they have disappeared? As if in thin air? And you don't know where they are now? That's something! That could almost induce me to take up practice again. I thought it was only hogs. I see now it's worse. Well, well—and right here at my place, too. Well, well . . ."

His bone-dry irony made me furious.

I said, more harshly than politely, "So you don't believe it, sir? So you don't believe me? Perhaps you think my mind has snapped? Do you mean to say that? Well, Doctor, this time you're mistaken. If you don't believe me, I'll show you the mound right now, hardly a hundred yards away. I can also show you the thirteen stone steps leading up to the top of that little pyramid. What is more, I can even show you the cave I excavated. What do you say now, my good friend?"

He had let me talk without once interrupting me. Now he only grinned.

He nodded in a fatherly manner, as if listening to the report of a patient whom he knew to be lying terribly, and slowly fumbled his pipe out of his pocket.

In a very dry, almost sleepy tone, he said, "I, too, can show you a cave which I dug, around here some place. More than just one. In fact, I can show you several of them. But it can't happen to me any more. I am over it. I have been over it for a long time."

Now it was I who looked at him with questioning eyes. But he said no more about his own adventures.

He lit his pipe and puffed at it a few times, then took it from his mouth and rested his hand on his knee.

"Well, old fellow," he said, "here's my advice, as a good friend and as a doctor. You'd better go down to one of the villages, any of the villages will do, and hire yourself a cook. See to it that she is a good-looker, a young one, and not so very dirty. I can assure you, old man, that with a good-looking cook about your place, no dead Indians will ever bother you again. And no ornaments, ancient or modern, will make you get up at night and put your boots on. No charge for this advice, Gales. It's given free and out of long experience. Besides, I owe you something for minding my place while I was away. I brought you five pounds of the very best tobacco I could find. Take it. You are welcome."

23

"Welcome." The word lodged itself strangely in my mind. It would not leave me. It went on and on, pricking in my head. Welcome? Am I really welcome?

No. I was not welcome. I was not welcome there any longer. Something had been destroyed, inside of me, or outside of me, or somewhere in the far distance. I could not tell what had been destroyed, nor where. I was no longer the same—at least not to me. I felt horror where before I had felt heavenly quiet.

And suddenly I longed for a change.

He had seen three dogs, of the hairy Indian kind, two black ones and one yellow. I had seen, positively, three hogs, of the hairy Indian kind, two black ones and one yellow. The worst thing of all, however, would be if I were to happen to see exactly the same three dogs he had seen.

Should that happen to me, I would not have the strength to

survive the day. He had survived many such days. Of this I was sure. I could not. He was of another make, Doc was.

I asked him whether I might stay for another night with him in the bungalow.

This granted, I now asked him, "Listen, Doc, you're a heavy smoker yourself, aren't you?"

"Why—yes—eh—I don't quite——"

"I wanted to make sure of that, Doc," I said. "Good night. I'll turn in. Time for the little ones to go to bed."

"Good night," he answered. While I was fixing the mosquito bar, I noticed that Doc was rubbing his chin and watching me with a strange stare in his eyes.

Next morning, while we had breakfast on the porch, I said, "What do you say, Doc? Could I maybe sell you four pounds of that fine tobacco which you brought me from back home?"

"Why, man, I gave it to you. What's the matter with it? It's very good tobacco. The best there is. Don't you like it, or what?"

"You see, Doc," I said, "it's this way. I'd like to have you buy these four pounds for, let's say, twenty-five pesos, cash."

"Why, of course, if you wish to dispose of it that way and buy your native brand for the money, that's absolutely okay with me. Fact is, I'll be in dire need of good tobacco myself in a few weeks. I couldn't bring much along. You know, the duty is awfully high."

"I won't buy another brand for the money, Doc," I said. "It isn't that, you see. I'm satisfied with just one pound for the time being. What I really need is the cash I asked you for."

"May I ask what you need the money for, if it isn't a secret?"

"No secret. No secret at all, Doc. It's simply this way. I mean to clear out of here. I turned everything over in my mind last night. You see, Doc, that prescription of yours

concerning the good-looking cook won't do any good. It's too
late now. It might have worked six, even three, months ago.
Now it wouldn't work out. I know that. And no doubt about
it, either."

"Well, what about your farm? The money you've invested
in it and all your hard work is worth more than the money
you paid. You don't mean to tell me that you're leaving all that
for nothing?"

"That's about the size of it, Doc," I said. "Yeah, I'll leave it
for nothing to anyone who comes along and picks it up. The
bush may have it back. It belongs to the bush, anyway. Everything here belongs to the bush. I don't. And the bush is
welcome to it, and with my best wishes thrown into the
bargain. And I hope the bush can keep it until the world's end.
Congratulations."

"As you say, Gales. I certainly won't persuade you to stay
on and try just once more. You're old enough to know what
you want and what is good for you. You don't eat green apples
any more. Well, there's your money. If you mean to go by
rail, you can sell your pony down at the depot. Anyone will
take it for a fair price. I'm quite sure you'll get forty for it if
you start asking ninety."

I noticed that his face changed while he was talking, and
now he moved his lips as he usually did when he was thinking
hard.

He turned around and walked over to the corner of the
porch and gazed down over the jungle ocean.

He took a deep breath, then said, "I wish I could go with
you, Gales. I wish I could leave as easily as you can. Yet I
can't. I can't any more. I'm bound here, damn it. I'm buried
here, bone, soul, heart, flesh, everything. Only ashes it is that
you see. All of me is buried here. Only the mind is still alive.
Sometimes I think that even my mind has gone to sleep, too,
and only my former thoughts are still lingering about. I must

stay here where my bones and my soul are resting. I can't leave them behind and all alone. You see, the thing is that I'm buried here in more than just one way. Well, what I was going to—was going to–to——"

He stared out into the far distance as if he were looking beyond the world. And as I had thought several times before in the earliest days of our acquaintance, so I thought at this moment again: He has died long, long ago, the doc has, only he doesn't know it. And that's the reason, the one and only reason, why he is still hanging on.

He turned to face me. "Of course, I'll lend you a mule to carry your few things to the depot. Leave the animal with the Straddlers until I call for it. Well, if the Lord only would have mercy and grant me that I could go with you, be free and easy like you, going where you wish and where your lucky star will lead you. Well, Gales, it was a great pleasure to have known you. I mean it, old chap. Since it has to be this way, good luck and good-bye."

24

It was the next day, late in the afternoon, when I bounced ten pesos silver upon the narrow board over which a hole in the wooden wall signified the ticket-seller's window.

"Which way does the next train go?" I asked. "West or east?"

"Oeste. West, I mean," the man behind the window said.

"A ticket for ten pesos, please. Second class."

"What station?"

"Just a ticket for ten pesos anywhere west. It doesn't make any difference."

The stationmaster looked up the list.

"There's one ticket for nine eighty-five and the next one is for ten seventy. Which will it be?"

"Make mine nine eighty-five, and that will be good enough for me any time now or tomorrow."

"There you are," he said. "Fifteen centavos change. There she is, pulling in, right on time. Rare thing, if you ask me."

I did not look at the station's name printed on the ticket. One station was as good as another as far as I was concerned. If you are to find a gold mine, you may as well wreck your house and dig up the ground below the basement. The place is as near to your fortune as any other if you're the guy to get what you want or what is meant for you to have.

I boarded the train. The conductor came up to me. He took my ticket, glanced at the name of the station, shook his head as though somewhat bewildered, stared at me for awhile without saying a word, and then crossed something out on the ticket with a thick blue pencil. He put the ticket away in his pocket and handed me instead a slip of paper on which he, with the same thick blue pencil, had written something in Chinese. When he saw me helplessly fingering that slip he pitied me with a deep sigh, took it away from me and pushed that slip into my hat ribbon. "That's your hat, mister, isn't it?"

I nodded.

"I'll call you in time to get off the train," he said. "Don't worry. Just keep quiet, take a nap, and don't worry a bit. Did you understand what I said?"

"You said something about worrying."

"The other way around, mister. I said you should not worry a bit. I'll see to it that you get off at the right place. So take it easy. Everything will be all right."

He gave me an assuring smile, nodded in a fatherly manner as if he were dealing with a little boy riding for the first time on a train all by himself, and went his way.

The coach was poorly lighted. There was nothing to do but doze off.

After I had slept what I thought must have been sixty hours

or more, I was pushed on the shoulders and I heard a voice. "Next station's yours. Got five minutes. Better shake out of it and get ready. We don't stop there, and if we've got a passenger the engine only slows down a bit. Far as I can remember . . . well, as long as I'm in service on this line . . . we've never had a passenger get off there. And neither has one ever got on. You'd better hurry, mister, and take care not to drop under the wheels. That would be just too bad. I'll throw your bags out of the window. You just pick them up once you're off and outside. Good night."

"What time is it, conductor?" I asked.

"Twelve. Middle of the night, you know. A clear beautiful night as far as I can judge. All the stars are bright like diamonds. Well, mister, there you are. Good night. Buenas noches."

The train slowed down. My bags were already out. I jumped off, keeping clear of the wheels.

Before I had come to my full senses and had realized what had happened and that I had jumped into darkness, the last car of the train had already passed by, and a few seconds later I could see only a little flicker of the red taillight.

Looking around from where I stood, I saw no building, no house, no shed; nothing. Absolutely nothing.

Nothing except a post with a piece of board nailed to it.

I went close, lit a match and looked at the board. There were a few blots which, a hundred years ago, might have been a name painted on the board.

No light other than that of the stars could be seen any-where, near or far.

I picked up my bags and sat down on one of them.

Less than fifty feet from either side of the track stood the wall of the bush.

A wall, dense, dry, dreary, greenish-gray, now looking black, looking in the darkness as though it were stooping slowly though irresistibly upon me where I sat, threatening to suck me into its fangs, intending to swallow me, to swallow all of me, bone, flesh, heart, soul, everything.

Who had said that to me many years ago, and where had it been said? My effort to remember this kept my mind busy for the next two or three hours.

The air was filled with chirping, whispering, murmuring, fiddling, whining, whimpering, now and then shrills and shrieks of fear and horror.

The bush was singing its eternal song of stories, each story beginning with the last line of the story just ended.

Effective Medicine

One afternoon, on coming home from the cotton field where I had worked all day long, I noted, outside the barbed wire fence of the bungalow I was living in, a Mexican peasant squatting on the bare ground. I did not know him because, as I learned later in the evening, he was from another village six or seven miles away. He was very poor and all in rags.

Having greeted me he waited patiently until I dismounted from the burro I had been riding home on. When I had taken off the saddle and the burro had gone its way looking for cornstalks in the yard, the Mexican entered the front yard, came close and began talking.

He talked rapidly and in a confused manner. For a moment I thought him to be on the high—that is to say, that he might have smoked more marijuana than he could digest. However, though he was now telling the end of his story, now the beginning, now the middle, all in confusion, I soon noticed that he was neither drunk nor doped, only very ignorant and evidently suffering from a nervous breakdown—as far as this can happen to a Mexican of his kind.

It was difficult for me to make sense of his story and for a long while I was unable to see which part of his story was the end and which the beginning or the middle. The farther he came in his story the more was he swept away by his emotion until he only blubbered or shouted absolutely incoherent phrases. Never once did he fully end his tale. Whenever I thought him close to the end and I was trying to catch up with the full meaning, I realized that he was already telling his story from the middle backwards to the start again. In this confused way he told me his story more than a dozen times and always with the same words, out of a vocabulary which barely consisted of more than three hundred different words. His mood changed constantly. Each time he started as if he were telling the story of somebody else, yet invariably he ended up crying almost hysterically.

"Look here, señor doctor, that old hussy and tramp that she is and always was, she is gone. She is gone with that ugly cabron and dirty son of a heathenish dog, that thief Pánfilo, you know him, señor, the one I mean, that would steal the horns of the Devil if they were not grown on, you know that housebreaker, and if you don't know him, so much the better for you because he steals barbed wire and cuts telegraph poles and the telegraph wire also and no hog is safe if he is around. I wish him the smallpox all over his face and the most terrible disease extra to make it worse for him. I come home. I come home from my work in the bush. In the bush I had to cut down hard trees for making charcoal; you see. I sell the wood and the charcoal if I have any to the agents—who are thieves, too. I come home tired and hungry. Home in my jacalito. I'm hungry more than a dog, that's what I am, from hard work in the bush. No tortillas ready. No frijoles in the pot. Nothing. I tell you the truth, señor doctor, nothing. I call my woman, that old hussy. My mujer I mean. No answer. I look around. She isn't at home, my woman isn't. Her sack with her dress in it, and her shirt and her torn stockings, which are in that same sack also, are all gone. The sack used to hang on a peg. My mujer has ran away. She doesn't ever return. Never, such what I say. And she is so full of lice too, my woman is. I've no tortillas for me to eat. Nor black beans for my empty belly. Off she went like the stinking hussy that she is. If I only knew who she ran off with, that useless old nag. I'll get *him*. And I'll learn him how to steal decent and honest women that belong to other men. He is a *mil* times worse than any dirty cabron." (*Mil* means thousand; to his kind, though, *mil* means anything between one hundred and one thousand billions.) "Now, I ask you, mister doctor señor, who will make tortillas for me? That's what I want you to tell me right now."

So he asked, but he did not wait for my answer and he went on with his story, hardly stopping to catch a full breath.

"Nobody is going to make me tortillas now. That's what it is, I tell you. She has ran away. I'll catch *him* and he won't live to tell who done it. I come home in my choza. I come home from the hot bush. Hungry and dying of thirst. I don't mind the thirst. I come home and no tortillas. No frijoles. She is gone. She has taken her sack with her dress and her stockings along with her."

At this point of his sad story he cried so bitterly that for the next three minutes it was difficult to understand what he was saying because it was all blubbering. Slowly he calmed down once more. Yet, crying or not crying, he talked on and on like a cracked phonograph record.

"I come home. From the bush I come home and I've worked all day long under that blistering sun and no——"

"Now wait a minute, manito." I interrupted him before he went into his speech again and made it impossible for me to stop him. "Let's talk this over quietly. You've told me your heartbreaking experience fifteen times by now. I admit it is

heartbreaking. But I can't listen to it a mil times because I've
got other things to attend to. All I can say is that your mujer is
not here in my jacal. Step in and look around and make sure."

"I know, señor mister, that she isn't in your house. A fine
educated doctor like you would never even touch such a filthy
one like her, and so full of lice that sometimes you might think
the wind is in her hair, so fast it moves from all the lice in
it."

The lice seemed to remind him once more of his loss and he
started telling the story again. The whole thing began to bore
me and I said: "Why, for hell's sake, do you have to tell all
that just to me? Go to the alcalde—the mayor, I mean—and
tell him your story. He is the proper person to attend to such
matters. I'm just a simple doctor here without any political
influence and no disputado backing me up. I've no power and
so I can do nothing for you. Nothing, do you hear? Nothing
at all. Go to the alcalde. He'll catch your mujer. It's his duty,
because he is the authority in this place."

"That alcalde, you mean, señor? I can tell you right now
and here that he is the biggest ass under heaven. That's why he
was elected alcalde. And he is a thief too, and also a woman-
raper. Just for his meanness and his stupidity it was that he got
elected because no decent and no honest person had any word
in that election, see? You ought to know that, señor."

"Anyway, amigo," I said, "he has to look after your
troubles. And as I said before, I've no power, no power at all,
to do anything for you. Get this in your mind, friend. I've no
power."

"But you're wrong, mister caballero. You've got all the
powers in the world. We know this very well. And no
mistake. You can pull bullets out of the bodies of killed bandits
with fishing hooks and make them live again. I mean the boys
with federal bullets in their bellies and legs. You understand

what I want to say and what I know and what the federales
would be so very eager to know also. Because you have all the
powers to do anything under heaven. That's why you know
where my woman is at this hour. Tell her that I'm hungry and
that I've come home from the bush after much hard work. She
has to make tortillas and cook frijoles for me. I'm very hungry
now."

"Now look here, friend. Let's be calm about it." I spoke to
him as I would have to a little boy. "See here, I've not seen
your woman go away. Since I've not seen where she went I
can't tell you where she is at present. I can't even imagine
where she perhaps might be. In fact, I know nothing, nothing
at all. I don't even know her face or what she looks like.
Please, amigo, do understand, I know nothing of her. And
that'll be all. Thank you for paying me such a delightful visit.
Now I'm busy. Good-bye. Adiós."

He stared at me with his brown dreamy eyes as if in
wonder. His belief in the infallibility of a white man, and
particularly in the immaculate perfection of a Norte-Ameri-
cano, had been shaken profoundly. At the same time, though,
he seemed to recall something which had evidently been
hammered into his head since he could speak his first words,
and that was something which, in his opinion, was forever
connected with the Americanos, as is the color green with
young grass.

So he said: "I'm not rich, señor. No, I'm not. I can't pay you
much. I've only two pesos and forty-six centavitos. That's all I
have in the world. But this whole fortune of mine I'll give you
for your work and for your medicine so that I can find my
woman and get her back to my side, that hussy, because I am
very hungry."

"I don't want your money. Even if you would give me mil
gold pesos I could not get your woman back. I don't know

where she is and therefore I can't tell her that you must have your tortillas and your frijoles. Can't you understand, man, that I don't know where your woman is?"

Suspicion was in his eyes when he looked at me after I had finished. He was quite evidently not certain whether it was the little money he could offer me which kept me from helping him or that in fact I might really not know the whereabouts of his spouse.

Gazing for a few minutes at me in this manner he finally shook his head as if full of doubts about something of which he had thought himself very sure before. Honoring me once more with that suspicious glance, he left my place but not until I had told him several times more that I had to cook my dinner and could no longer stand idly around and listen to his troubles, for which I had no remedies.

As I learned a few days later, he visited practically all the huts of the village, where he told his story and reported also that this white medicine man of whom they talked so highly was but a poor faker, ignorant of the simplest things of everyday life.

This low opinion of his was taken by the villagers for a grave insult upon themselves, since I was the pride of the whole community, who considered me one of the wisest and greatest medicine men that have ever walked the earth. I do not know, but I can fairly well guess, what the villagers recommended him to do so as to make my mysterious powers work in his favor.

Shortly after sunrise next day he returned to my place, placed himself outside by the barbed wire fence, and waited there peacefully until I noticed his presence and came out to speak to him.

The moment he saw me feeding corn to my burro he called me. "Just for a very, very little short moment, señor mister, please. Please, come here close to the fence and listen what I've got to tell you. And you'd better listen terribly carefully because I'm serious. As a plain matter of fact I'm extremely serious this morning, because I haven't slept very much."

On stepping up to the fence I noted that while I was approaching he picked up from the ground a long machete which as I could easily see had been sharpened with utmost care. It must have taken him hours to give that heavy sword-like bush-knife such an almost razor-like edge.

Nonchalantly, though meaningfully, he moved this machete up and down before my eyes while he was talking again. Occasionally, just as nonchalantly, he examined the edge with his wetted thumb, and now and then pulled a hair out of his thick black scalp and cut his hair softly, practically by only touching it with the edge. Whenever he did so he looked at me as if to make sure that I was observing how sharp that machete really was.

"So you won't tell me where my esposa is, señor?"

"It seems," I answered with dignity, "that you have a very good and very excellent machete. Looks like well-tempered steel to me."

"And good steel it is. And it has been made in your country: There you may be assured that it is the finest and the best steel we can buy down here. You'd better not make the mistake thinking that it might be German-made, because a German-made is no good, you cannot even cut cheese with it; if you try that the edge is gone for good. But they are very cheap. Only you cannot cut trees with them, not the sort we have got here in the bush. But the one I have got here will do anything I want it to do."

"Let me have a close look at it," I pleaded.

He put it through the fence but held the haft fast in his hand.

"This won't do at all. I must get a swing at it to see how good it is. I know something about steel."

"Oh no, señor mister, I won't let you have it. This excellent machete won't leave my hands, not before I know where my woman is. Just touch the edge. See. Now I think you'll understand that with one single stroke I could chop off the head of a burro from its trunk like cutting through wet mud. But should it be the head of a man, even that of a gringo, instead of that of a poor burro, I tell you, señor, I wouldn't need to make half so hard a stroke as I would have to use for a burro, with a machete having an edge like this one, and made in your own country, where the best steel comes from. What do you think, señor?"

"Since you ask me, friend, I think a bullet is even quicker than a machete, and more certain too."

"Maybe. Surely it is. But a bullet, without a gun to fire it, is not much to compare with such a good American-made machete. Everybody here in the village knows very well that you haven't got a gun, not even an old Spanish muzzler. I know this or I wouldn't perhaps bring my fine machete along with me. Understand, caballero mister?"

"I understand all right, manito. I see you want to cut my fence posts and carry them away. But you won't do that. You know that would be plain robbery. The federales would shoot you for banditry as soon as they come to this village again. It won't be long now and they will be on their way here once more looking for bandits."

"I don't need your fence posts. I wouldn't take them, not even for a gift. They're all termite-eaten anyhow and no good. I can get them better in the bush."

"Then what do you want? I've got to get breakfast ready because I must ride to my field and look after my tomatoes. I mean that I've got to go now, see, right now while the day is still cool and fresh."

"Mil times I have told you, señor mister, what I want. That's why I sharpened my machete. I want my woman back. You will now tell me where she is so that I can catch her and give her a terrific thrashing before I'll let her cook frijoles for me."

"And mil times I've told you that I don't know where your mujer is."

"So you still insist on telling me that you can't find her for me?"

"That's what I'm saying all the time and I don't know what to say any more. So what are you going to do about it?"

"Maybe you don't know where she is. What I know for sure is that you can find her if you wish to. I can't give you mil gold pesos for I haven't any. I suppose I've got to speak frankly with you, señor. In other words, if you don't tell me right away where my woman is I will be very sorry, and sorry for *you*, I mean, because in such a case I am desperate and I must chop off one head. I won't promise whose head it might be which is to be chopped off, and I can't promise either that it might not be your head which is going to be cut off with one single stroke and with that fine American-made machete too. Perhaps it will be done by mistake, so to say. In other words, señor mister, it will be your head, and no mistake about that, I am sure."

He raised his machete high up and swung it around above his head as a drunken pirate would his cutlass. It looked dangerous enough. I was cornered. I might, of course, try to escape into my bungalow. Sooner or later, though, I would have to come out and there he would be waiting for me. I had to get to my field to look after the crop, but he'd sneak up on me from behind or lay in ambush somewhere. His kind is patient. They will wait for days and weeks until they get their man. What does he care about killing somebody? He hides in the jungle. If he should finally be caught and fusilladed he will

consider it his fate, which was his since he was born and from
which he, in his opinion, could not have escaped. Right now
he is desperate. Without thinking of any or all the consequences which his murder will have afterwards, he, like a
stubborn child, wants his wish to come true immediately.

Again I told him the same thing I had told him twenty times
the afternoon before. "I haven't seen the way your woman
went. Therefore I don't know where she is now."

But my answer had lost its power. When he had told the
villagers what sort of answer I had given him the day before,
they had suggested what he ought to say if I were to tell him
again that I had not seen his woman go away. He himself alone
would never have come upon the answer he had in stock now,
for his mind was not developed highly enough for such mental
exercise. I was sure that the whole village was as much
interested in the kind of medicine I would give him as he
himself was.

At that hour I did not know that he had talked to the
villagers about our discussion the previous afternoon. But from
the way he now presented his answer I knew immediately that
it could not be his own, and that he had memorized it after
being taught what to say, because he not only used words
entirely new to him, but also spoke like a bad amateur actor.

"Listen here, señor," he said, "if I'd seen the way my mujer
went when she left I would have no need to trouble you, for
in that case I could do well and perhaps better still alone than
with the help of a medicine man. All people in the village here
have told me that you are a far-seer. They have told me that
you have two little black tubes sewn together to make them
appear like one. They say, because they know, that if you look
through these tubes you can see any man or woman or dog or
burro which might walk on that faraway hill yonder, and you
can see an eagle perching on a high tree a hundred miles away.
You have told the folks in this village that there are people

living on some of the stars, because this earth we live on is also but a star only we can't see it as a star since we are on it. All people here have watched you often when, by night, you look with your black tubes up to the sky so as to see the people on the stars and what they were doing at that time of night and how they lived there and how many cattle they had."

I remembered I had said something to this effect to a few of the younger men of the community.

"You've also told here that wise men in your country to the north have another black tube, by which they can look straight into the inside of any man or woman to see if there is a bullet there and where it is located, so that these medicine men of yours can get the bullet out without cutting open the wrong part of the body. More you have said. You have said that white men can talk to other white men who are mil and more mil miles away and they can talk to one another without shouting just the way as I talk to you now, and that they don't even need a copper wire on which their words run along, as do telegraph wires in our country. I want you to talk right now and before my eyes to my woman, and tell her that I am hungry and that I've no tortillas and no frijoles to eat. And I want you to tell her to come right home, and that she has to come home on one of those air-wagons you have said your people ride on when they are in a hurry. And I am in an awful hurry now."

Having finished his speech with the difficulty an urchin has saying his catechism at Sunday school, he began again swinging his machete pirate-fashion, obviously with the intention of making his demands more imperative.

What was I to do? If I got the better of him and clubbed him down, everybody in the village would accuse me of having killed a poor, ignorant, but honest Mexican peasant, who had done me no harm and had never meant to do me any, and who had not even insulted me, but had only come, a very humble human, to another human, asking for help which no good Christian would have denied him.

I had to do something to get me out of the hole I was in, and in which I did not feel very comfortable. As I was considered one of the greatest medicine men, there remained nothing else for me to do but to rely on medicine. The only question was, what sort of medicine I was to use to cure myself of his desperation, and of his machete which, as he demonstrated over and over again, would cut a hair as if by magic. The medicine to be served had to be of a special kind—that is, it had to be effective enough to save both of us at the same time.

At this precious moment, when I was thinking which of the gods I might call upon for a good idea and a better medicine, there flashed through my tortured mind a mental picture of two black tubes sewn together in such a way that they might look like one.

"With your kind permission and just one minute," I said to him and went into my bungalow.

Out I came, carrying in my hands my modest fieldglass. I carried it before me with a great solemnity, as if it were the holiest object under heaven.

I stepped close to the fence where the Mexican stood, high expectancy in his eyes.

In a mumbled voice I now spoke to the glass, moving it at the same time around over my head, now to the left, now to the right, also moving it towards the man who was watching me with an ever growing bewilderment.

Now I pressed the glass firmly to my eyes. I bent down and searched the ground while walking round and round, slowly lifting up the glass until it was at a level with the far horizon. For many minutes I scanned the horizon, searching every part of it while moving round in a circle. And I said, loud enough so that he would understand it: "Donde estás, mujer? Where

are you, woman? Answer, or I'll make you by hell's or
heaven's force!"

Another idea came to my mind at this minute. I whispered
to him: "Where's the village you come from?"

He tried to answer. His excitement did not allow him to
speak, though he had his mouth wide open. He swallowed
several times and then pointed, with one arm only slightly
raised, towards the north.

So I knew that I had to find his woman towards south to
make my medicine work properly for his benefit and mine.

Now, all of a sudden, I yelled: "I see her. Ya la veo. I see
her. There she is now, at last. Poor woman. Oh, that poor,
poor woman. A man beats her terribly. He has a black
moustache, that man who beats her has. I don't know who he
is. I am sure I've seen him once or twice in this village here.
Oh, that devil of a man, how he beats that poor woman. And
she cries out loud: 'Ay mi hombre, my dear husband, come,
come quick and help me; fetch me away from that brute who
has taken me by force and without my will; I want to come
home and cook frijoles for you because I know you must be
hungry after so much hard work in the bush; help me, help
me, come quick!' That's what she cries. Oh, I can't stand it
any longer; it's too terrible."

I was breathing heavily, as if entirely exhausted from the
trance I had been in.

No sooner had I stopped and taken the glass off my eyes
than the man, sweat all over his face, shouted as if going mad:
"Didn't I tell you, señor? I knew all the time that it must be
that dirty dog Pánfilo who has raped her. He has got a black
moustache. I knew it all the time. He was after her since we
came to this part. Always after her and always around the
house whenever I was working in the bush. All the neighbors
knew it because they told me so. I haven't sharpened my
machete just for the fun of it. I knew that I would need a

sharp edge somehow, somewhere and for someone, to cut off
his stinking head. Now I'll have to hurry to get her and get at
the same time that Pánfilo cabron. Where is she, señor, quick,
quick, pronto, pronto, say it. Ask her. Tell her that I'm on my
way already."

I looked through my glass once more and mumbled something as if asking someone a few questions. Now I said: "She is
mil miles away from here, your woman is. The man with the
black moustache has carried her far away, I think with an air-
wagon, perhaps. She says that she is in Naranjitos. That's way
down in that direction." I pointed towards the southeast. "It is
only mil miles from here and along a trail not so very hard to
go by."

"Well, then, señor mister, excuse me, but now I have got to
hurry to fetch her and leave my marks on that Pánfilo dog."

He picked up his morral, a little bag, from the ground. It
contained all he possessed on earth, a fact which made his life
and his goings so easy, and it would have made him a truly
happy man had it not been for women who would never be
satisfied with such a little bast bag instead of some solid furni-
ture or an electric refrigerator.

He became extremely restless now, so I thought it a good
opportunity to give him another shot of the medicine.
"Hustle, amigo, hurry up, or, dear God in heaven, you will miss
her. And don't you dare stop on your way. You know it's
more than mil days to walk. That rascal with the black
moustache is likely to carry her farther away still. You'd
better go right now, this very minute."

"This certainly I will do, señor, since you say so. This very
second I shall go. In fact, I'm running already." His feet were
dancing about as if the ground consisted of embers. I knew
that something still held him back, or he would have been a
quarter of a mile off already.

It was his courtesy, the courtesy of the primitive man, that

kept him still here. After a few wrong starts which seemed not
to satisfy him, he at last found the right words. "Many, many
thanks, señor, mil, mil gracias for your magnificent medicine."
The word magnífica appeared to be one of the new words he
had heard last night from the villagers, for he stumbled on it,
but he would not lose the opportunity to use it for me. "The
people in the village," he continued, "are right about you.
Truly and verily you are a great medicine man. You know all
the hidden secrets of the world. You found her so quickly,
much sooner than I could ever have expected. Of course, the
two pesos and forty-six centavitos I promised you for your
medicine, señor, I cannot pay now. I am very sorry for that.
But you are a great doctor, surely you are, therefore you will
understand that I cannot pay for the medicine now. You'll
have to be satisfied with my thanks, which are honest by all
means. You see, señor mister, the money I need for my trip.
That's why I cannot part with my money and pay you off.
You surely will understand this easily since you're such a very
wise man. Adiós, señor, adiós, and again mil, mil gracias."

And he was off like a hunted deer, without looking back.
One minute later the bush had swallowed him up.

Never have I cheated a Mexican. I did not cheat that man
either. The medicine I gave him is the best he could ever get.
No other doctor would have prescribed him such a good
medicine.

The village I named is about five hundred miles from here.
He is without funds, save those two pesos and forty-six
centavos. So he will have to walk the whole way. No hitch-
hiking for him, because there is no highway. As there is no
highway there cannot be motorcars. Even if there were
motorcars none would pick him up. Latin Americans are not
dumb enough to pick up strangers parked along the highways.

It is an excellent medicine for him and for me. It saves me
from the surprise of finding myself with my head chopped off.

He is a strong and healthy fellow, and he is used to hard work. He won't go fifty miles, and he will find some work or a job. Or he will steal a stray cow and sell it to a butcher in one of the villages through which he passes. In the meantime, and more than a half dozen times, he will have had his belly filled with tortillas, frijoles, and green chili. His belly satisfactorily full, he will forget his grief. Once he has found some work, he will stay on in a village in the end. Once there, it won't be one week before a woman will believe herself fairly lucky if allowed to cook frijoles and toast tortillas for him, and also hang her basket, or a sugar sack with her Sunday dress in it, at a peg inside the jacalito he will eventually, and quite predictably, occupy.

Assembly Line

Mr. E. L. Winthrop of New York was on vacation in the Republic of Mexico. It wasn't long before he realized that this strange and really wild country had not yet been fully and satisfactorily explored by Rotarians and Lions, who are forever conscious of their glorious mission on earth. Therefore, he considered it his duty as a good American citizen to do his part in correcting this oversight.

In search for opportunities to indulge in his new avocation, he left the beaten track and ventured into regions not especially mentioned, and hence not recommended, by travel agents to foreign tourists. So it happened that one day he found himself in a little, quaint Indian village somewhere in the State of Oaxaca.

Walking along the dusty main street of this pueblecito, which knew nothing of pavements, drainage, plumbing, or of any means of artificial light save candles or pine splinters, he met with an Indian squatting on the earthen-floor front porch of a palm hut, a so-called jacalito.

The Indian was busy making little baskets from bast and from all kinds of fibers gathered by him in the immense

73

tropical bush which surrounded the village on all sides. The
material used had not only been well prepared for its purpose
but was also richly colored with dyes that the basket-maker
himself extracted from various native plants, barks, roots and
from certain insects by a process known only to him and the
members of his family.

His principal business, however, was not producing baskets.
He was a peasant who lived on what the small property he
possessed—less than fifteen acres of not too fertile soil—would
yield, after much sweat and labor and after constantly worrying over the most wanted and best suited distribution of rain,
sunshine, and wind and the changing balance of birds and
insects beneficial or harmful to his crops. Baskets he made
when there was nothing else for him to do in the fields,
because he was unable to dawdle. After all, the sale of his
baskets, though to a rather limited degree only, added to the
small income he received from his little farm.

In spite of being by profession just a plain peasant, it was
clearly seen from the small baskets he made that at heart he was
an artist, a true and accomplished artist. Each basket looked as
if covered all over with the most beautiful sometimes fantastic
ornaments, flowers, butterflies, birds, squirrels, antelope, tigers,
and a score of other animals of the wilds. Yet, the most
amazing thing was that these decorations, all of them sym-
phonies of color, were not painted on the baskets but were
instead actually part of the baskets themselves. Bast and fibers
dyed in dozens of different colors were so cleverly—one must
actually say intrinsically—interwoven that those attractive
designs appeared on the inner part of the basket as well as on
the outside. Not by painting but by weaving were those
highly artistic effects achieved. This performance he accomplished without ever looking at any sketch or pattern. While
working on a basket these designs came to light as if by magic,
and as long as a basket was not entirely finished one could not

perceive what in this case or that the decoration would be like.

People in the market town who bought these baskets would use them for sewing baskets or to decorate tables with or window sills, or to hold little things to keep them from lying around. Women put their jewelry in them or flowers or little dolls. There were in fact a hundred and two ways they might serve certain purposes in a household or in a lady's own room.

Whenever the Indian had finished about twenty of the baskets he took them to town on market day. Sometimes he would already be on his way shortly after midnight because he owned only a burro to ride on, and if the burro had gone astray the day before, as happened frequently, he would have to walk the whole way to town and back again.

At the market he had to pay twenty centavos in taxes to sell his wares. Each basket cost him between twenty and thirty hours of constant work, not counting the time spent gathering bast and fibers, preparing them, making dyes and coloring the bast. All this meant extra time and work. The price he asked for each basket was fifty centavos, the equivalent of about four cents. It seldom happened, however, that a buyer paid outright the full fifty centavos asked—or four reales as the Indian called that money. The prospective buyer started bargaining, telling the Indian that he ought to be ashamed to ask such a sinful price. "Why, the whole dirty thing is nothing but ordinary petate straw which you find in heaps wherever you may look for it; the jungle is packed full of it," the buyer would argue. "Such a little basket, what's it good for anyhow? If I paid you, you thief, ten centavitos for it you should be grateful and kiss my hand. Well, it's your lucky day, I'll be generous this time, I'll pay you twenty, yet not one green centavo more. Take it or run along."

So he sold finally for twenty-five centavos, but then the buyer would say, "Now, what do you think of that? I've got

only twenty centavos change on me. What can we do about
that? If you can change me a twenty-peso bill, all right, you
shall have your twenty-five fierros." Of course, the Indian
could not change a twenty-peso bill and so the basket went for
twenty centavos.

He had little if any knowledge of the outside world or he
would have known that what happened to him was happening
every hour of every day to every artist all over the world.
That knowledge would perhaps have made him very proud,
because he would have realized that he belonged to the little
army which is the salt of the earth and which keeps culture,
urbanity and beauty for their own sake from passing away.

Often it was not possible for him to sell all the baskets he
had brought to market, for people here as elsewhere in the
world preferred things made by the millions and each so much
like the other that you were unable, even with the help of a
magnifying glass, to tell which was which and where was the
difference between two of the same kind.

Yet he, this craftsman, had in his life made several hundreds
of those exquisite baskets, but so far no two of them had he
ever turned out alike in design. Each was an individual piece
of art and as different from the other as was a Murillo from a
Velásquez.

Naturally he did not want to take those baskets which he
could not sell at the market place home with him again if he
could help it. In such a case he went peddling his products
from door to door where he was treated partly as a beggar and
partly as a vagrant apparently looking for an opportunity to
steal, and he frequently had to swallow all sorts of insults and
nasty remarks.

Then, after a long run, perhaps a woman would finally stop
him, take one of the baskets and offer him ten centavos, which
price through talks and talks would perhaps go up to fifteen or
even to twenty. Nevertheless, in many instances he would

actually get no more than just ten centavos, and the buyer, usually a woman, would grasp that little marvel and right before his eyes throw it carelessly upon the nearest table as if to say, "Well, I take that piece of nonsense only for charity's sake. I know my money is wasted. But then, after all, I'm a Christian and I can't see a poor Indian die of hunger since he has come such a long way from his village." This would remind her of something better and she would hold him and say, "Where are you at home anyway, Indito? What's your pueblo? So, from Huehuetonoc? Now, listen here, Indito, can't you bring me next Saturday two or three turkeys from Huehuetonoc? But they must be heavy and fat and very, very cheap or I won't even touch them. If I wish to pay the regular price I don't need you to bring them. Understand? Hop along, now, Indito."

The Indian squatted on the earthen floor in the portico of his hut, attended to his work and showed no special interest in the curiosity of Mr. Winthrop watching him. He acted almost as if he ignored the presence of the American altogether.

"How much that little basket, friend?" Mr. Winthrop asked when he felt that he at least had to say something as not to appear idiotic.

"Fifty centavitos, patroncito, my good little lordy, four reales," the Indian answered politely.

"All right, sold," Mr. Winthrop blurted out in a tone and with a wide gesture as if he had bought a whole railroad. And examining his buy he added, "I know already who I'll give that pretty little thing to. She'll kiss me for it, sure. Wonder what she'll use it for?"

He had expected to hear a price of three or even four pesos. The moment he realized that he had judged the value six times too high, he saw right away what great business possibilities this miserable Indian village might offer to a dynamic promoter like himself. Without further delay he started exploring those possibilities. "Suppose, my good friend, I buy ten of these little baskets of yours which, as I might as well admit right here and now, have practically no real use whatsoever. Well, as I was saying, if I buy ten, how much would you then charge me apiece?"

The Indian hesitated for a few seconds as if making calculations. Finally he said, "If you buy ten I can let you have them for forty-five centavos each, señorito gentleman."

"All right, amigo. And now, let's suppose I buy from you straight away one hundred of these absolutely useless baskets, how much will cost me each?"

The Indian, never fully looking up to the American standing before him and hardly taking his eyes off his work, said politely and without the slightest trace of enthusiasm in his voice, "In such a case I might not be quite unwilling to sell each for forty centavitos."

Mr. Winthrop bought sixteen baskets, which was all the Indian had in stock.

After three weeks' stay in the Republic, Mr. Winthrop was convinced that he knew this country perfectly, that he had seen everything and knew all about the inhabitants, their character and their way of life, and that there was nothing left for him to explore. So he returned to good old Nooyorg and felt happy to be once more in a civilized country, as he expressed it to himself.

One day going out for lunch he passed a confectioner's and, looking at the display in the window, he suddenly remembered the little baskets he had bought in that faraway Indian village.

He hurried home and took all the baskets he still had left to one of the best-known candy-makers in the city.

"I can offer you here," Mr. Winthrop said to the confectioner, "one of the most artistic and at the same time the most original of boxes, if you wish to call them that. These little baskets would be just right for the most expensive chocolates meant for elegant and high-priced gifts. Just have a good look at them, sir, and let me listen."

The confectioner examined the baskets and found them extraordinarily well suited for a certain line in his business. Never before had there been anything like them for originality, prettiness and good taste. He, however, avoided most carefully showing any sign of enthusiasm, for which there would be time enough once he knew the price and whether he could get a whole load exclusively.

He shrugged his shoulders and said, "Well, I don't know. If you asked me I'd say it isn't quite what I'm after. However, we might give it a try. It depends, of course, on the price. In our business the package mustn't cost more than what's in it."

"Do I hear an offer?" Mr. Winthrop asked.

"Why don't you tell me in round figures how much you want for them? I'm not good in guessing."

"Well, I'll tell you, Mr. Kemple: since I'm the smart guy who discovered these baskets and since I'm the only Jack who knows where to lay his hands on more, I'm selling to the highest bidder, on an exclusive basis, of course. I'm positive you can see it my way, Mr. Kemple."

"Quite so, and may the best man win," the confectioner said. "I'll talk the matter over with my partners. See me tomorrow same time, please, and I'll let you know how far we might be willing to go."

Next day when both gentlemen met again Mr. Kemple said: "Now, to be frank with you, I know art on seeing it, no getting around that. And these baskets are little works of art, they surely are. However, we are no art dealers, you realize that of course. We've no other use for these pretty little things except as fancy packing for our French pralines made by us. We can't pay for them what we might pay considering them pieces of art. After all to us they're only wrappings. Fine wrappings, perhaps, but nevertheless wrappings. You'll see it our way I hope, Mr.——oh yes, Mr. Winthrop. So, here is our offer, take it or leave it: a dollar and a quarter apiece and not one cent more."

Mr. Winthrop made a gesture as if he had been struck over the head.

The confectioner, misunderstanding this involuntary gesture of Mr. Winthrop, added quickly, "All right, all right, no reason to get excited, no reason at all. Perhaps we can do a trifle better. Let's say one-fifty."

"Make it one-seventy-five," Mr. Winthrop snapped, swallowing his breath while wiping his forehead.

"Sold. One-seventy-five apiece free at port of New York. We pay the customs and you pay the shipping. Right?"

"Sold," Mr. Winthrop said also and the deal was closed.

"There is, of course, one condition," the confectioner explained just when Mr. Winthrop was to leave. "One or two hundred won't do for us. It wouldn't pay the trouble and the advertising. I won't consider less than ten thousand, or one thousand dozens if that sounds better in your ears. And they must come in no less than twelve different patterns well assorted. How about that?"

"I can make it sixty different patterns or designs."

"So much the better. And you're sure you can deliver ten thousand let's say early October?"

"Absolutely," Mr. Winthrop avowed and signed the contract.

Practically all the way back to Mexico, Mr. Winthrop had a notebook in his left hand and a pencil in his right and he was writing figures, long rows of them, to find out exactly how much richer he would be when this business had been put through.

"Now, let's sum up the whole goddamn thing," he muttered to himself. "Damn it, where is that cursed pencil again? I had it right between my fingers. Ah, there it is. Ten thousand he ordered. Well, well, there we got a clean-cut profit of fifteen thousand four hundred and forty genuine dollars. Sweet smackers. Fifteen grand right into papa's pocket. Come to think of it, that Republic isn't so backward after all."

"Buenas tardes, mi amigo, how are you?" he greeted the Indian whom he found squatting in the porch of his jacalito as if he had never moved from his place since Mr. Winthrop had left for New York.

The Indian rose, took off his hat, bowed politely and said in his soft voice, "Be welcome, patroncito. Thank you, I feel fine, thank you. Muy buenas tardes. This house and all I have is at your kind disposal." He bowed once more, moved his right hand in a gesture of greeting and sat down again. But he excused himself for doing so by saying, "Perdoneme, patroncito, I have to take advantage of the daylight, soon it will be night."

"I've got big business for you, my friend," Mr. Winthrop began.

"Good to hear that, señor."

Mr. Winthrop said to himself, "Now, he'll jump up and go wild when he learns what I've got for him." And aloud he said: "Do you think you can make me one thousand of these little baskets?"

"Why not, patroncito? If I can make sixteen, I can make one thousand also."

"That's right, my good man. Can you also make five thousand?"

"Of course, señor. I can make five thousand if I can make one thousand."

"Good. Now, if I should ask you to make me ten thousand,

what would you say? And what would be the price of each?
You can make ten thousand, can't you?"

"Of course, I can, señor. I can make as many as you wish.
You see, I am an expert in this sort of work. No one else in the
whole state can make them the way I do."

"That's what I thought and that's exactly why I came to
you."

"Thank you for the honor, patroncito."

"Suppose I order you to make me ten thousand of these
baskets, how much time do you think you would need to
deliver them?"

The Indian, without interrupting his work, cocked his head
to one side and then to the other as if he were counting the
days or weeks it would cost him to make all these baskets.

After a few minutes he said in a slow voice, "It will take a
good long time to make so many baskets, patroncito. You see,
the bast and the fibers must be very dry before they can be
used properly. Then all during the time they are slowly
drying, they must be worked and handled in a very special
way so that while drying they won't lose their softness and
their flexibility and their natural brilliance. Even when dry
they must look fresh. They must never lose their natural
properties or they will look just as lifeless and dull as straw.
Then while they are drying up I got to get the plants and roots
and barks and insects from which I brew the dyes. That takes
much time also, believe me. The plants must be gathered when
the moon is just right or they won't give the right color. The
insects I pick from the plants must also be gathered at the right
time and under the right conditions or else they produce no
rich colors and are just like dust. But, of course, jefecito, I can
make as many of these canastitas as you wish, even as many as
three dozens if you want them. Only give me time."

"Three dozens? Three dozens?" Mr. Winthrop yelled, and
threw up both arms in desperation. "Three dozens!" he re-

peated as if he had to say it many times in his own voice so as to understand the real meaning of it, because for a while he thought that he was dreaming. He had expected the Indian to go crazy on hearing that he was to sell ten thousand of his baskets without having to peddle them from door to door and be treated like a dog with a skin disease.

So the American took up the question of price again, by which he hoped to activate the Indian's ambition. "You told me that if I take one hundred baskets you will let me have them for forty centavos apiece. Is that right, my friend?"

"Quite right, jefecito."

"Now," Mr. Winthrop took a deep breath, "now, then, if I ask you to make me one thousand, that is, ten times one hundred baskets, how much will they cost me, each basket?"

That figure was too high for the Indian to grasp. He became slightly confused and for the first time since Mr. Winthrop had arrived he interrupted his work and tried to think it out. Several times he shook his head and looked vaguely around as if for help. Finally he said, "Excuse me, jefecito, little chief, that is by far too much for me to count. Tomorrow, if you will do me the honor, come and see me again and I think I shall have my answer ready for you, patroncito."

When on the next morning Mr. Winthrop came to the hut he found the Indian as usual squatting on the floor under the overhanging palm roof working at his baskets.

"Have you got the price for ten thousand?" he asked the Indian the very moment he saw him, without taking the trouble to say "Good Morning!"

"Si, patroncito, I have the price ready. You may believe me when I say it has cost me much labor and worry to find out the exact price, because, you see, I do not wish to cheat you out of your honest money."

"Skip that, amigo. Come out with the salad. What's the price?" Mr. Winthrop asked nervously.

"The price is well calculated now without any mistake on my side. If I got to make one thousand canastitas each will be three pesos. If I must make five thousand, each will cost nine pesos. And if I have to make ten thousand, in such a case I can't make them for less than fifteen pesos each." Immediately he returned to his work as if he were afraid of losing too much time with such idle talk.

Mr. Winthrop thought that perhaps it was his faulty knowledge of this foreign language that had played a trick on him.

"Did I hear you say fifteen pesos each if I eventually would buy ten thousand?"

"That's exactly and without any mistake what I've said, patroncito," the Indian answered in his soft courteous voice.

"But now, see here, my good man, you can't do this to me. I'm your friend and I want to help you get on your feet."

"Yes, patroncito, I know this and I don't doubt any of your words."

"Now, let's be patient and talk this over quietly as man to man. Didn't you tell me that if I would buy one hundred you would sell each for forty centavos?"

"Si, jefecito, that's what I said. If you buy one hundred you can have them for forty centavos apiece, provided that I have one hundred, which I don't."

"Yes, yes, I see that." Mr. Winthrop felt as if he would go insane any minute now. "Yes, so you said. Only what I can't comprehend is why you cannot sell at the same price if you make me ten thousand. I certainly don't wish to chisel on the price. I am not that kind. Only, well, let's see now, if you can sell for forty centavos at all, be it for twenty or fifty or a hundred, I can't quite get the idea why the price has to jump that high if I buy more than a hundred."

"Bueno, patroncito, what is there so difficult to understand? It's all very simple. One thousand canastitas cost me a hundred times more work than a dozen. Ten thousand cost me so much time and labor that I could never finish them, not even in a hundred years. For a thousand canastitas I need more bast than for a hundred, and I need more little red beetles and more plants and roots and bark for the dyes. It isn't that you just can walk into the bush and pick all the things you need at your heart's desire. One root with the true violet blue may cost me four or five days until I can find one in the jungle. And have you thought how much time it costs and how much hard work to prepare the bast and fibers? What is more, if I must make so many baskets, who then will look after my corn and my beans and my goats and chase for me occasionally a rabbit for meat on Sunday? If I have no corn, then I have no tortillas to eat, and if I grow no beans, where do I get my frijoles from?"

"But since you'll get so much money from me for your baskets you can buy all the corn and beans in the world and more than you need."

"That's what you think, señorito, little lordy. But you see, it is only the corn I grow myself that I am sure of. Of the corn which others may or may not grow, I cannot be sure to feast upon."

"Haven't you got some relatives here in this village who might help you to make baskets for me?" Mr. Winthrop asked hopefully.

"Practically the whole village is related to me somehow or other. Fact is, I got lots of close relatives in this here place."

"Why then can't they cultivate your fields and look after your goats while you make baskets for me? Not only this, they might gather for you the fibers and the colors in the bush and lend you a hand here and there in preparing the material you need for the baskets."

"They might, patroncito, yes, they might. Possible. But then you see who would take care of their fields and cattle if they work for me? And if they help me with the baskets it turns out the same. No one would any longer work his fields properly. In such a case corn and beans would get up so high in price that none of us could buy any and we all would starve to death. Besides, as the price of everything would rise and rise higher still how could I make baskets at forty centavos apiece? A pinch of salt or one green chili would set me back more than I'd collect for one single basket. Now you'll understand, highly estimated caballero and jefecito, why I can't make the baskets any cheaper than fifteen pesos each if I got to make that many."

Mr. Winthrop was hard-boiled, no wonder considering the city he came from. He refused to give up the more than fifteen thousand dollars which at that moment seemed to slip through his fingers like nothing. Being really desperate now, he talked and bargained with the Indian for almost two full hours, trying to make him understand how rich he, the Indian, would become if he would take this greatest opportunity of his life.

The Indian never ceased working on his baskets while he explained his points of view.

"You know, my good man," Mr. Winthrop said, "such a wonderful chance might never again knock on your door, do you realize that? Let me explain to you in ice-cold figures what fortune you might miss if you leave me flat on this deal."

He tore out leaf after leaf from his notebook, covered each with figures and still more figures, and while doing so told the peasant he would be the richest man in the whole district.

The Indian without answering watched with a genuine expression of awe as Mr. Winthrop wrote down these long figures, executing complicated multiplications and divisions and subtractions so rapidly that it seemed to him the greatest miracle he had ever seen.

The American, noting this growing interest in the Indian, misjudged the real significance of it. "There you are, my friend," he said. "That's exactly how rich you're going to be.

You'll have a bankroll of exactly four thousand pesos. And to show you that I'm a real friend of yours, I'll throw in a bonus. I'll make it a round five thousand pesos, and all in silver."

The Indian, however, had not for one moment thought of four thousand pesos. Such an amount of money had no meaning to him. He had been interested solely in Mr. Winthrop's ability to write figures so rapidly.

"So, what do you say now? Is it a deal or is it? Say yes and you'll get your advance this very minute."

"As I have explained before, patroncito, the price is fifteen pesos each."

"But, my good man," Mr. Winthrop shouted at the poor Indian in utter despair, "where have you been all this time? On the moon or where? You are still at the same price as before."

"Yes, I know that, jefecito, my little chief," the Indian answered, entirely unconcerned. "It must be the same price because I cannot make any other one. Besides, señor, there's still another thing which perhaps you don't know. You see, my good lordy and caballero, I've to make these canastitas my own way and with my song in them and with bits of my soul woven into them. If I were to make them in great numbers there would no longer be my soul in each, or my songs. Each would look like the other with no difference whatever and such a thing would slowly eat up my heart. Each has to be another song which I hear in the morning when the sun rises and when the birds begin to chirp and the butterflies come and sit down on my baskets so that I may see a new beauty, because, you see, the butterflies like my baskets and the pretty colors on them, that's why they come and sit down, and I can make my canastitas after them. And now, señor jefecito, if you will kindly excuse me, I have wasted much time already, although it was a pleasure and a great honor to hear the talk of such a distinguished caballero like you. But I'm afraid I've to attend to my work now, for day after tomorrow is market day in town and I got to take my baskets there. Thank you, señor, for your visit. Adiós."

And in this way it happened that American garbage cans escaped the fate of being turned into receptacles for empty, torn, and crumpled little multicolored canastitas into which an Indian of Mexico had woven dreams of his soul, throbs of his heart: his unsung poems.

The Cattle Drive

Next to me in the snack bar was an American, an elderly man, and obviously a rancher.

"Are you looking for something?" he asked.

"Yes, the sugar!" And he passed me the enamelled bowl.

"I didn't mean that," he said, smiling. "What I meant was, would you like to earn some money?"

"I always like earning money," I replied.

"Have you ever cut out cattle?"

"I grew up on a cattle farm."

"Then I've got a job for you!"

"Really?"

"A thousand head of cattle, sixty heavy bulls among them, to be driven three hundred and fifty miles overland.

"Agreed!" I shook his hand. "Where shall I meet you?"

"Hotel Palacio. At five. In the lobby."

These cattle couldn't be transported by rail for there were no facilities for that. And as to overland drive there existed only few roads, many mountain ranges had to be crossed, swamps by-passed, rivers forded. Grazing pasture and water had to be found every day.

"Three hundred and fifty miles?" I asked the rancher when we met to talk it over. "As the crow flies?"

"Yes, as the crow flies," said the rancher. Mr. Pratt was his name.

"Dammit, boss, that might turn out to be six hundred."

"Not so unlikely, but as far as I've figured, it might be possible to keep a fairly direct route."

"What about pay?"

"Six pesos a day. I provide horse, saddle, and equipment. You got to cook your own food on the way. I'll send six of my men to whom the animals are well used along with you. Indians. The foreman, a mestizo, will also go with you. He's quite a good man. Reliable. I might perhaps trust him with the herd. But no. If he sells the herd on the way, and bolts, I could do nothing about it. His wife and children live on my ranch, but that's no security!—you could search for the likes of him forevermore in this country. Besides, I wouldn't like to give him so much money to carry about. On the other hand, I couldn't send him off without money. There are so many expenses on the drive, it's not fair to tempt any man that way. As for me, I can't stay away from the rancho that long . . . the bandits'd be around the place before you could say *knife*. That's why I'd like to get hold of a gringo like you to take over the drive."

"Well, I don't know if I'm as honest as you think. Not yet, anyhow," I said with a laugh. "I, too, know how to bolt with a herd. After all, you've just picked me up in the street."

"I judge a man by his face," Mr. Pratt went on. Then, after a pause: "To be perfectly honest, I'm not trusting entirely to luck. I know you."

"You know me? I can't imagine how."

"Didn't you work for a farmer Shine?"

"Yes."

"I saw you there. And I have Mr. Shine's word that I can rely on you. So you'll have the contract, you'll drive the herd, and I'll advance you money to pay your daily expenses."

"Very well! But what about the contract bonus?"

Mr. Pratt was silent for a while, then took out his notebook, made a few calculations, and said: "I've leased pastureland near the port, two miles from the main terminal market. It's well fenced. There, I can wait for cattle-buyers to come to me, and I'll probably get orders for several shiploads. If not, I'll sell the herd in small lots. I've got a good and very reliable agent there who's been working with me for years, and has always got good prices . . ."

"That's all very well," I interjected, "but what about my contract and bonus?"

"All right, for each head that you drive through, sound from horn to hoof, I'll pay you sixty centavos extra. If your losses are less than two per cent, I'll give you a hundred-peso bonus on top of that, plus your pay."

"What about the losses?"

"I'll deduct twenty-five pesos for every head lost above two per cent," said Mr. Pratt.

"Just a moment," I broke in. I made a few quick calculations myself on the margin of a newspaper. "Sold," I agreed. "Let me have a note of the contract."

He tore a leaf out of his little notebook, wrote the conditions of our contract in pencil, signed it and handed it to me. "Your address?" he asked.

"My address? That's an awkward point!" (I really didn't have an address.) "Let's say right here, Hotel Palacio."

"Okay. All right."

"How do matters stand at present? Has the herd been cut out?"

"No, not a single head has been cut out, yet. There'll be a

few yearlings, but most of the herd'll be two- and three-year-
olds. Yes, a few four-year-olds, too. I'll help you cut them
out."

"All branded?"

"All of them. No trouble there."

"What about the leader bulls?"

"That's your problem. You'll have to see about them."

"All right by me. I can manage to pick them."

Mr. Pratt got up. "Now let's have a drink, and then you're
going to have dinner with me. Afterwards, I've got some
private business to attend to, before we leave for the ranch."

What his private business was, that was no concern of mine.
I'm not curious when it comes to private business. One of the
many reasons why I am still alive.

The following morning, after breakfast on his ranch, we
saddled up and rode out to the prairie to see if I could pick out
a horse for myself. These horses were born, bred, and raised
out in the wide open; there was no horse stable on Mr. Pratt's
ranch, and so these horses were wild. They were shaggy, long-
maned and long-tailed, though rather small; and they galloped
off at the mere scent of man.

Two or three times a year these horses were rounded up,
and driven into a corral close to the ranch. Here they were
fed, and watered, so as to get used to man; they were tied up,
bridled, saddled, and eventually mounted before being turned
loose again on the range. And thus, with patience and care, the
horses were kept this side of remaining wild. The trainers
were careful never to break the horse's spirit, nor hurt his
pride, nor curb his natural mettle.

I picked out a horse, neither the wildest nor the tamest, but
one which looked as if it would stand the strenuous trek. We
closed in on him, lassoed him, and took him back to the ranch,
where I left him to his peace, tied to a tree. Later, I threw him

some grain, which he ignored. Then some fresh grass, which he likewise declined. So I let him go hungry and thirsty overnight. In the morning, I brought him more grass; but he shied off, to the end of his rope. Then I put some water in front of him, which he immediately tipped over as he wasn't used to drinking from a bucket, for he'd drunk only from streamlets and rain pools.

In time I made him, or rather his hunger made him, feed and drink; and so he came to associate food with my presence. Within two days I could come up to him and pat him gently on the back. He trembled, but after a while the trembling ceased. I could not, of course not, spend all my time with the horse, only moments when we came to the rancho for meals; meanwhile we were very busy cutting out the herd.

When the horse had become used to me, I put a bitless bridle on him, with a bridle strap fastened outside around his mouth. If a horse hasn't been ruined by rough handling, you can ride him without any iron in the mouth. In fact, he responds wonderfully; the assumption that you can master a horse only if you tear its mouth open, or dig its sides raw with a spur, is utterly false.

At last I saddled him. And every time I came to the ranch to eat, I tightened the straps. At the same time I pressed the saddle and put weight on it as if I was going to mount. Then I let down the stirrups, so they dangled freely and knocked against his flanks. Now I moved about as if to mount by putting a boot in the stirrup. At the first attempt, he kicked and danced away; but in a few days he was well accustomed to the knocking and dangling of the stirrups. Then I jumped on, got one leg over the saddle, and jumped off again.

All this time, the horse had been tied, sometimes on a long rope, sometimes on a short one. At last I ventured to mount. I blindfolded him and got into the saddle. He stood still and trembled all over his body. Quickly I jumped off, patted his neck and back, and kept up a flow of smooth talk. I mounted again. He turned, quivered, but danced and bucked only slightly; now he bumped against the tree, and so stopped altogether. I remained in the saddle and pressed my heels into his flanks. He became restless, but by now he realized that there was nothing to be afraid of, so I removed the blindfold. He looked about him. I, still in the saddle, spoke to him, patted him, reassured him.

Next, I had to discover whether or not he was suitable for riding. From the first day I had been tapping him gently on the rump with a switch, to accustom him to this signal. One day I mounted him, and winked to a boy nearby to untie him. The horse stood still, having no idea of what was expected of him. I tapped him with the switch. Nothing doing. Then he got a good sharp blow, and lo! he started off. I kept him under control, out on the prairie, where he could run freely. He ran, and even galloped, but I kept holding him back more and more, until he realized that this was a signal to stop or fall into a different gait. Through all this time of training, I managed to keep my patience, never to break his pride, and so this strong, shaggy three-year-old became a good horse. I called him Gitano, which means Gypsy.

Whether in the long history of mankind a colt had ever been trained for riding in a similar way before, I don't know. Anyhow the way I had done it produced lasting results so my training system cannot have been so very wrong, after all. And now the herd had to be cut out. I possessed not the slightest notion what was meant by that and how it had to be done. Never in my life had I driven even as few as fifty cattle from one pasture to the next. Now, since Mr. Pratt was hawk-like, watching every move I made preparing the herd for the long march, I was forced to show off here and there. If you wish you may call it bluffing shamelessly. Perhaps you are right. If I had never tried bluffing at some critical occasions in my existence on earth I would have lost my life long, long ago.

My idea (if it was good or wrong, this I did not know) was to form a little group of the animals, sort of a family center of the whole transport around which smaller groups might gather and thus keep together more naturally—since cattle belong to the species of animals who for many good reasons prefer to live in groups or herds, as do dogs, horses, wolves, elephants, antelope, zebras, also fish.

Meantime, we had started cutting out the herd. First, I cut out the bulls, looking for a leader bull. We cut and drove into the cattle corral the bulls I had picked, and I let them go hungry. I continued putting the herd, the two- and three-year-olds and the oxen, as well as the rest of the eighty bulls, into another enclosure. I examined every one to make sure that it was healthy enough for the long trek; and all these were fenced into a field so that they might get the herd feeling. When I had three hundred head in that enclosure, I believed the bulls were ready.

We drove them into the field with the picked herd, and the battle for leader began. The bulls who were indifferent to the honor got by themselves as far out of the way as possible, and the battle soon centered on five of them. The victor, still bleeding profusely, charged towards one of the cows in heat who pushed her way towards him. We attended to all the wounded bulls immediately; and after the victor had spent himself and returned to his herd senses, he too got his medicine. For if the wounds weren't treated promptly, they'd soon be full of maggots, and it'd be a long and tedious job getting them out.

Worms, maggots, and ticks are a big problem with any herd, anywhere, but worst of all in the tropics. And if cattle start losing weight, their skin dries out, and deadens, and the lean

cattle are in danger of being eaten alive by worms and ticks.
Healthy animals, however, are attacked only by limited numbers of pests which can easily be kept under control.

Once we had cut out the thousand head of cattle, Mr. Pratt,
a very generous man, gave me five extra healthy ones as
replacements for those five in a thousand who were certain to
fall sick or fail to survive the long drive.

Then I was given a hundred pesos cash in silver for transport expenses, besides some checks I could cash in case of
emergency, and I was also given the delivery note to the
terminal pasture. Then Mr. Pratt handed me a map.

The less said about this map, the better. You can put
anything you like upon a map: roads, rivers, villages, towns,
grasslands, water pools, mountain passes, and plenty more.
Paper is patient, it won't refuse anything; but though a river
or a bridge appears on a map it doesn't mean that you're going
to find it where it is supposed to be.

It was a real joy to hear Mrs. Pratt swearing; every other
word was "son-of-a-bitch," "bastard," or "f——ing," and
more in the same beautiful strain. On a rancho like theirs, it
could be damned lonely, and the nights were long, so you
couldn't blame her for living her life as intensely as existence
on a cattle rancho permitted. How else was the poor woman to
use up the surplus energy, which, had she lived in a village or
town, would have gone into chatting and gossiping with the
neighbors all day? To her, everything was son-of-a-bitch; her
husband, I, the Indians, the fly that dropped into her coffee
cup, the Indian girl in the kitchen, her finger that she cut, the
hen that fluttered on the table and upset the soup pot, her
horse that moved too slowly; yes, every object between
heaven and earth was to Mrs. Pratt a son-of-a-bitch.

They had a phonograph and we danced nearly every evening. For a number of reasons, I preferred to dance with the

Indian kitchen-maid; but Ethel, Mrs. Pratt, danced far better and we got onto such good terms that one night she told me quite frankly in her husband's presence that she'd like to marry me if her husband should die or divorce her.

She was a fine woman, Mrs. Pratt, she certainly was, and I wouldn't hear a word against her. A woman who can handle the wildest horse, swear to make a sergeant major wince, a woman before whom tough Indian vaqueros trembled and with whom bandits kept their distance, a woman who in the presence of her husband (whom she seemed to love) could quite soberly declare that she'd like to marry me if he died or left her—damn it, a woman like that could stir you even if you didn't care much about the so-called weaker sex.

As we were leaving, Ethel Pratt stood on the long veranda and waved good-bye. "Good luck, boy! You're always welcome on this rancho. Hey, Suarez, you dirty dog, you filthy son-of-a-goddamned-old-bitch, can't you see that black one is breaking out, the son-of-a-bitch of a bull. Where are your f——ing eyes? Well, boy, good-bye!"

I waved my hat, and Gitano swept off with me.

Yes, we were off. We broke out. The yelling, the shouting, the calling, the high-pitched shrieking of the Indians; the sound of the short-handled whips cutting through the air; the trampling of hoofs and all the uproar as a column of beasts shied off, rushed away and had to be blocked in, lest it lost contact with the main herd.

The first day is always one of the hardest, so Mr. Pratt came along with us. The herd is still only loosely knit and a sense of belonging together does not develop until the transport has been under way a few days, until the herd knows the leader bull and gets the smell of mutual kinship. Then the family feeling, rather the herd feeling, emerges and the animals want to stay with their herd.

But they didn't stay together like a flock of sheep kept in order by a shepherd and a dog. For these cattle, born and raised on vast ranges among Mr. Pratt's twelve thousand-headed herd, were accustomed to space, and they wanted to spread out, run loose. The dogs we took with us couldn't make much of a showing, for they tired easily and could be used only for small jobs. Thus, it was a constant galloping back and forth, shouting and yelling.

I had a police whistle with me as a signal for the boys, the foreman had an ordinary whistle, easily distinguished from mine. I put the foreman at the head and I took the rear, as it afforded a better view of the field of transport, and it seemed easier to me to direct operations from there.

What more beautiful sight could there be than a giant herd of healthy half-wild cattle! There they were ahead of me, trampling and stamping, the heavy necks, the rounded bodies, the proud, mighty horns. It was a heaving sea of gigantic vitality, of brute nature herded along by one single purpose. And each pair of horns represented a life in itself, a life with its own will, its own desires, its own thoughts and feelings.

From saddle-height I surveyed the whole of this ocean of horns and necks and rumps. I could perhaps have walked on the broad backs of the animals across the entire herd up to the belled bulls in front.

The animals bellowed singly and in chorus. They quarrelled and pushed each other around. Shouts and calls went up. The bells clattered. The sun smiled and blazed. Everything was green. The land of perpetual summer. Oh, beautiful, wonderful land of everlasting springtime, rich with legend, dance and song! You have no equal anywhere on this earth.

I couldn't help singing. I sang whatever came into my head, hymns and sweet folk airs, love songs and ditties, operatic arias, drinking songs and bawdy songs. What did I care what

the songs were about? What did the melody matter? I sang
from a heart full of joy.

And what magic air! The hot breath of the tropical bush,
the warm sultry sweat of the mass of moving cattle, the heavy
vapors from a near-by swamp, wafted to us by the wind.

Thick droves of buzzing horseflies and other insects circled
over the trotting herd, and dense clouds of glittering greenflies
followed us to settle on the dung. Blackbirds accompanied us
in whole flocks, lighted on the backs of the beasts to pick ticks
and bugs from their hides. Untold thousands of creatures lived
off this mighty herd. Life and life! . . . everywhere nothing
but life.

Our march took us over country roads for a few days, with
fields and pastureland on either side fenced in with barbed
wire. Of course such pastures can't be used without the
owner's consent, so our herd had to graze along the roadsides,
which proved to be ample, and there were sufficient water
pools still filled from the rainy season.

When cars or trucks or pack caravans passed along the roads
there was quite some performance, for we had to push the
herd to one side; but the cattle would break away, wheel
around, and hightail it singly or in groups for several miles.
Then we'd have to give chase and round them up, drive them
into the herd again.

It was even more complicated when we came to open
pastures where other cattle were grazing in herds, often without herders. Sometimes these herds mixed in with ours, and
had to be sorted out again; on one occasion, this took practically a whole day, for we couldn't drive off a single head of
another rancher's cattle. Had we done so, it would have led to
unholy difficulties for which I, and in the last resort Mr. Pratt,
would have been held responsible.

Sometimes, we couldn't get rid of straying animals. They

insisted on following us, because they took a liking to our bulls perhaps, or liked the smell of our herd. I was always supposed to know at a glance if a stray animal got in with our herd, or one of ours lagged behind; but the brands and markings were often very similar and almost illegible. The foreman with an Indian driver was supposed to chase other herds away before our herd approached them; but it often happened that a few dozen head of our own would manage to scamper off with the other herd. Then the mix-up would be hell on hooves, and we'd be soaked with sweat and have throats like sandpaper before we got them all sorted out again.

For a general to take an army overland is child's play compared with the task of transporting a thousand head of half-wild range cattle across undeveloped, half-civilized country. Soldiers can be told what's expected of them. Herds of cattle cannot; you have to do everything yourself. You are the superior and the subordinate in one.

At around five in the afternoon we usually called a halt, depending on whether we'd reached grazing land and water. The animals could hold out without water for one day provided they had fresh grass; two days, if they had to; but on the third day water had to be found. If I couldn't find water, I'd often let the herd run freely and they'd find it by themselves; but such water might be so far off our main line of advance that we'd lose a day or so.

We set up two camps at night, one in front and one in the rear. Fires were lighted, coffee made, beans or rice cooked, camp bread was baked, and dried meat eaten with it. Then we wrapped ourselves in our blankets and slept on the bare ground, with the sky for cover, our heads upon our saddles.

I posted two watches, with reliefs, to keep jaguars away and to keep the herd together. There are cattle who like to nose around at night just as some men do; and of course all the animals are up long before dawn, grazing. We gave them plenty of time for this, as well as a long rest at high noon.

After several days, I had lost only one bull. He had been fighting and got so badly gored that we had to slaughter him. We cut out the best meat, sliced it thinly, and dried it in the broiling hot sun. To make up the loss of this one bull, a cow had calved the night before, and this presented us with a new problem. The little calf couldn't make the trek, but we didn't want to kill it. We wanted him to keep his noisy young life, and we felt sorry for the mother cow who licked her baby so lovingly. So I took the calf first on my own horse, then passed it to other riders about every halfhour.

This little calf became our pet. He was a joy, and it was always a touching sight when we handed him down to his mother, who always ran near the rider holding her calf. There was always a great licking, mooing and lowing at these re-unions, where the little calf went at her udder and she was almost beside herself with joy. When he got heavier we had to load him onto a pack mule.

If too many cows had calved, it would have been impossible to show the mothers this consideration; but it happened three times more and I could never bring myself to kill the little ones.

Ingratitude is so much a part of human character that it is best to take it for granted and not feel hurt by it. Nature on the other hand is grateful for the smallest services we render her. No animal or plant ever forgets the drink of water it receives at our hands, or the handful of fodder that we may give it. And so did the little calves and their mothers present their gratitude, although unknowingly, to us for the charity we had shown them.

We came to a large river and neither we nor the guide could discover a ford. Farther downstream we found a ferry. But the

ferryman demanded so much a head that the crossing would
have been too costly; and I had yet to face the cost of other
rivers, ferries, and toll bridges that had to be used, regardless.
While I was bargaining with the ferryman, the herd rushed on
upstream for another three miles. Here we stopped for two
days, because the grazing was very good. Here they bathed,
standing in the water for hours on end, ridding themselves of
the various vermin that perished in water.

After two days of rest, we still had to cross the river. We
started to drive them over, but as soon as they felt the incline
of the river bed, they turned back; though the river wasn't
very wide, there were deep channels.

At last I hit on an idea. Taking our machetes, we chopped
down some small trees and made a raft. We tied the lassoes
into one long line and an Indian swam across with one end of
the line. We tied the other end to the raft, as well as a second
lighter line for pulling it back. I packed one of the calves onto
the raft, the Indian pulled it over and landed the calf. We
pulled the raft back and we sent a second calf over; in a few
minutes we had all the four calves on the other side.

They stood over there alone, pathetically wobbling on their
spindly high legs and set up a chorus of wretched mooing. It
sounded pitiful. And if the mooing of those small, helpless
creatures went straight to our hearts, how much more did it
affect the mothers. The little ones had cried out only a few
times when one of the mothers took to the water and swam
across. Soon, the other three mothers followed. There was an
affectionate reunion. But we hadn't time to watch it for much
hard work awaited us.

Now the mother cows were mooing, because they were
separated from the herd; they were afraid, and longed to be
reunited with their kith and kin. The bulls listened to the
mooing for a while and then began to swim over. The leader

bull was not among them. Only younger bulls had crossed over, probably thinking they now had a chance to found a new empire on the other side away from any interference from the older bulls. The jealousy of the older, bigger bulls was thus aroused, including the leader bull. They snorted and rushed over to teach those precocious young greenhorns a lesson.

The water cooled them down, however, and by the time they got to the other side they lost the urge to fight, although they had been snorting so fiercely from the opposite bank. Now that the bulls were over, the cows had no intention of spending the rest of their lives with no bulls around; as they were in the habit of following the bulls everywhere, they followed them now. Soon the water was full of snorting, splashing cattle doing their best to swim across. It was a fine confusion of horned heads and of thrusting, monstrous backs.

When the going got perilous, some of them turned back, and this was the moment when we had to take a hand. If we let the timid ones turn back, half the herd might follow; they were all fighting, unable to keep a straight course in the swift water, and milling about and heading for any bank. So we went in with our horses, shouting, using our whips, heading them all across, across, and across to the other side. Three of them swam too far downstream, drifted out of our reach, and were swept away, lost to us.

These three were the sum total of our losses at this crossing. It was cheap at the price, for they weren't much good anyway, they'd made trouble on the transport, they were slackers, and the fewer slackers in any troop, the better. Now we let the herd have a good rest while we made camp for the night. That night one of my two-year-olds was killed by a jaguar, though none of us heard a sound of it. The carcass and paw-marks told us the story next morning.

In every respect, I got off lightly. Crossing by means of the small ferry would have taken a week, and would have cost hundreds of pesos; and even at that, I'd have suffered losses. Cattle might have jumped off the ferry or fallen victim to more jaguars or alligators had we stayed so long by the river. Thus, the pesos I saved went towards my earnings and bonus.

What I had saved at this river-crossing, I owed to my dear little calves. The love we had shown to them and their mothers had been bountifully repaid.

The cattle drive would not have seemed the real thing without bandits or rustlers. In fact, as each day passes, you feel rather surprised if they don't show up. A big cattle transport like ours can't take place in a vacuum. Dozens of men see it; it gets talked about, and you never know what pair of eyes is a scout for a band of cattle-thieves or bandits.

One morning we met them. They came riding along quite innocently and might have been ranch hands riding to market or looking for work. They approached from our flank.

"Hello!" called the leader. "Any tequila?"

"No," said I. "No tequila. But we've got some tobacco. You can have some."

"All right. We'll take it. Got any maize leaves?"

"We can spare two dozen."

"We'll take them too. Well, now, what about money? The transport must have money for ferries and toll bridges."

Things were getting hot. Money. "We've no money with us, only checks."

"Checks rubbish. Can't read."

They talked among themselves, and then the spokesman came riding alongside. "About the money. We'll look into that."

He searched my pockets, the saddlebags, saddle, and gear.

No money. He found only the checks, and had to admit that I spoke the truth.

"We could do with some cows," he decided.

"I could do with some myself," I said, "I'm not the owner, I'm only in charge of transporting these cattle."

"Then you won't be hurt if I take out one or two for myself."

"Go ahead," I agreed, "help yourself. I've one good cow, but with a lame foot. She'll be in milk in three months. You can cure the hoof, it's not bad."

"Where is she?"

I had her driven out, and he liked her. All this time, the transport had been moving on, for it couldn't be halted by a word of command, like an army, particularly since there was no grazing. The rustlers obligingly rode along beside me.

The leader said: "Well, you've given me one, and now it's my turn to pick one out for myself."

He picked one, but he didn't know much about cattle; and I didn't mind losing the one he picked.

"Now you can pick one out for me," he granted.

I did so. Then he picked himself another one.

This time he took one of the milk cows.

"Now it's your turn again, señor!" he called.

I had to have my little joke. I called the man who was carrying the milk cow's calf on his saddle. "Here you are, the little one in the bargain," I said, handing the little calf over to him. He was well satisfied with the bargain, and let the calf pass for a fully grown animal. But he wasn't acting out of generosity. Oh no. Many Indians can't milk cows; or they can milk the cow only if the calf is sucking. The milk must practically flow by itself, as if she's giving the milk to her calf. So, the calf was a welcome gift to that man. He could now get milk from the cow for his family, or for sale.

It was his turn to pick out another cow.

When they rode away, they had seven cows and one calf. Which cost me a hundred and seventy-five pesos. Of course, the possibility of bandits was duly considered when I made the contract with Mr. Pratt; and it was only a question of how I'd deal with the bandits. It's best to bargain with them, as with businessmen, and employ diplomacy, too, for they might well have driven off with fifteen, instead of seven and a half.

It all counts up as business expense; like freight demurrage. It was a business risk, such as a derailed train, a ship wrecked or burned, which would be the end of the transport. In this country, at that time, no rancher insured his herd, and no insurance company would issue a policy except at impossible rates. Bandits were a business risk, just as depot, freight, feeding, watering, taxing and licensing might be in other regions. Here, the total risks are rivers, mountains, mountain passes, gorges, sandy regions, waterless routes, bandits, jaguars, rattlesnakes, copperheads, and, if worst comes to worst, a cattle epidemic which might be caught from contact with other cattle met on the march.

Here, the cost was borne by the vastness of everything: the land, the herds, the breeding, the increase. Mr. Pratt's twelve thousand head were not among the largest herds of his region. Bandits and rustlers were just another factor. Of course, one can shoot at bandits, or threaten to call the military. Some fools may do that. You can always see it done very nicely, in films: three dozen bandits fleeing from one smart cowboy. In the movies, yes; in reality, no. In reality, it's quite, but quite, quite different.

In reality, bandits do not gallop off so easily. It is the birthright of bandits to take what they need. Three hundred years of slavery and subjugation under Spanish overlords and Church domination and torturers couldn't but demoralize the most upright people on earth. My bandits were pleased that they got everything so easily, so pleasantly, with such genial conversation, including my little calf-joke. So we all were pleased.

Now we had to make a long detour, for a biggish town lay on our route, and no grazing ground near it. We had to make our way up a river cut, and then cross a range of mountains, la Sierra.

Here, it was getting cool. There was plenty of water about, but grazing was getting tight and the animals were eating leaves from the trees. Tree foliage was as filling as grass, and seemed to make a pleasant change for the cattle. As I watched them stripping the leaves off trees so neatly I couldn't but believe that cattle in ancient times may not have been prairie and steppe beasts, but beasts of the forest, living off shrubs and low-branched trees, in woods that have nearly disappeared while tall high-growing trees have survived.

The moutain-crossing was laborious, for these range cattle were not used to mountain trails. Two lost their footholds, one of them a magnificent young bull. He went down with his cow just as they were merrily copulating. A tragedy of love. We could see them lying in the gorge below, smashed. For all that, I'd anticipated more falls.

We had two cases of snakebite, too. One morning we noticed that two of the cows had swollen legs; examination showed the fang-marks. But the cows had been lucky, evidently not fatally infected with the venom. We treated the wounds by cutting them open, bathing them in pure alcohol, and applying tourniquets above the wound. We had a two-day halt, once that crossing was behind us, and the cows picked up well. I was glad to be able to save them.

That evening two Indians started a terrible argument as to what kind of snakes those had been. One maintained for rattle-snakes, the other insisted on copperheads. I settled the dispute, which threatened to become serious, by drawing a parallel: "Castillo, if you were shot at, or worse, shot dead, it wouldn't matter to you whether you were shot with a revolver or a rifle, would it?"

"Seguro, señor, this doesn't matter. Shot is shot."

"There you are, muchachos, the same goes for cows. They've been bitten by posionous snakes, by rattlers or coppers. It hurts. As for the rest, they don't give a damn."

"You're right, señor. A poisonous snake. Who cares what kind?"

They found my dictum so clever that they turned from snakes to curability of snakebites, discussing all kinds of herbs and Indian remedies, and so their quarrel petered out.

One day at sunrise when we were calling the signal to start off, I rode up onto a hill to see beyond the herd, and decide on our direction. From hilltop, I could see church spires in the distance.

Laid about with dawn's shimmering gold, the end was in sight!

Our troubles were over. In that town over there, bathed in golden sunlight, joy awaited us. I left the herd on the prairie, ordered camp pitched, galloped into town and wired Mr. Pratt. It was evening when I got back to camp, where the fires were blazing and the two vaqueros on guard watch were riding leisurely about singing the animals to sleep.

To man, who has always been a diurnal creature, there is something indescribably uncanny about the tropic night; and tropic nights are also uncanny to diurnal animals. In the evenings, small herds gather round the rancho house to be near man, knowing that man is their protector. During the weeks after the rainy season when mosquitoes and horseflies zoom through the air, thick as swirling dust, the cattle come home from the prairies to congregate around the rancho house, expecting help. But you can't help them because you've wrapped your own face and hands in cloth to protect yourself against the evil sprites of the tropical hell.

Even great herds on their home ranches get restless at sundown. They surround the huts of the vaqueros, and the watches ride around them, singing, throughout the night, and the animals lie down to sleep. Some of the big breeders leave it to the vaqueros to sing or not, for some think it's unnecessary. But cattle not sung to sleep are restless the whole night through, lying down for ten minutes, then getting up to prowl around and rub against the others for companionship. The cattle are then sleepy next day, and feed less than cattle sung to sleep, and hence take longer to fatten into shape. During transports, singing is even more essential, for cattle are even more restless, having to lie as they do on strange earth.

So I had my men sing every night, and they did it willingly. As the men rode slowly around them, singing, the cattle would lie down with a feeling of absolute security; drowsily the cattle would follow the singing rider with their eyes, moo and low, sigh gigantically, and settle to sleep. The more singing through the night, the better. For the cattle felt reassured that nothing could happen to them, as man was near to shield them from all dangers, including jaguars and mountain lions. I might add that my own kind of cowboys' singing would keep away anyone who adored music. My own singing, for instance, was regarded as the eighth wonder of the world, but not as music.

A front watch was no longer necessary as the river guarded us and the flanks needed only the two regular watches; I took the foreman from the front, so we could all spend the last evenings together. Later, while the men smoked and chatted around the big fire, I saddled up and rode watch along the herd, singing, whistling, humming, calling to the cattle.

Clear as only the tropic night can be, the blue-black sky arched over the singing prairie along the river. The glittering stars studded the velvet night with gold. Dozens of falling stars streaked the heavens, as if winging from the high lonely dome in search of love or to give love, so unobtainable in those lonely heights where no bridge spans the void from one star to the other.

On the grassy flats, only glowworms and fireflies were visible. But invisible life sang with a million voices and made music like that of violin, flute, and harp . . . and tiny cymbal, and bell.

There lay my herd! One dark rounded form next to the other. Lowing, breathing, exhaling a full warm heavy fragrance of natural well-being, so rich in its quiet earthiness, such balm to the spirit, bringing with it such utter contentment.

My army! My proud army which I'd led over river and mountain, which I'd protected and guarded, which I'd fed and watered, whose quarrels I'd settled and whose ills I'd cured, which I'd sung to sleep night after night, for which I'd grieved and worried, for whose safety I'd trembled, and whose care had robbed me of sleep, for which I'd wept when one was lost, which I'd loved and loved, yes, loved as if it had been of my own flesh and blood!

Oh, you who took armies of warriors over the Alps to carry murder and pillage into lands of peace, what do you know of the joy, the perfect joy, of leading an army!

The next morning, the salt transport came out. I'd given them salt only once during the whole march; for it's not wise to risk salting unless you've plenty of water for them the same day, and the next. Now, however, they took salt and drank water to their fill, so they took on such a magnificent plump appearance, like soldiers with new uniforms. Their hides, well-rubbed, gleamed, as if lacquered. Yes, I was proud of my transported herd.

In a few days, Mr. Pratt arrived with his cattle-agent.

"Damn it all, man," the agent kept saying. "That's some cattle. They'll sell like hot cakes in cold season."

Mr. Pratt kept shaking my hand. "Boy oh boy, how did you do it? I didn't expect you until the end of next week. I've already sold four hundred head. There's another breeder on the way, and if you'd have been late, the price would have been lower, for this market can't take two thousand head in one week. Come on, I'll drive you into town. The foreman can manage the herd now."

In town, we settled accounts, and I had hundreds of pesos in hand. Still, he stood me to a real dinner.

"If I get a good price," said Mr. Pratt, "I'll give you another hundred pesos as an extra bonus. You've earned it. You got off lightly with those damned bandits."

"I must tell you, honestly," I admitted, "one of the bandits I knew personally, a certain Antonio. Once I picked cotton with him. He saw to it that I got off lightly."

"That's just the point. You must have good luck. Everywhere. Whether you breed cattle, drive them, or take a wife . . ." He burst out laughing. "Tell me, boy, what did you do to my wife?"

"Me? To your wife?" The food stuck in my mouth, and I thought I turned pale. Women! They can act so irresponsibly! They get all sorts of notions into their heads; out of the blue, they may get a confession jag. Could she possibly have spilled the beans? She didn't seem the type . . .

"When your wire arrived, she really raved. 'There you are! See what a wash-out you are! A dead loss. But that boy gets the herd over, as if he was carrying it in a hamper slung on his pommel. Just like you couldn't ever do. This fellow's got something, the f——ing son-of-a-bitch!' "

"For goodness' sake, Mr. Pratt, you're not thinking of divorce?"

"Divorce? Me? Whatever for? Because of a trifle like that?"
He gave me an odd smile. If only I knew what it meant.

"No. Why should I get a divorce? Are you afraid I might?"

"Yes," I confessed.

"But why?"

"Because your wife said she'd marry me . . ."

"Oh. Yes, I remember her saying that, and if she says she's
going to do a thing, she does it. But why are you squirming
like that? Scared? Don't you like my wife? I thought that
. . ."

I didn't let him finish that one. "I like your wife very
much," I confessed rapidly. "But . . . please don't get a divorce! If I did marry her, it wouldn't be a bad thing, perhaps,
but I really don't know what I'd do with a wife, I beg your
pardon, what I should do with your wife . . ."

"What you'd do with any woman!—Give her what she
likes."

"That's not the point. It's something else. I don't know how
I'd get on as a married man." I tried hard to make it clear to
him. "Understand, I'm only a vagabond. I'm incapable of
staying put on my arse. And I couldn't drag my wife along on
my travels. Nor could I stay put, and sit at a proper table with
a proper breakfast and a proper dinner every day. No! My
stomach wouldn't stand it, either. Now, if you'd like to do me
a favor . . ."

"Anything you like. Granted," he said, good-naturedly.

"Don't divorce your wife. She's such a good wife, such a
beautiful, clever, brave wife! You'd never get another like her,
Mr. Pratt."

"I know that. That's why I wouldn't get a divorce. I never
thought of such a thing. I don't know how you got such
nonsense into your head! Come off that, now, and we'll go
celebrate the end of your cattle contract."

And off we went.

When the Priest Is Not at Home

The good padre of a village populated entirely by
Indian peasants had to leave for the capital of the state to
attend a conference called by the bishop. There were no trains
and no buses and so our good padre had to travel by mule.
Because he did not want to overexert himself he only rode by
day, from one hacienda where he had spent the night to the
next, where he would remain until the following day. Everywhere he was of course well received and treated with the best
of food and drink.

No wonder he considered this trip a well-earned vacation
after three years of doing his duty as village priest to peasants
whose homes were scattered over a vast region. The round
trip would take from four to six weeks. Consequently, before
leaving, he blessed the community, warning the faithful
against the slings of Satan and of the ever and ever expected
return of the ancient Indian gods, more feared by him than
Satan himself.

He called in Cipriano, his sacristan, and officially turned the
care of the church over to him. Cipriano was by profession a
woodchopper and charcoal-burner, and as a human being he

was neither better nor worse than any other man in the village.

Extremely proud of his duties as sacristan, he took his job very seriously. In his opinion, there existed only two persons of real importance in the region: el padre and el sacristan, and he realized well enough that without the help of a sacristan a padre isn't much to speak of.

Frequently he had let his friends know confidentially that a sacristan was perhaps even more important than a padre, but this of course he would never say out very loud for surely that might be considered sinful. Truth was, if the padre was respected in the community, it was the sacristan who was feared. The padre was a Mestizo whereas Cipriano was a full-blooded Indian. For that reason his position was more or less like that of a medicine man, or *brujo*, among his people. And that was easy to understand. Cipriano was as close to the saints as was the padre. He, Cipriano, knew all the secrets of religion just as well as the padre. He had access to the most Holy. He could chant and conduct the ceremonies of the Mass out of memory better than the padre, who sometimes would forget certain lines and had to consult the book.

He had been sacristan for thirty years and during that long time had served under four different priests. Not only did he know every line of the liturgy by heart, but he also knew every single glass pearl on every one of the many holy images which crowded the church; he knew every holy day and every saint's day without ever making a mistake. In fact, the members of the community, especially the children and ado-lescents, thought that Cipriano was more important in carry-ing out the many intricate ceremonies than the padre himself.

Just as all Indians first appeal to the saints when they want something from God, so the members of the parroquia first appealed to Cipriano when they wanted something from the padre. Whether it was a marriage, a baptism or a funeral, they first came to Cipriano for advice. Even when the girls and

boys went to confession they inquired first of Cipriano
whether this or that was a deadly sin if one did not confess it,
or how to indicate this or that without expressing it directly.
Cipriano counselled everyone and he had help for all. He was
the confidant of every single member of the community to a
much greater extent by far than the best priest could ever
be.

For all these reasons Cipriano was comparatively well-off.
He got a chicken here and a rooster there, here a bottle of
tequila and there one of rum. And on his saint's day he got so
many good things that he could live on them for a whole
month.

When the señor padre was ready to depart for his trip, he
said to Cipriano: "You know very well what to do around
here. I don't have to tell you anything about that. You will
open the church early in the morning, see to it that the bells
are rung rightly and at night you will lock up the holy place as
always. Sunday mornings and Wednesday and Saturday evenings you will sing the service and say the prayers. You know
them all well enough. And don't forget to fill the fonts with
the blessed water when you see them empty. That you also
know. And then there is something of great importance. Clean
all the saints, dust them and remove the droppings of the birds.
It's a shame to see how they look. You know the señor bishop
might perhaps pay us an unexpected visit any day. I would be
embarrassed to have all the images so dirty and the church so
full of sh— Well, Cipriano, you know yourself how dirty the
whole place has gone during the years, what with those
terrible dust storms we've had."

"Si, Padre, the place is in a horrible state and 'specially the
poor santitos."

"Now that's exactly what I'm telling you. You clean them
well, all of them. Where the paint has come off, put on some
new. But don't paint the Mother of God over the altar. Just

wash off the dirt and then cover Her with colorless varnish. I'll show you how to use it."

"I'm sure I can do it fine, Padre."

"So am I, Cipriano. Now, tomorrow morning I'll buy all the material you need. And from there I'll be on my way to the conference."

The various paints and the varnish had been bought and the use of it explained by the merchant.

Then, before taking his leave, the padre took his money belt and shelled out eight pesos in silver.

"There, Cipriano, take this money so that you won't have to work in the bush but can take full charge of cleaning up the holy place instead, so that when I come back I can be proud of our church. May the good Lord and the Holy Virgin bless you and help you in your pious task. And now, Cipriano, let's have a drink together and wish me good luck on my trip."

The drinks—it wasn't just one—consumed, the padre went on his way, his simple suitcase tied on behind the saddle.

Cipriano rode home on his burro content with the world and in particular with religion. He arrived just in time for the vespers service.

Next morning he started cleaning up the church and beautifying the saints, washing them with tender care as he would babies. Though he was no expert in using paint, instinctively, with the inborn love for colors of the Indian, he felt sure he would do a satisfactory job.

The paint he had at his disposal was rather limited because it was expensive and the padre was a poor man who could not afford to spend more on anything even for his personal wants than was absolutely essential.

In consequence of that, Cipriano handled Judas Iscariot first, who anyway in his opinion was really only a half saint because his true relationship to Christ had never been made clear. Some say he betrayed the Lord and for that he is roasting in hell for two thousand years already.

Others maintain that God ordered Judas Iscariot to betray the Lord. For if he had not betrayed Him, Christ would not have been taken prisoner and Christ could not have been crucified and so He would not have died laden with all the sins of the world to redeem humanity. But since Judas Iscariot was absolutely necessary to fulfill the miracle of redemption, the Indian looks upon him as a half saint who now and then can perhaps put in a good word for him in heaven.

One should not blame an Indian peasant for such a strange attitude, because among the ancient Aztecs the evil gods who could do much harm to men were worshiped as devotedly as were the good gods. By all means it is considered wise to stand on a good footing with all and every personage mentioned in the Bible. You can never know for sure whether a certain patriarch was not perhaps God's tool even if he behaved himself badly on earth.

Now as to Judas Iscariot, he always stood in a dark corner of the church like a schoolboy who has put a frog into the teacher's handbag. There he will stand, Judas will, all during the whole year until Holy Week when he is taken out, dusted off and cleaned, and set at the table of the Last Supper put up in the church. At this table Judas Iscariot must not be missed even though other saints as for instance San Augustin or San Jerónimo may be substituted for some of those originally present at the Last Supper.

Like anybody else Cipriano had to learn by practicing. And Judas to practice on was as good as anyone on whom to try out how much and how well one might wash without harming the original paint still good and how much new paint to use. He, Cipriano, could to his heart's content paint and lacquer on Judas to find out how the paint took and how it came out without overdoing it. If he spoiled something on Judas it was

but of little importance. Judas would be put into his dark
corner again until Easter Week and by that time enough dust
would have accumulated to hide Cipriano's miscalculated artistic efforts. The principal idea was to keep the beard and the
money bag intact so as to recognize the image as Judas Iscariot, for it had happened, and might happen again any odd
day, that he was taken for St. Joe and given presents such as
candles or trinkets of silver.

Cipriano painted Judas Iscariot with real zest, almost with
devotion, and when he had finished he could hardly tear
himself away. He hated to put him into his dark corner again
where rats and mice would molest him. At this moment
Cipriano felt a profound pity for Judas that he had allowed
himself to be bribed and that he had betrayed the Lord. Had
he, Judas, only not done it so openly Cipriano might have been
able to put him in front so that everybody could see him shine.
But that could not be done because all the faithful, especially
the women, knew the story of that infamous betrayal and they
would object violently.

Cipriano even had a blasphemic intention to change the beard
of Judas, take away from him his money bag and make a St.
Marcus out of him. But this change of course would have been
detected very soon, as the features of Judas Iscariot were
better known to all members of the community than those of
any other image.

The thought of making such a change had occurred to
Cipriano because on Judas he tried out all the colors and saw
their effects. As for the other images he had to keep to the
original basic colors so that they would be recognized by the
worshipers whereas it did not matter much where Judas was
concerned.

The next few days Cipriano put all his work and effort into
cleaning and repainting the images but constantly his thoughts
would return to the beautiful artistic expressions he had be-

stowed upon Judas. No doubt since he was no longer under
the padre's protection he must have worked under Satan's
influence to perform such a remarkable job, and of all images,
on that of the greatest sinner that ever walked on earth. In no
other way could it be explained why, in the course of time, all
that occurred thereafter might well be traced back to the fact
that Cipriano had wasted his talents so lavishly on that arch-
villain Judas. What now happened showed plainly and unmis-
takably how smartly Satan works, that even such a good man
as was Cipriano fell into the abyss.

On purpose he had kept the Virgin waiting to be the very
last of the images to be handled so that in the meantime he
would become a great expert in cleaning and repainting the
holy effigies.

At last Cipriano arrived at the task of cleaning and varnish-
ing the adored statue of the Holy Virgin enthroned over the
altar. He realized that this was the holiest of all his tasks which
could have been conferred upon him. The different likenesses
of the Lord he had handled easily and with no more particular
respect than he gave the saints. But the Holy Virgin was the
holiest of the holy, to him, the simple-minded Indian peasant,
more important than God the Father Himself. To him, the
way he had been taught, the Virgin was the very essence, yes,
the fundamental base of the only true religion.

Before taking Her likeness down from the little stage on
which it stood he kneeled down and said two dozen Ave
Marias besides various other prayers by which She usually was
addressed. He crossed himself several times and finally he
brought down the image and set it on the floor. He took off
Her mantle to dust and wash it. Then he washed Her face
while he mumbled prayers incessantly. Now he rubbed and
polished the figure with soft cotton rags. Then he carefully
applied the varnish. The body was made out in such a manner

that the inner garments appeared to be carved woodwork. The Virgin's garments he laid out in the yard to dry.

On the brick floor of the church Cipriano had kept a small fire burning for warming the water a little and also to keep the glue liquid with which he repaired broken parts of the images. On this same fire he now boiled some coffee and heated his frijoles and tortillas because he did not want to lose time going home to eat.

His meal finished he left to sit in the sun for a short rest. While he smoked a self-rolled cigarette his thoughts again turned to Judas Iscariot, how he might perhaps paint him better still since he discovered that he had some little paint left over. He hoped that perhaps even the padre would be pleased with his great work of art and give Judas a better place to live than the darkest corner of the church where he was condemned to contemplate his unforgivable sin. He thought that after all a big injustice had been done to Judas, making him atone for two thousand years because of a lousy thirty pieces of silver which he surely must have needed to pay his back rent or buy his daughter a much needed dress or maybe even medicine for his sick wife. With the heavy strain of these thoughts over such complicated problems and questions concerning religion, and at the same time thinking that the relations of the señor padre with doña Elodia and doña Agapita, both good-looking widows, might fairly well be interpreted in more than one way, Cipriano fell asleep. That was only natural because at the moment he had nothing else to do but wait for the sun to dry the Virgin's mantle. He was just dreaming that Judas Iscariot had come to life complaining to him that the thirty pesos he had received for his job had turned out all counterfeit and caused him lots of trouble when the ferocious barking of several dogs, fighting inside the church over some tortillas Cipriano had left, brutally awoke him. He hurried into the church and drove the dogs out by the back door.

When his eyes got used to the darkness inside the church and he approached the image of the Holy Virgin, cold shivers ran up and down his spine. He had to look several times before he could convince himself that what he saw was real and not a dream.

The dogs in their fighting for the tortillas had pushed the Most Holy Mother of God into the fire, where She lay helplessly and with the same natural consequences as any other piece of wood when tossed into any fire. Cipriano, without being told so, knew at once that Satan had sent the dogs to keep him out of heaven.

With a resolute grip he rescued the Godmother from the fire. Her left hand was held pressed to Her heart hanging outside the center of her body from where rays of gold, red and bronze radiated in all directions. Her right hand was raised to the level of Her chin with the palm down in a gesture as if to bless someone, or cover the head of an invisible child. This hand the fire had completely charred. The right side of the image was blackened in a most ugly way.

Cipriano extinguished the still burning parts of the figure with the last few drops of his coffee. When this did not altogether help he used his spit. Not for one moment did he consider this spitting on the Virgin an act of disrespect. In spite of all his education as a faithful Christian he, without realizing it, turned heathen again when confronted by reality.

Now he had to think of what to do. He completely forgot that he held in his hands the Mother of God who was worshiped and prayed to as if she really was the Mother of God alive and in person and not just a wooden figure.

Automatically he closed the church so that nobody should come in to witness the damage that had been done. He was aware of the fact that there was no excuse for his negligence.

He would lose his position and, what was a hundred times worse, he might even be excommunicated. Not that his job brought in much money, ten centavos for a baptism, twenty-five centavos for a good wedding, fifteen centavos for a funeral. But what bothered him more than the possible loss of his job as sacristan was to lose the respectful position he now held. If the disaster for which he alone was to blame should become known he no longer could be the one closest to the padre, no longer would he be allowed to attend to all that was holy, no longer would he substitute for the padre during his occasional absences, nor would he have the envied privilege to light the candles in the presence of the whole community, nor would he have the unbelievably great honor to hand the wash basin and towel or the chasuble to the padre. Nobody would ask or heed his advice, there would not be any more chicken or rooster on his saint's day, no tequila here or pumpkin cooked in wild honey there. In other words, life would not be worth living anymore. In his thirty years of service he had become so involved with the church that nobody could even imagine the church without him. The present generation had been raised in the belief that his person was irreplaceable. Perhaps, so he thought, he might pray very ardently and a great miracle would happen, and the hand of the Mother of God would grow again. But Cipriano's belief did not reach out that far. He was too much Indian to know that charred wood does not grow under any circumstances, no matter how much you pray for that to happen.

After hours of thinking and speculating he contemplated the idea of sawing off the charred hand, carving a new one and gluing it onto the stump. He then would apply a thick coat of paint, and once the image was again set up over the altar nobody would notice the difference. The carving of the hand would take a day. During this time the Virgin would have to be in Her place or the worshipers who come to pray would surely miss her immediately. Without the image before him, an Indian cannot concentrate on his prayers but thinks of his corn, his goats, his sheep and his wife instead.

Cipriano clothed the Virgin again in her dark-blue velvet mantle and put Her back on Her little stage over the altar once more. He arranged the candles in such a way that in the twilight of the church one would not easily notice the charred hand. He draped some folds of the cloak over the hand in such a smart way that no one could easily distinguish the charred hand from the dark cloth. Before the padre returned, a new hand perfectly well painted would have been glued onto the arm.

Meanwhile it became late, Cipriano opened the main door and a few elderly women entered to pray. When it was time to close he locked the church and went home reassured that during the night nothing would happen to make the calamity known. He looked for a piece of wood and started to carve the hand as best as he could. The finer points he would do in full daylight during the next forenoon. He worked fast and figured that he would have his job finished by noon the following day.

While he was busy carving a terrific storm broke loose. Thunder rattled from all sides, lightning flashed over the skies and tore the black night into flaming shreds. A more pious person than Cipriano would have connected the storm with the Virgin in disgrace. And surely the padre would have said: "There you are, Cipriano, see what you did, the wrath of God Almighty is over you. Repent, Cipriano, repent!"

Capriano was pious but not pious enough to believe for one moment that the storm happened in consequence of his carelessness in regard to the Virgin's image. As an Indian he was well acquainted with nature and he had already seen in the early afternoon how heavy storm clouds gathered far out on the horizon. In fact he had told his neighbors Mateo and

Eusebio when they came visiting for a while in the church-yard: "Watch out, you cuates, we'll have a severe storm such as we haven't had for a long time. Who knows whether or not a few jacalitos might not burn down." And that happened at least one hour before the hand of the Virgin was lost. So what had the thunderstorm to do with that lamentable mishap?

The padre though would have said: "The Virgin knew all this long before and therefore arranged the thunderstorm beforehand." And Cipriano would have answered: "Si, Padre, that's so." For he had been taught as a little boy that one commits sin arguing with a priest. What a priest says is the truth of God. But to himself Cipriano would have said: "If the Virgin had known all this beforehand, She would also have known that a few hungry village dogs would throw Her into the fire. Would She really have allowed those dogs to do that to Her for no other reason but to cause me trouble? I can't believe that, so help me the Lord."

Cipriano rolled himself a cigarette and waited, for he knew that, in his situation, praying would not help anyway. The tempest would wear itself out. He remembered doña Lucina, the wife of Pancho Lazcano, who was killed by lightning while fingering the rosary. So it was better to roll a cigarette and stand in the open door to watch the splendor of the storm.

While he so watched the sky, a tremendous burst of thunder exploded right above his head which shook him so that he had to hold fast to the doorpost of his choza to avoid dropping to the ground. At the same fraction of a second he saw a flash hitting the roof of the church. Roof tiles crackled all over and he expected the church to go up in flames at any moment. But nothing happened. The dark outline of the church stood out quietly against the night. Slowly the thunders began to retreat, the flashes quivered away and a heavy rain started pouring down. After half an hour the rain stopped, the storm had abated, and only in the far distance could one see an occasional flash.

While Cipriano was still standing in his door, a few men came running, shouting: "Don Cipriano, did you see that last flash which hit the church? Quickly, bring your keys and open up. We must see if something is burning inside. Still time to put out any fire that may have caught on somewhere."

When they arrived at the church many people were waiting already and many more were coming fast, men, women and children. Everyone had seen the flash strike the church straight over the altar and they now wanted to see what damage had been done.

Cipriano opened the door, the men went in and looked around but could see no fire anywhere. Until midnight they searched around. When finally they had made sure that not even a glimmer had been overlooked they all went home satisfied.

Very early next morning Cipriano opened the church and women entered to pray.

Having lighted the candles as usual, he stood near the door filling the font when suddenly two women right in front of the altar let out a shriek, crossing themselves violently at the same time.

Cipriano turned around, terribly frightened. He knew that everything had been discovered and that he only had to wait for the padre's return to be dishonorably discharged from duty. Other women in the church also were running now toward the altar to see what had caused that horrifying shriek. Hardly had they come close when they stopped, screaming and crossing themselves.

Cipriano heard a word here and a scream there but finally he could make out what they were shouting: "A miracle has happened! A great miracle! Blessed be the Mother of God.

Glory to the Holy Virgin! A great miracle!" The women
hurried toward Cipriano, dragging him to the altar.

He had become entirely indifferent. He would have liked
best to go home, lie down in bed and say that he was deadly
sick. But they pulled him along, shouting at the same time:
"Look, Don Cipriano! Have you no eyes for the great miracle
that has happened? A lightning struck the church. Up there
the tiles have fallen out from the roof. A great miracle has
happened to our church. The hand of the Holy Virgin caught
the flash! La Madre Santísima sacrificed Her adored hand to
protect the holy flesh of Christ our Lord. She saved our
church! Be She blessed for ever and ever, She kept the fire
away that would have destroyed our church. A miracle! A
great, great miracle has happened. Glory be to God!"

In less than three days the church was surrounded by
Indians and Mestizos alike, thousands of people. Cipriano could
not do anything anymore. He had become convinced that
there surely must be a higher power which determines fate on
earth, in particular his own.

In no time the church became an important source of
income in solid cash and it has stayed so to this very day
because faithful pilgrims adore that Virgin, praying for her
protection against injuries lightning might cause.

It was only human that Cipriano never said anything. How
would he dare tell the princes of the church, archbishops and
bishops who came to celebrate Masses here, that a little error
had occurred? These dignitaries would have laughed out loud
and told him that he was getting too old and a little weak in
the head.

A true Indian, he was endowed with an inborn worldly
wisdom and knew when and how to hold his tongue. After
all, he did not believe it his duty to reform religions. Less so as
they were good enough for him the way they existed. Everything concerned, he thought it most beneficial for him to leave

matters as they stood, because soon he learned that a sacristan of a rich church can live much better than one of a poor Indian community. No longer did he have to go out, cutting wood and burning coal in the bush under a tropical sun. And for this convenience he remained forever grateful to his half saint, Judas Iscariot.

Midnight Call

One certain night there was a hard knock on the light wooden wall of the weather-beaten bungalow in which I lived. I had no watch, but from the position of the moon I judged that it was about midnight. It happened in a village populated by Indian peasants which was known in the region as a *nido de bandoleros*, or as we would say, a nest of bandits.

Those were revolutionary times; scores of small semimilitary groups that had lost contact with their regiments and whose little properties had been devastated had to keep alive with their families as best as they could.

Fact is, and I ought to know, that one can live securely in the countryside of the Republic in the very midst of so-called bandits if one is neither Indian nor Mestizo and does not care what the people there are doing or how they make their living. In addition I had learned from experience that one can live peacefully and happily in such a neighborhood if every inhabitant of the place knows that one owns only one pair of shoes with holes, a few worn shirts and one pair of pants which can no longer serve even to repair another pair of ragged pants.

129

Aside from this, one may safely own a few pesos, some books, and a dilapidated typewriter without a Spanish type body.

The people of this village, bandoleros or no bandoleros—what did I care—would not let me starve. After I had lost my beautiful cotton because of the boll weevil, and so all the proceeds of my hard work of nine long months, I stared at the world discouraged and utterly dejected. Yet no sooner had I asked myself, What shall I eat, what shall I drink, to whom shall I turn now? when two men of the village appeared at my bungalow with an express desire to learn English and asked how much I would charge. I told them twenty centavos each for one lesson. They paid me ten hours in advance and so I was able to buy corn seed to plant in my ruined cotton field. It was just the right time to plant corn because the rainy season was to start in less than four weeks.

Through those two pupils I got five more within two weeks, because for some reason not clear to me at that time, several villagers had suddenly decided to study English. They all came regularly and paid for their lessons punctually. So all of us were satisfied with one another. Under such conditions I had no reason to bother about whether they were bandoleros or not. They let me live undisturbed and I left them alone. No better way to live on this earth.

Now, if someone in the countryside in the Republic knocks on your door around midnight, experience, advice, good taste and manners demand that you keep quiet, that you don't answer and that you hold your breath as long as possible, because it might just so happen that at the very moment you open the door to see who is there—you wishing it might be the telegraph boy bringing you a hundred-dollar order—you have two or a dozen shots fired at you, and you withdraw safe and unharmed or filled with lead, alone or followed by some men who push you farther inside and not exactly in a friendly way.

There are people who don't know better and who will claim that bravery is a great virtue on the battlefield, but bravery in certain places at certain times and in certain circumstances in the Republic is usually a sign of incurable and innate stupidity. No one around there is expected to be a juggler or to catch revolver bullets with his teeth. To see that you pay for it in a circus.

Because many years had elapsed since I traveled with a circus, I had, as is only natural, lost the ability to catch bullets with my hands open or with my teeth closed, so I kept as quiet as a buried chest full of money when I heard the knocking on my door. Whether I began to tremble and break out in a cold sweat I no longer remember now, but I don't believe I did. If things have already gone so far that you hear a violent knocking on your door at night and the knocking gets more vehement every second, it will no longer be of any use to sweat from fear. Whatever is going to happen, whatever it may be, that has already been decided outside without consulting you and so you'd better save the cold sweat.

After several more of those violent knocks I heard half-loud voices. There were at least three men as far as I could distinguish from the different voices. The voices carried a strong and merciless tone, as of men who knew precisely why they had come and what they wanted.

Then I heard shuffling close to the door. They left the porch and I could catch their heavy steps on the sandy ground. From the sounds their feet made I gathered that two of them were wearing boots and one huaraches. I realized that my life was prolonged by the amount of time it would take them to decide what to do next.

Naturally I thought of escaping. The one-room bungalow had, like most houses in the country in that part of the Republic, two doors, one at each side. But I had barricaded both doors with beams. The loosening of these beams could

not be done without noise, and with the least little noise I
made the men would immediately be at the door through
which I wanted to escape.

In spite of having just come out of a deep sleep, I tried to
think of some medicine or trick by which I might save myself.
However, at that precious moment I could not concentrate
sufficiently on any sort of medicine that might be useful. After
all, I had first to see the men and how they looked so that I
could select the right medicine.

I had no gun. Anyway, a gun would not have helped me in
such a situation as I was in. One might be lucky and shoot all
three men. But it would be difficult to get out of a village in
which one has shot three of its citizens, especially if the place
is a hideout for bandoleros. Actually I was better off without a
gun. What's more, it eliminated any obligation to be brave.
Always and everywhere bravery is badly rewarded. It's always
and forever the cowards who survive the wars. The really
brave fall on the battlefield for the glory of those who march
home under showers of confetti and ticker tape.

By now the men had returned to the door. Because of the
annual tropical rains, the bungalow was built on posts and
several steps led up to the doors.

I heard the men stamping up and, as the steps were narrow,
only one could be at the door while the others had to remain
on the lower steps.

The fellow at the door knocked hard with what seemed to
be the butt of a revolver or a shotgun.

When the knocking had no effect, he yelled. "Hey, hombre,
abre, levántate, we got the goddamn hell to talk to you."

That proved they knew perfectly well that I was in the
house, for otherwise they wouldn't have called.

Stubbornly they continued knocking and calling. But I
didn't move a lip, that is, not voluntarily. My lips quivered all
right. Whose wouldn't?

Now they talked again to one another. Then they stamped down the stairs and shuffled over the sand. I thought that at last they were convinced that I was not at home. My mistake. Miscalculating things mostly happens when one wants to believe something to be of some benefit to himself.

For half a minute or so they walked about as though not knowing what to do now and then stopped exactly at that part of the wall against which the cot on which I slept was set up. They knocked on this wall with full force and continued to call: "Abre, señor, abre!"

Now I realized that among them must be one who knew the inside of my bungalow very well; otherwise he would not have known where I slept. I was cornered perfectly and had to admit that I was in.

I got up, prepared to look cold death in the face without moving an eyelash. It wouldn't be a glorious death with no one to take notice of the sneering and cold laugh with which I accepted, even welcomed death, because there was no newspaperman present to tell posterity how bravely and nobly I had behaved during the last hour of my life. Bandoleros don't care much whether or not one trembles and shakes from cold fear. Neither does a hangman care. It is business, sober and plain business, not a bit sophisticated as some other business.

Although they obviously had expected me to jump up quickly, I did not move. Every minute I gained was wrested from old man death. So I said sleepily: "Hey, you, out there, what's the matter? You goddamn muledrivers, stinky arrieros, can't an honest man sleep one single night in this here godforsaken burg of whores, thieves, and violators of decent womenfolk? What kind of a drunken lousy pack of cabrones is there shuffling at my door? Not a single stinking goddamn drop of tequila have I got here in my house. To hell with you, you filthy worm-eaten dogs. Hear me! I want to sleep."

I got talking louder and louder on purpose, trying to get as angry and beastly furious as I possibly could, for if these had to be my last words on earth I wanted them to be added to my last prayer so that eternity should be less boring.

Anyhow, by now it had become obvious these fellows out there wanted very much to get me up. But for what reason, this I could not even guess.

When they heard me answer their harsh tone changed immediately into a very mild one. Perhaps they had imagined until now that I was not at home and that they would have to leave unsuccessfully.

One of them spoke up: "Please, señor, por favor, come to the door just for a moment. We got to talk to you very urgently. It's a serious matter." There was a tone of pleading in his voice. Almost pitiful.

Indios and medium-Indios have no conception of time. When their heart is full of sorrow they will come to you at any time be it day or night. In this particular case it might of course have been a trick to lure me to the door and whatever they had in mind doing would thus have been easier to accomplish. But no matter what there was in store for me I had to open the door at last. They could have broken in anyway, had they wanted to.

"Hello, there, señores!" I said sleepily, leaning against the open door. "Welcome. Bien venidos, amigos. What can I do for you on such a night of romantic love?"

Because the moon shone so brightly I could see them very clearly, though I did not recognize one of their faces, shadowed by big palm hats. They were robust types, without coats, clad only in white pants and white, very clean cotton shirts open at the neck. One wore as far as I could make out in the semidarkness of the night leather leggings and yellow boots with high heels, which were completely run down. The second wore brown leather boots that were torn at many places. The third wore—as I had concluded before by hearing his

light step—huaraches. The two men with boots on each carried
a rifle of the kind used by the army and which they held ready
to shoot. Of these two one had, besides, a revolver stuck into a
shabby holster. Both wore belts adorned with a full row of
cartridges. The man with huaraches on his feet had for his
whole armament only an ordinary machete.

It was this man with the machete who seemed to know me. I
thought that several times I had seen him around the village.
The other two were complete strangers to me.

Instinct told me that the man with the machete had peaceful
intentions toward me, and that the other two were not after
my riches or my life, but needed help instead. The one holding
the machete said: "Would you be so very kind, señor, as to
come to our house? My nephew is lying there, sick. I don't
know what ails him. They brought him in, awfully sick. He
won't wake up. He will not come to. So we ask you, very
much, please, go with us. Perhaps you can help him. We're
sure you can. We know you're a very wise man, in fact a great
doctor."

"What's the matter with him?" I asked.

"That's exactly what we don't know and why we ask you so
very much, please, do come and see what's the matter with
him."

The nearest doctor lived about forty miles away. The round
trip on horseback would take him three days at least and he
would charge no less than one hundred pesos, a sum that had
to be put on the table before he would even saddle the horse.
Who of these villagers to whom one hundred pesos was a
fortune could pay such a sum? No doctor comes without
previous payment. He, the medico, is primarily a businessman.
No mistake about that. In this world in which he lives he has
to be a businessman. No one will give him credit for his rent,
and if he does not pay his bill the baker or the grocer, medico
or no medico, neither will lend him the following month as

much as a pound of potatoes. He who cannot pay has no right
to live; he must either die or try to live without a medico.
That is the reason why most people of the Republic stay alive
for more than ninety years unless someone shoots them.

In my possession I had an old cardboard case in which, once
upon a time, shoes had been packed. This cardboard affair
served me as my medicine chest. It contained some medicine,
if you will call a few aspirin tablets medicine. But besides
medicine there were sewing implements, trouser buttons, a
torn typewriter ribbon, a few used razorblades, an empty tube
of toothpaste, one big fishhook, two small fishhooks, five
newspaper clippings, a pocketknife with a broken blade, the
other small blade rusty but otherwise in good shape, strings in
different thicknesses, four different screws, a few nails, a pencil
stub, a leaking fountain pen, the tooth of a donkey, the tail of a
rattler, and some few other things which I no longer remember.

During my early youth I carried all my earthly goods in my
pants and coat pockets, that is when I had a coat, because I had
to be ready to travel at any hour no matter where I happened
to be, mostly on account of merciless truant officers. Since
then, having become in the meantime well-to-do, I carried all
my earthly riches in that shaky cardboard box. It makes you
wonderfully independent.

Even had these good men not asked for it, even had they not
so highly solicited my medical knowledge, I would still have
taken the medicine box along with me. This I did entirely
instinctively and out of long and often very bitter experience.
For it had often happened to me in the past that, when I
thought of leaving my residence for only one hour, upon
regaining full consciousness I discovered that I had landed on a
different continent. Through such experiences one learns to
become careful, so that toothbrush, shaving kit and a little
pocket compass were constantly buttoned up inside my back

pants pocket. How would I know where I might land if I flew away with these three nightbirds?

"Is this your doctor box?" asked one of them.

"Sí, señor, this is my medicine box," I confirmed, and the men murmured something which sounded like satisfaction.

"Then let's go," said another one.

I bolted my door and off we went.

Quite naturally I had not the slightest idea of where we were going. Nothing was said about that. After all it was useless for me to ask such a question, for if we were marching to Honduras or to Sinaloa, it was not up to me to decide. Whether I liked it or not this was determined by those who carried guns. He who carries a gun always has the right to give orders, and the one who has no gun always has the damn duty to obey. And that has been the law since that memorable day when the archangel Gabriel with his flaming sword in hand chased two naked people out of the Lord's vegetable garden. Had they had a machine gun, everything would have turned out entirely different and giving orders or obeying them would have taken a different road. It was for that difference that anyone will understand why I wandered along with these three men through the night without complaint, without one word to ask where we were going.

We did not trudge through the center of the village, but kept along the periphery instead. On all sides dogs barked furiously. And those dogs that could not see us barked too, barked themselves hoarse so as not to make the impression they had not noticed us or to leave the pleasure of barking exclusively to the other dogs. There was a hellish noise in the whole village. Because of that horrible barking most of the roosters woke up and began crowing lustily, and then the sad braying of lonely donkeys fell in. Not a single living soul came out of his hut to see what was going on. Once these village dogs start barking they will stay noisy half the night through, whether there is a gang of bandits sneaking around or a mule wandering sleepily along the road or one cat chasing another, or whether nothing happens at all.

We left the village behind and marched a fairly long time through underbrush, then for a while through bush-land, when finally we reached a frame house. It had a well-kept, fenced-in flower garden in front, and on both sides there were vegetable patches which I could distinguish clearly in the moonlight. The house was not decrepit or covered with rags and reed mats like most of the homes in the village. From the outside it made a good impression. On the porch were innumerable plants and flowers, in pots and cans and pails, so-called macetas.

The good impression I had received from the outside was increased when I entered the living room. Neither in this village nor in the whole region had I ever seen such a clean and well-furnished house. The living house on a farm in Texas or Arizona, Coahuila or Sonora could not look more agreeable than this one. I had not known nor would I have believed that in this neighborhood there was a family able to keep a house in such fine order and pleasing shape.

The beds were of white lacquered iron. There were real chairs and even some rocking chairs. Large framed pictures adorned the wall. Lohengrin with his Elsa sitting on the bed, Othello holding forth speeches about his adventures in foreign lands. The march of the hero Hidalgo leaving the town of Dolores surrounded by Indian peasants swinging machetes. The Virgin of Guadalupe and a group of small and enlarged photographs of uncles, aunts, grandfathers, children carrying Communion candles, obviously all members of one great family. One could not think of a more respectable and honorable family than that living in this house. People who kept such a house and in such order and cleanliness could not but be citizens who fortified and preserved the pillars of the state and at the same time the columns of the only church which guarantees you a seat in heaven.

But a life full of experience teaches you not to take anything at its face value. There are beautiful plants in the Republic which tempt one to look closer, but if one only touches them or brushes against them with the naked arm one gets a rash which takes months before it can be cured, if at all.

In spite of being at this moment in this respectable looking house I did not forget for one minute that three men had brought me there and that these three men were armed. Neither did I allow my face to express my wonderment that the house and the appearance of the men were in sharp contrast. I accepted everything as if it could not have been otherwise. I looked with great interest at the pictures on the wall, and so as to make these people believe that I admired the pictures I said: "Very fine paintings, made by great artists."

But while I said this, I looked sidewise at everything in view. The windows were well barricaded and covered. No ray of light could escape out into the night. Little hope there was to escape through one of those windows if it should become necessary. Two doors led into two other rooms. Both men with the guns seated themselves near the entrance door in such a way that nobody could enter or leave without being carefully scrutinized by them. Putting the guns between their knees, they rolled themselves cigarettes.

"Sit down, señor, por favor," said one of them and motioned me with a nod to an empty chair. I sat down and again looked around. The floor was covered with thick petate mats, fresh and yellow. Where the floor showed, I could see that it was scrubbed clean like freshly washed linen. In the farthest corner, in a sort of niche, there was a picture of *La Virgen del Perpetuo Socorro* with a small candle burning in front of it. Placed around it there were rosaries and cheap pictures of a dozen or so saints. On the table, which was covered with a multicolored cotton cloth, there stood a kerosene lamp, lighted.

I had not seen such a lamp for at least fourteen months, nobody in the village had one, nor had I. It was this kerosene lamp which had given me the first impression on entering that I was in a house of honest people well-off. On the table there was also a glass bowl of the kind one can win for ten centavos at a fair by throwing balls at objects until they are hit and fall.

When we entered the house the fellow with the machete immediately stepped into another room, closing the door tightly behind him. Since the walls were of rather thin wood I heard now and then voices in an undertone emanating from that room.

After a while the man came back with a glass and a bottle.

"First let's have one," he said and filled the glass.

"Salud!" I said and shot it down. It made me feel warm and I thought to myself that where such good tequila is offered there certainly would not be murder back of it. No one wastes such good Añejo on someone he wants to get rid of.

The two at the main door remained where they were sitting. Suddenly I had the impression that these men were not watching me to prevent my escape but rather sat armed close to the door to protect the people in the house against possible harm coming from the outside. Of this I became even more convinced when the two whispered to each other and one left to sit on the stoop outside, while the other took up a position inside in such a way that he could not be seen immediately by someone entering but could cover any intruder with his gun.

The glass was filled again. I was offered and accepted another drink. No one else got a second. Closing the bottle, the man said: "Now, let's get down to business." He rose and motioned me to follow him.

We entered that other room, where a very small lamp gave

little light. The man returned to the main room, picked up the kerosene lamp and brought it in. Now I could see more clearly. Two women were sitting in rocking chairs, their rebozos wrapped around their heads and necks. Both were Indians, cleanly dressed, and in their speech and bearing not different from any woman of a ranch-owner. One of them was comparatively young, about thirty or so, and as I learned later she was the wife of the man with the machete. The other was older and could well have been the mother of either the man or his wife. Obviously the room was the bedroom of the couple. Judging from the two beds in the main room, several persons seemed to live in the house.

Both women got up and greeted me courteously. They shook my hands lightly and sat down again. A young man was lying on a bast mat, covered up to his chin with a white cotton blanket. His face was pale but full and I concluded that he could not have been sick very long but had probably been seriously injured. He did not move and appeared as if dead or nearly so.

"This is the boy I told you about," said the man and put the kerosene lamp on a chair near-by.

"I'm sure you can help the boy," the young woman said. "He's my nephew and we don't want him to die. Since our own son lost his life in some silly shooting, this one has been like our own. We would really be very grateful if you could do something so he won't die. He's the last young one of the whole family left. All the others have been shot or stabbed to death at election time, even though none of them wanted a job for themselves. They just got mixed up for the sake of others." The woman did not cry but spoke with touching emotion while the older woman now and then sighed.

The election fights took place in the city of the district to which men and women, young and old, went to enjoy the shootings and the yellings of "Viva" and "Muera." Of those who went, not all returned; usually two or three, sometimes a dozen, fell and stayed on the battlefield.

There had been no election for some time, so it could not have been in an election fight that this young fellow got hurt.

I knelt down and began to examine him. His eyes were closed. On lifting the lids I saw that the eyes were sleepy but not dimmed and they reacted to light. The heartbeat was regular but very faint. The breath was slight yet fair enough.

"What's the matter with him?" I asked.

"That's just what we don't know," the woman answered. "They brought him to the house unconscious and he hasn't come to since then. Do you think he will die, señor?"

"Sorry, I can't tell that at this moment. Hasn't he said something about what's wrong with him?" I asked.

No one answered, and I looked up to see why there was no answer.

I noticed that the man shot a quick look at his wife, put a finger slightly on his lips and shook his head.

Immediately I looked away pretending not to have seen anything and let my eyes rest on the boy. I gave them time enough to finish their secret language. Then I asked: "Has he eaten something which did not agree with him?"

"I don't believe so," the man answered.

I sat down on a chair, my elbows on my knees, and buried my face in my hands as if lost in deep thought exactly the way all really big doctors do. In other words, I would not know anything until the sick himself would tell me where it hurt and what the matter was. After all I was no veterinarian.

Now I said the same thing all doctors say: "This is a very serious case, but I shall do my very, very best and I'm sure we can pull him through."

At that very moment the two armed men came in to see how I was doing.

"Where is my medicine chest?" I asked.

One of the two bolted immediately into the main room and returned with my cardboard box.

What I was to do with it, I did not know at that moment.

However, I was sure a good idea would come to my mind. By all means I had to do something, for I had been dragged here as a doctor and I was expected to behave and act like one. So I had no other choice but to please these people. No doubts puzzled my senses as to what would happen to me should I fail.

It was obvious by now that the two men with guns were in the room for no other reason than to watch my performance, and because they didn't let go of their guns I was convinced that any minute they might point their guns at me and order: "You goddamn gringo, you save that boy at once and if he isn't up and around in ten minutes you'll lie next to him deader than a curbstone." Such things really happen to doctors in the Republic and since I had been brought here to work as a doctor, there was no reason they should make an exception with me.

An able-bodied doctor, one who has studied medicine successfully, can now and then, if lucky, prolong the expiring of a dying human for a good length of time. And if it finally happens he can still excuse himself by saying that against the will of God nothing can be done. So often are people made to believe that cheap explanation without questioning it that perhaps they will believe me, too, I thought. After all, these good people are Christians, good Christians with lots of rosaries, and are well supplied with all kinds of images of saints as I can see all around me.

Now I started working.

"Do you have Cafion in the house?" I asked the woman with an expression on my face as serious as that of a clergyman anointing and blessing a corpse.

"Yes, we've got a full bottle of it."

"Three tablets and one glass of water."

I dissolved the tablets in the water and let the boy swallow the mixture. He took it perfectly without anything going into his windpipe.

Quietly I sat down, smoked a cigarette and asked for another shot of tequila.

After about ten minutes had gone by I examined the lad again and I discovered that the medicine had had an excellent effect. The heart had begun to beat more strongly. Though the tablets could easily have stimulated the heart so violently that it might have stopped beating altogether, I had luck— which, by the way, every doctor needs if he wants to be a successful one.

Of course I knew quite well that a real doctor would have done everything I did entirely differently. For that reason he has a license and a partnership in an undertaker's establishment. I, however, had to do with the knowledge and medicines that were at my disposal. I couldn't make a camphor or adrenaline injection in the heart because I had no tools for it nor camphor either.

By now the heart was beating strongly and satisfactorily but the boy refused, sternly refused, to wake up. I couldn't find anything on his head. I slapped his cheeks, palms and wrists. No success.

Now I untied my medicine box. All people present saw the contents of course. However, I could not make out whether or not they were surprised at the different kinds of medicines in my box because no one made a single sound of surprise. They might have thought that the fishhooks in the box served to fish objects out of stomachs—the scorpions perhaps that fall into the big earthen vessels from which people take their drinking water. The broken rusty pocketknife might, in their opinion, serve to amputate feet or arms or to take out an appendix. In any case, the respect toward me and the confidence in my abilities as a medico did not seem to grow less, but, as I could see and feel, increased immensely.

I took a tube of mentholatum half used up and smeared a thick layer of it in the fellow's nose to help him breathe more easily. Now I asked whether they had ammoniac in the house. They had a little bottle of it and after having given him a few strong doses he sneezed and woke up. Vigorously I now fanned air at him and soon he began to breathe deeply, almost normally. But when he came to, he began to sigh pitifully as if from the bottom of his very being.

Now I knew what was wrong and what I had not been told. If I spoke frankly of what I now knew, then to be sure there would easily happen what I had expected since someone had knocked on my door. The knowledge I had gained in a roundabout way had made me a very unwanted witness. And that almost surely could be reason enough for the men to snuff me out.

I looked at the boy's aunt. Tears were in her eyes and I knew that she spoke seriously of her feeling toward the boy as though he were her own. The boy would perhaps recover without my help, yet not in less than two days. And in the meantime the soldiers would come, and he who could not get away safely would be shot right outside at the gate. No doubt he would be shot.

Again I looked at the woman who questioned me with her eyes. I don't want to say that I acted because of exaggerated philanthropy. That would be incorrect. Besides I don't want to appear better and nobler than I really am. To tell the truth, I am very much like any other ordinary man—endowed with wickedness, baseness, but also with an earnest willingness to help my fellow creatures. In this case, out of sheer curiosity, I decided to find out what would happen to me if I did what I considered the most stupid and dangerous thing.

I looked steadily at the man with the machete and said in a

short and loud voice: "Where then is that goddamn hole?
How can I bring him around if you don't tell me where he got
the shot?"

All present, even the old woman, were startled, uttered
short exclamations, paled, and looked with fright in their eyes
from one to the other until they all focused their eyes on me.
The uncle regained his composure first and said to the other
two men in a tone as if he was ready to give up everything: "I
told you before, but you didn't want to believe me, we can't
bamboozle that cabron of a gringo. The hell of it is he's a
doctor through and through."

Now I didn't wait any longer. Resolutely I pulled the
blanket back, looked quickly at the boy's chest and stomach
and there I noticed a heavy blood stain on the petate. Examining the poor lad closer I discovered two gun wounds, one in
his thigh, the other in his left calf. The latter was not serious.
A bullet had just grazed it. In contrast, the shot in the thigh
had caused a heavy wound. Doubtless the bullet was out, for I
noticed two holes, one where the slug had gone in and one
through which it went out again. Judging from the size of the
holes, it must have been a forty-five apparently fired from an
automatic, the kind only the army is allowed to use. The bone
was not damaged but the bullet had obviously torn several
veins, which was the cause of so much loss of blood and it was
also the reason for the weakened condition of the chap. The
whole leg was sticky with dry blood and a light crust had
already begun to form around the wounds. Very dirty rags
had been used for a hasty bandage. The only danger for the
youngster consisted in the possibility of an infection and, as a
possible aftermath, gangrene.

Now, the blood of the Indians in general is very healthy; an
infection sets in only when all and every ordinary precaution
has been disregarded. I ordered them to boil quickly some old
linen rags. Strange as it was, so I thought, they had plenty of

packages of clean cotton. In my box I carried a few sterilized, still unused gauze bandages. First I washed the wound with hot water and soap. Then I took a very strong disinfectant from my medicine box, the kind that had saved tens of thousands of American soldiers during the war. This stuff I poured undiluted directly into the wound and the poor boy practically jumped high up. He must have felt as if someone had pierced him with a red-hot iron right through the wounds. But he could be sure that this would save him. I let it dry, put some Bismuth-Jodoform over it and bandaged the whole with gauze. He sighed deeply but now with a definite expression of relief. I gave him a four-finger-high dose of tequila and within a few minutes he had fallen asleep soundly and quietly.

I imagined what question would come up now. So I said right away and without waiting: "When you put him on a horse tomorrow morning to make his getaway, it will be highly advisable to apply a bandage made of an old rubber hose or rubber belt or elastic braces to avoid another bleeding, for then he easily might bleed to death."

I showed the men how to apply that safeguard, told them to boil each new bandage before using it, gave them the rest of my powders and disinfectants, asked for another tequila and bade them good night. I shook hands with all of them—the boy's aunt bent down and kissed my hand—and then I made my way to the door.

I surely must have given them the impression that what I saw and did here was to me a daily occurrence. But the truth is, I now expected any moment that one of the men would say: "Wait a minute, mister gringo, you just wait a minute, you cannot go away like that. We first got to have a word with you before you leave this neighborhood. And we got to have that word outside, you understand. Best place is behind the vegetable patch."

The fact that I did not say a word as to how the boy might
have got his wounds or even let on that I knew they were
gunshots, the fact that I behaved as if I were a bandit myself
and a close friend of the family and that it was immaterial to
me what my neighbors thought of me and I of them as long as
they left me alone, all this quite obviously upset their plans and
made them puzzle. And so as to lay still more emphasis on all
this, I said nonchalantly: "Should he get worse you may call
me any time. I will be only too glad to be of help to you."

By appearance the last words decided the outcome. No one
will slay the only doctor in the vicinity; because of his not
being licensed he has no professional duty to inform the
authorities of gunshot wounds he has attended.

However, it was not so easy to get away. When I had
reached the door, the uncle said: "Excuse me, mister, but we
cannot let you go home alone, something might happen to you
on the way and besides you might not find your way back.
You may easily lose your way in the underbrush. We brought
you here and it would be impolite not to see you back home."

And so I saw before myself the prospect of marching again
at night through underbrush, with three men, two carrying
guns and the other a machete. Three men who would be
happier to have one certain man less in this world, one who
knew too much for their comfort, even though they might
have a good opinion of this doctor and his willingness to help.
Only one of them needed to entertain such a thought, and
before the other two could prevent it, it would be all over.

Sharply and significantly I looked at the aunt. Out of
politeness she had not taken her seat again, but was waiting
instead to do so until I had left the house. She contemplated
me with gratitude in her eyes. As if by a sudden impulse she
now came close, took my hands, kissed them again and with a
smile on her lips went to a little cupboard, took out a jar of
honey and gave it to me, saying: "This is very good for baking

little cakes. It doesn't make them taste so dry. Tomorrow I'll
send you two dozen eggs and a few pounds of good beef. And
again many, many thanks for coming."

"No hay porqué, señora, not worth mentioning. By the
way, when the boy wakes up give him a good strong meat
broth with two, or better still, four eggs whisked in. It will put
him fast back on his feet. Good night, señora."

The woman knew very well what might happen to me on
the way back home should the men feel that their safety was at
stake. But I had won her sympathy and thankfulness. She, as I
learned later, played a more important part in the business than
what would be guessed from the surface and from what her
honest appearance covered.

Reflecting on the look of this sweet, sweet home where even
a huge heavily framed picture of the Pope in full regalia was
not missing and where a candle before an image of the Virgin
was burning day and night, I could tell who was in command.
Since this woman doubtless was more intelligent than any of
the men I had met so far, I also knew who was the brain of the
enterprise. There is not much difference between an intelli-
gently led band of robbers and certain types of banking
institutions whose presidents ride in custom-built cars. Today
as always the best mask behind which to cover deeds and
misdeeds successfully is still an innocent appearance, a plain
face, and an ostentatious display of believing in God and in the
holiness of His servants. And that smart and intelligent
woman, when she told me in the presence of those men: "I'm
sending you in the morning meat and eggs," was in effect
saying: "Woe to these mugs if you are not safe and sound at
your house tomorrow to enjoy what I'm sending you."

The men understood the command. And they also understood the doctor had to be preserved for the good of the
flourishing business.

We arrived peacefully at my bungalow. When we parted

with a well-meant "buenas noches," I felt three pesos pressed
into my hand by the uncle. "Please, take this, mister, for a
small reimbursement."

"Excuse me," I said, "I don't ever take anything from my
friends for assistance which I give for purely humane reasons
and I'll always do the same whenever an opportunity presents
itself."

For a while he held the three pesos in his hand, most likely
believing that it was only out of politeness that I refused the
money and that in the end I would take it anyway. He, like
everyone else in the village, knew how badly I could use three
pesos. But again I resolutely said: "You don't want to offend
me, do you, señor?"

"Definitely not," he answered, "most definitely not," while
at the same time replacing the three pesos in his pocket. Then
he added: "Let me see, maybe I can send you two more
fellows tomorrow who want to study the English language."

"That's better," I said. "Tomorrow morning I'll come to see
how your boy is getting along."

"Well, well," he muttered, "I don't know, but if you insist,
all right by me."

Next morning about nine or so I went to see the lad.
Scarcely had I passed the last house of the village when I met
the uncle and immediately I had the feeling that he had been
waiting for me because he did not want me to come to his
house in daylight. I was not even sure that I would find the
house again. In fact one week later when I tried to find it out
of pure curiosity, I lost my way so completely that it took me
hours to get on the trail back to the village and then only with
the help of a man I met in the bush. During that eventful night
I had been taken through underbrush and thickets in such a
way that while I thought I knew where we were going I only
learned later that I had been wrong all over.

The uncle told me the boy had been up very early and had gone away with the others.

"We put the bandage on as you told us to and everything went very fine. The wound is healing already. And here are the meat and the eggs the woman promised you last night. And, by the way, mister, you'd better not talk much about all this in the village. You know people might think there was a sort of brawl or what have you and that would give the boy a bad reputation. He's going to get married, see. You understand that, don't you, mister?"

"I understand perfectly," I said. "I've no reason to talk about anything. Not anything at all. But I would very much like you, please, to buy for me the medicine I used up last night when you get to town."

"Of course, of course, it will be a pleasure," he said and took the note on which I had scribbled the name of what I wanted, and we parted.

When I got home two men were sitting at my door steps. They wanted to learn English and they paid me ten hours in advance.

Early in the morning, two days later, I noticed that the village was surrounded by soldiers. Nobody was allowed to leave the village, but those coming from the outside could come in. A few houses were searched and on the main square all men, women and children were questioned by officers of the district police.

I soon learned what had happened.

A few nights ago bandits had attacked a hacienda, bound the owners and had taken all the money they could lay their hands on. Thirty thousand pesos had been stolen. Every child of course knew that this was a lie. No owner of any hacienda would ever have that much money in his house. Two thousand pesos might have come closer to fact.

The soldiers, all Indians themselves, had traced the bandits to this village. Since the place was rumored to be a nest of bandits, the soldiers would have come here anyway.

I walked slowly toward the center of the plaza to watch what was going on, when a man from the village stopped me and said: "There's not much to see. They'll soon go away again without having caught any bandit. They are only looking for an hombre who helped a wounded bandit to get away. When they find that man, the soldiers will shoot him immediately after he has dug his own grave at the cemetery. The officers say that men like these are by far more dangerous to mankind than the bandits themselves."

"What did the man do, how did he help the bandit to make his getaway?" I asked. "Bandits are big and clever enough to help themselves."

"This is a different case," the man said. "It happened this way, you see. At the hacienda that was robbed a young bandit was shot in the leg, maybe he got two shots. He bled profusely, but his friends got him away, and they reached this village. Someone had seen them carry the wounded man on horseback. Where they took him, nobody knows. Then they got hold of a doctor, not a real one, you know, but as you know, señor, one who can do just as well. Now you see, yesterday morning the man, actually a mere boy, was well enough to ride away. The bandits were seen by peasants working in the bush, but the doctor who cured the boy was not with them. They would not have gotten away. The soldiers would have found the boy and then found out who he was, to what family he belonged, and so they would have caught the whole gang."

"Highly interesting," I said. "And now it seems there isn't much hope to catch them?"

"Very little. Since they know that the wounded boy escaped, they are only looking for the doctor who cured him and helped him get away. The officers say that the doctor lives in this village. They have surrounded the whole place so now he cannot get out. They are searching all the houses and as soon as they find the medicine they will know right away who he is. Then they will shoot him on the spot."

"That serves him right," I said. "No decent person should ever help a bandolero."

"You have medicine at your house, too, haven't you?" my neighbor asked.

"Yes, a little for emergency cases. As we call it, First Aid."

At that very moment one officer accompanied by three soldiers came out of the house opposite from where we stood and where they had searched for medicine. I had no liking for being searched and questioned by police, so I walked on, but the neighbor said: "Stay quietly where you are, señor, they won't do anything to us."

I also thought it best to stand still as the officer with his men approached me. Since I was completely innocent, never having attended wounded bandits, never having helped bandits to get away, I had no reason to feel embarrassed.

"Which of the huts over there is yours, señor?" the officer in charge asked.

"That one there, yes, that bungalow back there," I said.

"Have you got any medicine in your jacal?" he asked.

"Yes, a little."

"What kind?"

"A half-empty tube of mentholatum for colds, señor."

"Can you cure shotgun wounds?"

"Has one of your men been shot?" I asked sympathetically.

"Yes," said the officer.

"I'm sorry to hear that," I said, "but when I see blood I faint right away. It makes me awfully sick."

"That's exactly what you look like. You gringos, all of you, don't have the healthy strong nerves we have got. We can see blood and plenty of it. Of course no offense meant. Excuse us for bothering you. We're on duty here, you know. Adiós." He shook hands with me.

My neighbor followed the officer into another hut.

While I was standing there contemplating whether to disappear or remain where I was, a boy ran toward me, shouting before he even reached me: "Mire, señor, here is the medicine I brought from town. The señor said everything is paid already."

I took the package and put it into my pocket.

As soon as my corn was harvested and sold, I thought it wise to leave the neighborhood without waiting for any other thing to happen.

A few weeks later I was sitting in a train going to the capital. Railroad trips sometimes bring people together who have little in common and who under other circumstances would never speak to each other.

Two gentlemen, both natives, sat in front of me and asked whether I would like to play a game of *Siete y Medio* with them. I agreed. We played for beer which was served on the train and thus passed the time until we got tired of the game.

Now they wanted to talk, the kind of small-talk one indulges in on a train and, as always, the conversation very soon turned to Americans living in the Republic and, invariably, whenever a remark was dropped slightly offensive to an American, the gentlemen politely added: "You understand, señor, that was meant only in general, no intention of offending you or your compatriotas."

Then they laughed and I also said something critical of the natives and grinning I would add that one says things like that only for the sake of conversation and that I like every one of them very much as if they were my own countrymen and that all of us have our good and bad sides regardless of what nation we are citizens of.

"And right you are, mister," said one of the two. "We've got many Norte-Americanos down here who cause lots of mischief in our country."

"That I know, señor, there are for instance the big oil magnates, and the mining companies, and the chicle and fruit companies and the big bankers who would like nothing better than to annex one Latin-American country after another."

"Yes, of course, those too," he said, "but fact is I did not think of that sort right now. I was thinking of another sort of gringos. Oh, excuse me, please, what I meant to say is that it seems to me that all the bums and gangsters, gamblers and drug peddlers and hoodlums for whom it gets too hot up there in the States come down here and try their nasty tricks on our honest people here."

"Yes, there are that kind, too," I admitted, "and they believe they are safe down here."

"Not with me," said the little fat gentleman, "no, not with me. With me they don't get very far. In my district these godforsaken hoodlums don't exist. They simply cannot stay alive. I am on their trail immediately. And when I catch them I give them plenty. And when I say plenty I mean plenty. They get deported and take their rap at home."

"Seems you are an Attorney General?" I asked to please him.

"Not yet, but some day maybe, who knows? No, right now I'm only Chief of the Rural Police in the district of San Vicente Lagardilla. Do you know that district, señor? Ever been there?"

"Who? Me? Never in my life," I said truthfully. One must always tell the truth to a Chief of Police, a Judge or a District Attorney. Only then and then only can one pass life pleasantly and happily. I got somehow suspicious of these two gentlemen because San Vicente Lagardilla happened to be the very district where I had rented and worked a small cotton farm and where I had been living in a shaky bungalow in a village among people, all of whom, without exception, looked innocent like freshly washed angels decorating a saint's picture.

The Chief of course knew immediately that I had never been even near that neighborhood. That's why he felt that he could talk freely to me.

"There, in my district, a fair amount of Norte-Americanos are living, some are shopkeepers, some cotton-planters, others farmers and cattle-raisers. They are decent and honest people who pay their taxes punctually and live strictly by the law. None of them causes me ever any trouble. People with education, industrious, money-saving, progressive. People we are proud of, señor; countrymen of yours toward whom I feel a deep respect and we would welcome them becoming citizens, you know."

"Yes, I've met many such fine people from home. Too bad that they didn't stay home," I said with profound conviction.

The Chief seemed not to care much about my opinion; he wanted to talk and so I let him continue. The greatest pleasure one can give people is to let them talk all they want. One is respected much more if one lets people talk instead of talking himself. No one has the least interest in hearing somebody else's opinion. So he continued to tell about a poor fellow who as it seemed had lived in his district and had given him a lot of headaches. He swore that said fellow was wanted for murder, theft, rape, forgery, smuggling of narcotics, selling worthless shares of a gold mine, and a few other felonies.

"I never knew how he managed to come to my district or what he actually did there. He pretended to farm or search for oil, but in reality he was sort of a tramp who scarcely had rags on his back. He never paid for the lease of his farm or the rent for the elegant house in which he lived."

"Maybe the poor chap had no money," I replied.

"Perhaps you are right there and I don't hold that against him. Dios mío, any good man may have bad luck. But what irked me ferociously was what he did in my district. He was a quack. Not that I would have asked him for his license even if he operated on people's bellies, but what I hated most was that he cured all the bandoleros we shot and that made me really mad. Without him we would've shot them all to pieces. But through his activities we never could get a single one of those monsters. He protected them, all of them. He knew every single jacal where they lived and hid out. Worse thing was he not only cured them but he supplied them with a sort of magic potion which made them nearly invisible so that they succeeded in all their attacks. He worked with radio transmitters and light signals, so that these outlaws knew many hours before when the soldiers would arrive at the village. And what money this man earned! The heaps of pesos that the bandoleros brought to his bungalow. That man earned ten times as much as I do being Chief of Police. On top of all that he taught all of them English so that they could attack and rob the American farmers in their own language, his own countrymen. Madre mía, how I chased that man! Four times I was there with a whole company of soldiers to catch him. You being intelligent can imagine how much money all that has cost our government. You see, we can't do anything without money. Everything costs money and a Chief of Police has to live, too. He cannot work for peanuts just out of love for his profession. I received many reproaches from the government and several times I was threatened with dismissal if I would not bring law and order into my district. I reported everything in a sixty-page typewritten report. Now the government finally realizes that I did all that was humanly possible and now they know very well that if those goddamn lawbreakers have a smart gringo backing them what can I with only one company of soldiers at my command do against bandoleros? You're telling me, mister."

"Didn't you ever catch that gringo?"

"Never, no, never. He was so sly, so goddamn cunning we never could even lay an eye on him. Besides, being the doctor of the bandoleros, how could we get anywhere? They protected him because they needed him so very badly. The government knows all that by now. Some day they will get him. We've notified all the police departments in the Republic. Only trouble is we haven't got a picture of him."

"How much will he get, once he's caught?"

"Oh, he will either be shot or sent up for thirty years to the Islas Marías."

"Doesn't that gorilla live in your district anymore?" broke in the other gentleman.

"No, he left one night. We had made it so terribly hot for him that he at last simply had to take to his heels. And believe you me, señor, since he's gone, we've had no more attacks by bandoleros. The village is peaceful and quiet as it hasn't been for many years. So you will see how one man low as only a gringo can be—oh, excuse me, mister, please—may corrupt a whole district populated by law-abiding citizens and good Catholics besides."

When we arrived at San Juan del Rio, two deputies whom the Chief knew entered the train and right away they began a lengthy conversation with the other two gentlemen, now and then shooting a kind of investigating suspicious glance at me as if they had seen me before somewhere. So I thought it would be better for me to take advantage of their being engaged in lively conversation.

Knowing the ways and tricks of members of the police

force, especially the plain-clothed ones, I got off the train as unnoticed as possible at the last stop before it reached the Central Station of the capital, and for convenience' sake boarded a city-bound streetcar.

After all, how was I to know that my pupils wanted to learn English for no other reason than that they could make the cattle of American farmers obey and follow them in a language which the cows understood? And all I got out of my doctoring bandits was a jar of honey, two dozen eggs, a few pounds of beef and three pesos which I did not accept. This certainly was no just equivalent for a possible thirty-year stretch on the Islas Marías.

A New God Was Born

A few years after Hernando Cortes had conquered Mexico, he formed an expedition with the idea of discovering a seaway from the Atlantic to the Pacific. For in that period of history the Americas were believed to be huge islands and not one continental land mass extending from the Arctic to the Antarctic.

Cortes' expedition marched south with the hope of coming upon a strait connecting the two great oceans. The farther south they marched the more difficult became their situation, and they were close to complete exhaustion when they arrived at the great Lake of Peten, situated in what is today the Republic of Guatemala.

On the islands of that lake and along the shores the expedition found many villages inhabited by Indians of the most hospitable and peaceful nature. They were the first human beings Cortes had met for weeks on his arduous march through the immense jungle, which stretched out for hundreds of miles to the west and to the east of the mighty Usumacinta River.

After its tedious march through tropical areas, where the

trail had to be hacked out by Indian auxiliaries brought from Tlaxcala, the Cortes army was suffering from hunger and from all kinds of fevers and jungle diseases. The soldiers' bodies were covered with infected wounds caused by bites and stings of reptiles and insects. The expedition was considered even by its most optimistic officers to be a total loss. In its helpless condition, had it not come upon the hospitable natives of Peten, the so gloriously initiated enterprise would have ended in a huge disaster with no hope for any member of it ever to return to Mexico. Those Indians, had they been a warlike tribe, could have cornered and massacred the whole Cortes army.

(The expedition, by the way, was looked upon as a complete failure when it returned. It added little knowledge to what was known already. Its only achievement was its proof that, as far as it had ventured, there was no navigable strait between the Atlantic and the Pacific.)

The natives of Peten fed Cortes' men as they hadn't been fed since leaving the last populated region in Mexico many weeks before. They cured the sick and wounded, and they gave Cortes plenty of provisions so that the army could march without fear of hunger for the next few weeks.

In their fervor to please their uninvited guests even more and make them happier still, the Indian natives cheerfully agreed to be baptized by the visiting army. And so it was that all of them became good Christians.

The monks who accompanied the expedition saw to it that everything was done properly, according to the established rules. The peaceful natives appeared to have no objection to the destruction of their gods and images, to the cleansing of the Indian temples and the installing of new images brought by the strangers—images of the Holy Virgin, of Santiago, of San Antonio, and half a dozen more.

Because the monks hadn't time enough to baptize each

native individually, they used another method. The baptismal ceremony was turned into a great fiesta, and all the natives of that region were directed to meet on a vast plain where their foreign guests would offer them a show such as they had never before witnessed.

They came, a thousand or so of them. They were asked to kneel down. Then the monks, with hands raised up as if in prayer, bestowed upon them the benediction and declared them Christians, good and true Catholics, who must obey their superiors in Rome.

Those kneeling near the monks, who had been touched personally upon their heads, were ordered to confer that touch upon any man or woman they were to meet.

Now the real show commenced. And what a show! Bugles and trumpets blared. Cannons and muskets were fired. Horsemen performed tournament feats, as knights used to do centuries ago.

These natives of Peten had never seen or heard cannons fired or trumpets sounded. Nor had they ever seen a horse before. So it was only natural that they believed every rider to be physically united to the steed he straddled. The fiesta was an awesome display of powers and happenings strange to the Indians. Of course they were confused. They saw the whole expedition army on their knees singing the *Te Deum*, the monks chanting and performing strange rites, the trumpets and bugles raised up and blaring, cannons and muskets spitting fire and thundering, and horsemen jousting and riding wildly upon the plain.

That whole show was such that even today anywhere on earth it would attract huge crowds and satisfy their craving for excitement. The natives received an impression which would live forever in their memories.

It was part of the clever policy of the conquistadores to impress natives with their power and make them believe that

the white men of the expedition were gods of a kind. It was
for that reason that it had been possible for such a ridiculously
small number of Spanish soldiers to march on and on, leaving
their rear unprotected, because the Indians whom they met on
the way would never dare to raise arms against such divine
beings.

Fortunately, those peaceful natives of Peten owned no
jewelry of gold or silver, possessions which would have made
the Spaniards believe the natives knew of gold or silver mines.
To discover such mines and deposits had been the second
reason—and for most members the first and only reason—that
this costly expedition was undertaken. Nor did the Indians
have pearls or precious stones. Not even the surrounding land
was tempting to the Spaniards, who could lay their hands on
better, more fertile properties in Mexico. The lake was the
principal source of native income, an income which couldn't
be earned just by loafing on the shore and looking dreamily
across the water.

It was natural for Cortes to leave that unfertile area as soon
as his army was well and on its feet again.

For all the services the Spaniards had received from the
natives they paid nothing. Cortes considered them well rewarded in that their sins (of whose existence the Indians
formerly had known nothing) had been cleansed by the
monks and all obstacles to their admission into heaven had
been cleared away. In fact, Cortes left these people in a state of
poverty such as they hadn't known for generations. He took
full advantage of the Indians' natural generosity. All their
stock of fruit, dried fish, dried meat, salt, medicinal herbs and
roots, corn, chili, and cocoa beans (which served them for
money) was carried off by the army for provisions.

On the day of his departure, however, Cortes decided to
show the natives of Peten his gratitude by leaving them a royal
gift. He presented them with a horse—which, as he well knew,

would be accepted by them as the most precious payment they might have hoped to receive. The horse was of no further use to Cortes, since one leg was so badly injured and swollen that the poor animal would only have been a burden to the soldiers if taken on the return march. So it is a fact that this single sign of gratitude and generosity on the part of Cortes was given exclusively in his own interest.

The natives received the horse with all the excitement which such a kingly gift merited. Then the strange visitors disappeared as mysteriously as they had arrived. Had it not been for the horse they now possessed, and the vanished stock of food and supplies they no longer possessed, the peaceful hosts might have believed the whole adventure was a sort of mass hallucination.

Cortes had left a horse with the natives. What he, that mean trader, hadn't left with them was instructions on how to take care of that strange animal.

Now, every Indian the Spaniards met in peace or in battle since their arrival in America had always professed more fear of horses and horsemen than of cannons and muskets. The Spaniards were soon exploiting this fear and took the utmost care never to let Indians go near the horses in camp or at rest sites. Thus, Indians never got a chance to see horses fed. The Spaniards even spread the story that horses and horsemen were invulnerable. In those days horses and riders were heavily armored when in battle, and the Indians, with their primitive arms, couldn't kill or wound the horses or their riders. For this reason the Indians came to believe horses were war gods of a kind they could never defeat. In the siege of Mexico City, however, this belief was badly shaken when Indians managed to kill several horses and their riders too.

The natives of Peten now had a horse. Word spread, and thousands came to see with their own eyes that strange crea-ture the bearded white men had left behind in payment for services received. Because the exotic animal seemed related not only to the white men but also to the fire and thunder of cannons and muskets, the natives looked at the horse in constant awe. Soon they declared it a god.

They brought it the most beautiful flowers and the choicest fruit for gifts, just as they had brought offerings of flowers and fruit to their gods in the temples. The horse sniffed at the flowers in hopes of finding some fodder among them, for it had become very hungry since the conquerors' army had left.

The Indians noted this gesture of the horse and believed that the animal had graciously accepted the offering. Yet, after sniffing the flowers, it turned around and stared longingly across the plain, where in the near distance a huge patch of the finest grass and fields rich with young green corn could be seen. But to these riches the horse couldn't go because it was firmly tied to a big tree.

The natives grew very sad, thinking they had offended this divine creature who refused to accept the flowers and fruit and turned its head aside in open disgust.

The oldest medicine man of the tribe was now sent for. He came, looked the horse over, and said: "You stupid tribesmen, can't you see that this godly being is very sick? Its leg is terribly wounded. See, it has a horrible looking lump there. Treat its ailments and it will be well again in no time, and then it will bless our lake, our fields, and our hunts."

It was then a custom with Indians, as it still is today in remote regions, to feed a sick person only wild turkey, in the belief, based on ages of observation, that the meat of wild turkey has highly curative properties.

The horse's leg was doctored with mashed herbs and it was bandaged. This done, heaps of roast turkey, spiced with the finest aromatic vegetables, were arranged on large native jícara trays, decorated with flowers and fruit, and placed before the starving horse.

The poor animal, plainly at a loss as to how it was possible for human beings to be so utterly ignorant of what a horse likes to eat, began to trample and shy about, trying harder and still harder to free itself from the rope so that it might reach the green pasture from where a light breeze brought the sweetest of odors to its quivering nostrils.

With every hour the horse grew more restless, started to dance about and neigh unceasingly until it tired itself out. Again the medicine man was called. Said he: "Well, you boneheads, don't you see what he needs?"

The natives understood. A beautiful young maiden was chosen, adorned, and offered to the horse. The horse, though, had no interest in this sacrifice either, and didn't even sniff at such a rare gift.

The poor natives by now couldn't think of anything to do to make the horse happy. It dawned on them that this divine creature was sinking fast, and their gloom turned to terror.

Here was a situation where a horse might have led a life so sweet, so quiet, and so happy, a life such as no horse had ever enjoyed since the time horses were found useful to man. Since the natives had no domesticated animals except a species of dog, all the rich pastures in the whole region would have been at the disposal of that horse, to be shared only by an occasional antelope. But ill luck had it that this horse with the heavenly prospects around it was destined to perish by starvation amidst plenty.

There was no remedy for these misunderstandings between the horse and the Indians. The horse finally could do nothing but lie down and die miserably, with a last hopeless glance of its bursting eyes upon that huge crowd of humans, among whom there was not one individual with horse sense.

Horror and consternation seized the natives when they found the horse stiff and cold and dead. Superstitious as they were, they naturally feared the revenge of that godly being.

What better could they do to protect themselves against the wrath of the foreign gods than to bestow upon the dead horse all the honors which a deity had a right to expect from frightened men?

With great ceremony, the horse was buried, and on top of its resting place a temple was built.

Ninety-three years later, in the year of Our Lord 1618, two monks of the Franciscan order came to Lake Peten carrying the gospel to the natives living there. Since Hernando Cortes had left the region no white man had visited Peten.

The two monks entered a temple with the intention of dethroning heathen gods and setting up in their place the image of the Holy Virgin.

Inside the temple their sight fell upon a huge sculpture in stone, very crudely shaped. No matter which way they looked at it, there wasn't the slightest doubt that it was meant to be a horse. In the opinion of those monks the Indian artist had followed an inexplicable whim in making one of the horse's legs imperfect, exposing an ugly protuberance. Yet, from an artistic point of view, that imperfect horse leg was well done.

The monks had seen, heard, and read about very strange gods, but never had they expected to find a horse elevated to the highest worship, as this one was by the Indians of Lake Peten. That piece of sculpture was not only the natives' highest and most powerful creature god, but it was also their god of thunder and lightning, in whose honor, every year on a certain day, great celebrations took place.

The greatest surprise the monks received in their search of the temple, however, was a wooden cross so weather-beaten and decayed that they believed it to be easily a thousand years old. It was standing behind the stone horse and, according to the native folk tales, a white man with a long beard had either brought the cross or made it from a mahogany tree there in the area.

The monks' report on this strange find reached Spain and the rest of Europe and caused immense excitement among scientists and historians. The most fantastic speculations arose to explain the origin of that cross in such strange connection with the stone image of a horse, on a continent where, to the best knowledge of scholars, no horses had existed and no Indians would know anything of the shape or appearance of horses.

Just as speculations and theories had reached the stage where learned men seriously began to maintain that one of the apostles had come in person to the Americas during the first century, a certain registrar to the crown who was studying the archives of former Spanish kings stumbled upon a short note in one of the letters which Hernando Cortes had written to his sovereign, Emperor Charles the Fifth.

This note, relating the episodes of the so-called Hibneras Expedition, cleared up the event of the horse-god and the cross. Without the note, it would have remained one of the greatest mysteries of mankind.

Friendship

One early afternoon the French owner of a restaurant located on Bolivar Street in Mexico City noticed a medium-sized black dog sitting on the sidewalk near the open door of his establishment. Looking in at the Frenchman with soft brown eyes which sparkled with a suggestion of making friends, the dog put on that good-natured, innocent, somewhat tragicomic expression found on some old tramps, who, no matter what happens to them, always have a humorous answer in store, even if they are kicked down the porch steps and a bucket of water is thrown into their face.

For a moment the Frenchman glanced at the dog. Interpreting that look in his own way, the dog wagged his tail, cocked his head, and gave his open mouth such a quizzical twist that he appeared to be grinning at the Frenchman.

So he couldn't help but smile back, and for an instant he had the strange sensation that a little spark of the golden sun had crept into his heart as if to touch it and warm it.

His tail wagging faster now, the dog rose slightly, sat down again and, remaining in this sitting position, moved a few inches closer to the door, yet did not enter.

Considering this a very decent attitude for a hungry street dog, the Frenchman could resist no longer. From a half-empty plate, just taken from a table by a waitress walking past him toward the kitchen, he picked up a steak which the customer, obviously not hungry, had only nibbled.

Lifting that juicy steak with two fingers, holding it high for a few seconds, his eyes fixed on the dog, he waved it invitingly; and, by a move of his head, hinted at the dog to come inside and get it. The dog, wagging not only his tail but his whole hindquarters, closed and opened his mouth quickly, licking his lips with a rosy tongue. Still, he would not enter.

The Frenchman, becoming more interested in the dog than in his patrons, left his place behind the counter and took the steak to the door, playing it before the dog's nose for a few moments before he let it go to its final destination.

The dog caught it more gently than hastily, gave the donor a grateful look, stepped back from the door and lay down on the sidewalk close to the cafe. There he ate that big steak in the undisturbed manner that comes only from a clear conscience.

Done with his meal, the dog stood up, approached the cafe door, sat down and waited patiently until the Frenchman would once again notice him. As soon as the Frenchman granted him that hoped-for look, the dog rose, wagged his tail, put on his comical grin, shook his head as if in fun so that his ears fairly shook, turned and went on his way.

The Frenchman, naturally, thought that the dog had returned to face him hoping for another helping. But when he came to the door, holding between his fingers a chicken leg with lots of meat on it, the dog was gone. So he concluded that the dog had appeared a second time for no other reason than to say, "Thanks a lot, monsieur"; otherwise he would have waited until given another mouthful.

The Frenchman quickly forgot the incident, believing the

animal to be only another street dog that visited cafe doors, searching for food, begging diners or a roll or a bone, until driven away by the waitresses.

Next day, however, about the same time, at half past three, the dog was sitting again at the same place by the open door. The Frenchman, seeing him seated there, smiled at him as if he were an old acquaintance. The dog smiled back, with a very funny expression of silent laughter. When he caught the Frenchman's friendly smile of welcome, he got halfway up, just as he had done the day before, wagged his tail in greeting and widened his grin with his pink tongue dangling over his lower jaw.

With a backward jerk of his head, the Frenchman invited the dog to come inside and have his free lunch close to the counter. The dog, however, who clearly had grasped the meaning of that gesture, came only one short step nearer the door—but enter he would not. The Frenchman realized that the dog refrained from coming inside not so much out of fear as from the apparently inborn decency of intelligent dogs who sense that a room in which humans dwell is not the proper place for dogs living on and by the street.

The Frenchman raised his hand to the countertop, drummed his fingers, and looked at the dog, trying to make him understand that he should wait a few minutes for a plate with a tasty bone on it to come back from one of the tables. To the man's great surprise, the dog understood this finger language perfectly. He stepped back a little from the door, as if not to molest patrons coming in or going out. He lay down on the sidewalk, his head between his forepaws; and, with eyes half closed, he watched the Frenchman attending customers at the counter and collecting money brought by the waitresses to the cash register.

Five minutes later, when a waitress carried a tray of dishes from the tables, the owner winked at her, picked up a huge

leftover sirloin T-bone, took it out to the dog, played it before
his nose and let go.

The dog took it from the man's hand as gently as if it had
been offered by a child. And as he had done the day before, he
lay down on the sidewalk close to the cafe and there enjoyed
his lunch without hurry.

Now, remembering the dog's peculiar attitude of yesterday,
the Frenchman was anxious to learn what the dog would do
today, once he had finished his bone. He wished to know
whether yesterday the dog had acted in that particular way
only because of an occasional impulse or because of natural
good manners or by some sort of training.

He was just about to bet a patron that the dog would come
to the door to say "Thank you" when he noticed a shadow on
the floor near the entrance. He watched the dog from one
corner of his eye, purposely avoiding a full look at the animal
now sitting by the door and patiently waiting to be noticed by
the owner. But the Frenchman busied himself behind the
counter and at the cash register, all the while watching the dog
by stealth just to see how long he would remain sitting there
hoping to get his chance to say, "Thank you very much, until
tomorrow."

Three or four minutes had passed before the Frenchman
decided to look up and gaze straight at the dog's face. Right
away, and as if the dog had been ordered to do just that, he
rose, wagged his tail, put on his quizzical grin, turned around
and disappeared.

From that day on, the Frenchman always had a juicy piece
of leftover meat ready for the dog. And he came every day,
appearing at the door so punctually that one could set one's
watch by his arrival. Always at half past three the Frenchman
would direct a glance towards the door and see the dog sitting
there greeting the owner with his drollish grin.

And so it went for six or seven weeks without the slightest

change in pattern. In fact, the Frenchman came to regard the black street dog as his most faithful customer, and he considered him a sort of mascot.

In spite of the fact that the dog by now felt positively assured of the Frenchman's sincere friendship, he did not relax his formal manners. Never once had he come inside, no matter how often or how insistently the friendly owner invited him to enter.

The Frenchman grew very fond of the dog. He wanted him to hang around for good, make himself useful by chasing less decent dogs away, and guard the premises night and day—or just wait around and have a good time. He, of course, didn't know whether the dog had a master or lived on his own. Lately he had begun to caress the dog for a few moments when he gave him his lunch. It seemed the dog had never in his life known what love was, so he liked that sign of true affection. Yes, he relished the caresses. While he was stroked and patted he would wait patiently, a steak in his mouth, until the Frenchman ceased petting him and returned to his counter. Only then, and not before, would the dog step back from the door, lie down in his accustomed place on the sidewalk and eat his meal. When finished, he would come back to the door to wag his tail, grin at the Frenchman, thereby telling him in his own way, "Merci beaucoup, monsieur, same time tomorrow, bye-bye," and then turn and trot away.

Came a certain day when the Frenchman had a terrific argument with a patron who had been served a hard roll and who, setting his teeth into that roll for a hearty bite, had broken a tooth.

The Frenchman was angry with the waitress who, poor girl, was fired immediately and now crouched in a dark corner weeping bitterly. It hadn't been her fault, entirely. Of course she ought to have noticed that the roll was hard like wood, but so should the customer have noticed it. Anyway, it wouldn't be hygienic or mannerly for a waitress to take each roll into her hand and squeeze it to test its freshness before serving it. But she had served that roll and so she was blamed for what happened.

The real culprit, though, was the baker who had intentionally or carelessly thrown that hard old roll among the hot fresh ones. Anyhow, the damage was done.

The Frenchman, in a thundering rage, rang up the baker and told him that he was on his way, loaded gun in hand, to kill that careless dough-kneader like the rat that he was, for he never was anything else but a stinking sewer rat whose relationship to his father, to say the least, was questionable at all accounts; whereupon the baker told the Frenchman a few of those little mind-openers which, if uttered inside a church, would make its whitewashed walls turn deep red and stay red for keeps. This lively exchange of personal opinions ended with the Frenchman hanging up the receiver with such force that—had telephone engineers not foreseen attacks of this kind and calculated almost perfectly the force which a maddened telephone-user might employ—nothing of the apparatus would have been left intact. As it was, only the hook was bent and the wall plaster nicked.

His face red as a ripe tomato, two bluish veins protruding from his hot forehead, the Frenchman returned to the counter and, looking up, saw his friend the black street dog sitting by the door, grinning, amused as ever, patiently waiting for his lunch to be served.

Seeing that dog sitting there so quiet and innocent, apparently unbothered by any of the worries which make cafe owners appear to be twenty years older than their true age, gazing at the animal as if spying it for the first time in his life, seeing him eagerly wag his tail to greet his benefactor and put on his comical grin to please the friend who liked that doggy face so very much, the Frenchman—practically blinded with madness and driven by a sudden brutal impulse which he, who had no violent temper, later could never explain to himself—took that hard roll from the counter and threw it with all his force at the dog.

The dog had clearly observed the Frenchman's move. He had watched the angry man pick up the roll and had no doubt about the roll being aimed at him. He had seen it shooting through the air towards him. He could easily have dodged that roll had he wished to, for he was a dog that lived entirely on what the street offered him and he was used to the hard life without a master or with a master so poor that he could give little else to his dog but love. Surely the dog had cleverly dodged, perhaps hundreds of times, the sticks and stones thrown at him, and he certainly was an expert at avoiding any sort of missile.

A slight movement of the head would have sufficed to save him from being hit by that hard roll. Yet he did not move. Not an inch did he move. He kept his soft warm eyes fixed straight at the Frenchman's face without a flicker. And without a tremor he most bravely took the shot.

For several seconds he kept sitting in the same place as if stunned, not so much by the blow as by sheer bewilderment caused by a happening which he believed impossible.

The roll lay at the tips of his forepaws where it had dropped after hitting him between the eyes. He gave the roll a short glance, as though he thought it might be a live thing which might jump up and prove to him that he had been mistaken in believing his friend capable of doing such a thoughtless thing.

Now, raising his eyes from the roll, he let them wander across the floor and slowly up the counter until they ultimately came to rest on the Frenchman's frozen face. There they fixed themselves, as if held by magnetic power. No accusation was in the dog's eyes, simply a profound sadness, the sadness of one who infinitely trusts somebody's honest

friendship and then unexpectedly finds himself betrayed, and
cannot tell why it all happened.

The Frenchman, suddenly realizing what he had done, stood
aghast as though he, by accident, had killed a human being. An
involuntary shiver straightened his whole body, and he came to.

For a few seconds he stared at the dog with astonished eyes,
as if seeing an apparition. Now the dog slowly rose, shook his
head so that his ears flapped against his jaws, turned around,
and went his way.

On seeing the dog disappear from the door, the Frenchman
got irritated, looked around vaguely as if to find something
very quick, without for a moment knowing exactly what it
was; and looking down, his eyes came to rest upon a patron
sitting at the counter who was just sticking a fork into a steak
that had been placed before him by a waitress. Deftly, the
Frenchman snatched that steak from the platter of the astonished diner who, with an earsplitting yell, jumped from his seat
and loudly and energetically protested against the outrageous
violation of a citizen's constitutional right to eat his food in
peace.

Holding that steak between his fingers, the Frenchman
darted out of the door and ran along the street. He saw the
dog already trotting along in the next block, and he started
running after him, whistling and calling, not in the least
minding the people on the street who stopped to watch a
lunatic with a steak dangling from his fingers whistling for a
street dog to come and get it. When he reached the third
block and could no longer see the dog or make out where he
had gone, he let the steak drop and walked back to his
restaurant.

"Perdone me, señor, siento mucho," he said to the patron,
who in the meantime had returned to the counter where he
had been given another steak in order to calm him. "Excuse
me, friend, the steak wasn't good anyway, you see . . . besides I just wanted to give it to somebody who might need it

more than you! Please forget it, amigo. Order anything special, and whatever it may be, it'll be on the house."

"Caramba, such things don't happen in an ordinary day's work, so it's okay by me. Don't mention it. I got another steak, thanks to the elegant service you give in this here joint. And say, señor, as to that special order on the house, make mine a double-sized pie à la mode, see. Okay?"

"Right, mister, and a double-sized à la mode it'll be, and you're welcome to it."

Restlessly walking about the place, moving in a daze, here pushing a chair there a table into another position, pulling a tablecloth straight, he presently reached that dark corner where the waitress was crouched, still crying.

"It's all right, Bertha, you can stay on. It wasn't all your fault. I'll murder that baker some day even if I get shot for it. Well, anyhow, I'll change that baker instead of you. That's all. I just got upset with that guy hollering about his cracked false tooth like a monkey gone mad."

"Thanks, boss," Bertha sniffled. "I'm really grateful, really I am, 'n sure thing I'll make it up to you by being a real help around here. See, boss, I got a mother and two brats to care for, and I tell you it ain't so easy to land another job as good as the one I got here, tips and all . . ."

"For Christ's sake, stop talking and get to work. I told you it's okay, so what are you kicking about?"

"I'm not kicking, not at all. I only meant to say thanks, boss." Turning to an impatient patron, she said, "Yeah, yeah, mister, I heard you the first time. Just keep your shirt on and wait a second, okay?"

The Frenchman consoled himself that the dog would come again next day. He wouldn't miss his lunch for a little misunderstanding like that. Why, things like that can happen every day in a dozen places, most anywhere. Every dog is whipped by his master now and then if he deserves it, and the dog stays on, forgetting all about it in an hour or so, perhaps. Dogs are faithful, they stick to the one who feeds them.

Yet, despite reassuring himself, he couldn't feel at ease. For the rest of the day his conscience kept reminding him of the dog's habitual and quizzical grin which had amused him so much whenever he saw it, and he thought how it had died on the dog's face and changed into a desolate sadness, as though in that bad moment something had broken within the dog. The more he tried to forget the dog, the more frequently did he shoot a glance at the door, expecting to see him sitting there. Over and over he told himself that this dog was just a common mongrel, an ordinary street dog, living off the garbage cans, with no character or personality in particular. Yes, hand him a bone and you're his eternal friend. "Gosh," he finally muttered, "can I never concentrate on anything else but that stray dog which is not even mine? Why, I don't even know his name. Well, well. Let's forget it. He isn't worth the trouble, anyhow."

Next day, however, by three in the afternoon, the Frenchman had a good piece of steak ready, juicy and rare, with which to welcome the dog and to apologize at the same time for the insult he had given, and so renew the old friendship.

Half past three. And as if materialized by the striking of the nearest clock there was the dog sitting at his usual place near the door.

The Frenchman's heart leapt with joy. "I knew it, I knew he'd be there," he said to himself with a satisfied smile.

Yet while saying so he felt slightly disappointed that this dog should prove to be exactly like any other dog. As he had come to like the dog, if not to love him, he had expected him to be different from other dogs, more proud or distinguished. Anyhow, he was pleased that the dog had come again and had given him a chance to make the animal feel that only by mistake had he been ill-treated, and that he, Monsieur Leblanc, had never meant to hurt him at all. Generously he forgave the dog his apparent lack of pride, telling himself that man must accept dogs as they are made, since man has no power whatever to change either their physical make-up or their canine nature.

There the dog sat, almost motionless, looking at the Frenchman with its velvety warm eyes as though searching that man's mind.

Greeting the animal with a wide-open smile of welcome, the Frenchman expected the dog to wag his tail and put on his clownish grin as a sign that no bad feelings existed between them. Yet the dog kept his mouth closed and made not the slightest move, either with his head or with his tail, even when he saw the Frenchman pick up the steak and wave it at him from behind the counter. The Frenchman jerked his head to indicate to the dog that he might come in and eat his lunch close to the counter, and thus feel more at home.

The dog, however, remained quietly sitting at his usual place outside the door, looking in at the Frenchman without a flicker of the eye, staring him straight in the face as if he meant to hypnotize the man.

Once more the Frenchman beckoned, with the steak swinging from between his fingers. He smacked his lips at the dog and clucked struuush-struuush to arouse the dog's appetite and to make his mouth water. This time the dog answered by slightly moving his tail, but stopped abruptly when, so it seemed, he realized what he was doing.

Presently, the Frenchman, carrying the steak between his fingers, went out to the dog. Going close to him, he played the meat before the dog's nose, as he often used to do when he was in a mood to tease the dog a bit before letting him have the meal.

The dog, on seeing the Frenchman step up to him, raised his eyes, but otherwise did not move. When the dog refused the offered gift even as it dangled before his nose, the Frenchman, not losing his patience, laid the steak down on the pavement in front of the dog's forepaws. He stroked the animal, pulled one ear gently and patted him on the back while the dog wagged his tail now—but so slightly that the move was barely noticeable. Yet, no matter what the Frenchman did, the dog never let his eyes waver from the man's.

Nodding at the dog with a big smile on his face, the Frenchman returned to his place behind the counter and watched the dog from there, expecting that he would now pick up the steak and eat it as usual out on the sidewalk.

However, the dog didn't. He lowered his head, sniffed without interest the meat before him on the ground, raised his eyes again to the man's face, stood up, turned around, and left.

The Frenchman rushed out onto the sidewalk and saw the dog ambling alongside the buildings, with not one look back at the man staring after him. Soon he disappeared amidst the people walking along the street.

Next day, punctual as ever, the dog again was sitting by the door, gazing at the face of his lost friend. And again, just as on the previous day, when the Frenchman approached, with a huge calf's bone this time, the dog only stared at him without taking the slightest interest in the man's gift laid before him on the sidewalk.

The dog, not for a moment ceasing to stare into the man's eyes, now wagged his tail when the Frenchman stroked and caressed the animal's head and fondled his ears.

Then the dog rose, pushed the man's caressing hand from his head with his nose, licked that hand over and over again for a full minute, once more looked up into the man's eyes—and, without picking up the meaty bone or even sniffing at it, turned around, walked from the doorway and left.

This was the last time the Frenchman ever saw that dog. He never came back to the cafe, and never again was he seen anywhere in the neighborhood.

Conversion of Some Indians

An Indian chieftain named Pluma Roja came to see the Spanish monk, Padre Balmojado, who in the last decade of the sixteenth century came to the Americas to teach the natives the only true faith. Padre Balmojado soon became widely known as a great friend of the Indians and was loved by them for his kindness and his helpfulness.

The chieftain was accompanied by six men, elders of his tribe. These Indians had made a trip of some one hundred fifty miles to see the monk of whom they had heard so much in recent years.

Padre Balmojado received his visitors with the politeness and cordiality for which he was famed.

Pluma Roja greeted Padre Balmojado and said: "Holy white father, we have come for a visit and we want you to tell us about the new gods you brought with you from beyond the great waters. We have come to listen with patience to your holy words and to learn what better gods you have to offer. If you can convince us that your gods are greater and more powerful than ours, and that they really will help us in our many wants, our entire tribe is ready to accept your gods and

your teachings; if we were so convinced, your religion would
be ours, we would respect and honor it as we now do our own.
We shall listen to your words with care and with the greatest
attention, and whatever you tell us we shall carry in our hearts
and think over in our souls. In due time we shall give you our
honest answer. I have spoken, holy white father, and we are
ready to listen to you."

Padre Balmojado didn't use much adornment or pomp; he
preached the gospel in the form of simple stories, in such
manner that he thought even little children would understand
it. He spoke the language of the tribe to which Pluma Roja
and his men belonged. As he couldn't speak it fluently, and as
his pronunciation was poor, he had to speak slowly, distinctly,
and use the easiest words and the simplest constructions; this
was, in a way, to his advantage in the task he was confronted
with.

All details which were difficult to explain and which would
have made long detours in telling, such as the dogmas which
would have confused these children of nature, he left out,
thinking, and rightly so, that there would be sufficient time for
these intricate questions during the next five hundred years.

He devoted a whole day to teaching his visitors, for he was
eager to win that tribe for Christendom. His guests were no
less eager to accept the religion of the whites as the padre was
to persuade them of the superiority of the Catholic faith.

Not once did the Indians interrupt the padre, nor did they
ever ask questions or ask him to repeat something he had said.
They squatted like statues close to his feet. From their eyes,
though, he could see that they didn't miss a single word of
what he told them.

When night began to fall he ended by telling them the story
of the Saviour ascending to heaven and disappearing into a
cloud after having told his followers to go to all countries and
to all peoples and spread the gospel.

For more than twelve hours the Indians had remained seated on the ground without saying one word.

Padre Balmojado went into his little house to prepare supper. Supper ready, he came out and invited his visitors to share his simple meal. The Indians thanked him politely and declined the invitation, telling the monk that they had their own food with them, but that they would like to spend the night on the earthen floor of the padre's porch.

Next morning, Padre Balmojado stepped out to read Mass and found the Indians had risen long before. It seemed that they had been waiting for him some time already. He didn't ask what their decision might be, but before entering his little chapel he looked at them with a certain expectation in his eyes which they well understood.

So chief Pluma Roja said: "Holy white father, we have heard what you told us. We could give you our answer right away because we think our answer is ready. But you have told us your story so very honestly and with so much desire to win us for your faith that my heart would bleed were I to give you our answer at this moment. I might speak hastily and without proper courtesy. I might hurt your feelings and also the feelings of your gods who are so very good and have suffered so very much and have never done any harm to anybody.

"Far be it from us to make the hearts and souls of your gods ache. We, my counsellors and I, shall stay here in the vicinity for three days and sleep here for three nights, and in deep silence we shall listen during these three days and nights to what our gods, our hearts, and our souls have to tell us now that we have heard you. We must give our gods this hearing, too, before we can decide once and for all. After three days have passed we shall come back to you here and give you our answer. Then it will not be a hasty answer; and no god, no friend, no enemy can be hurt, for it is the gods who put into our hearts the thoughts we have. Is this all right with you, father?"

"Perfectly all right, my sons. I shall pray that God Almighty and the Most Holy Virgin may direct your thoughts properly toward your salvation and toward that of your people at home. God bless you, and may He be with you for ever and ever. Amen."

It was three days later.

Padre Balmojado had just celebrated Mass in the little chapel which he himself, with the help of natives, had built; and he was about to enter his house when he found the chieftain and his six elder counsellors waiting by the porch for him.

He wanted to speak with them right away and hear what they had to say. Chief Pluma Roja, however, said, "I see, holy white father, that your morning meal is waiting for you and that you must be hungry. Being hungry would make you hasty, for an empty stomach makes men impatient. In matters of religion, nothing must be hasty. For religion lasts long and the life of man is short. Therefore, have your breakfast first and when your stomach feels well satisfied, please do us the honor then of hearing what I have to say."

When he had finished his meal, the monk came out and led his visitors to the chapel yard where they sat down under a tree. He didn't ask and he didn't urge; he sat and waited for the chieftain to speak.

Half an hour the chieftain sat in silence before he began: "We have turned over in our souls and hearts every word you said to us. I think we haven't forgotten one single detail of the many that came from your venerable lips."

For a few minutes the chieftain hesitated. Then he went on: "Your god did allow men to whip him. Is that right?"

"Yes, that's right. He did so in order to take upon His sacred shoulders all the sins of mankind."

"Your god permitted men and women to spit into his face. He allowed the crowd to throw mud at him. He permitted people to make fun of him, parading him through the streets as a fake chieftain. He permitted persons to put on his head a warrior's headgear made of thorns so as to insult him even more. Is that right?"

"Yes, that's right. He let bad people, who didn't recognize His goodness, do all this. But He did so because He wanted to free all men on earth from their sins, so that they might get to heaven where they can see the glory of God."

"He allowed people to nail him to a wooden post, and he, remaining nailed to that post, died a miserable death there. Is that right?"

"Yes, He did so in order to save mankind from eternal pains in hell."

And the chieftain said: "Holy white father and most honest and kind messenger of your god, now I must tell you what our god has put into our hearts and souls during three days and three nights of fasting and thinking. A god who by his very personality as a god is not able to make men respect him so that people won't dare to spit into his face, whip him, throw mud at him and insult him in the meanest manner cannot be a god for us Indians. One who does not defend himself when being attacked or insulted cannot be a god for us Indians. Somebody nailed to crossed wooden posts who is not strong enough to free himself by his divine power from that post can never save any Indian from any evil or from any enemy."

The chieftain wanted to continue, but Padre Balmojado hadn't the power to keep as quiet and as solemn as the seven Indians had kept themselves for a whole day while he had been talking.

He interrupted the chief, and in an excited voice he said: "Everything you say, my son, is right, but you must see that Our God did these things to save men from the consequences

of sin. He wished to suffer so that men should not have to
suffer through all eternity."

The chief was far from being convinced. He went on: "You
said that he, your god, is an almighty and an all-powerful god.
You also said that he is a god of infinite and unlimited eternal
love and kindness."

"True. So I said, because this is true of Our God."

"Well then, holy father, if your god is really almighty and
all-powerful, why then does he not take all the sins away from
poor humans? If he, as you told us, is such a great god and so
full of eternal love and kindness, why does he allow persons to
commit sins and to make errors? Why didn't he, since he is so
very powerful, not make men perfect, so that they would be
without sins? Does he, your god, allow men to commit sins for
no other reason than to have a chance to save them later when
he thinks it time to do so?"

"Can't you understand, my beloved misguided son, that Our
God did all this so that all men might gain eternal life in
heaven on account of their own merits and on account of their
faith and their belief in God, so that they might have the great
opportunity to earn what they are going to receive from
God?"

"No, holy white father, this is something I can't understand.
Please forgive me if I fail in being polite. But why so roundabout? Why must men earn by a roundabout way that which
a god of eternal love and of never-ceasing kindness ought to
give them for nothing, out of his great love for them? Were
he such a great god of love and kindness, he should not even
ask people to believe in him and pray to him and worship him.
My own mother gives me everything she has to give out of
love for me, whether I believe in her or not, whether I pray to
her or not. She would, my beloved mother would, give me
everything she could; and should I be cruel enough to insult
her, a thing which my god may prevent me from doing even

in my dreams, even then she would give me everything in her power to give. Yes, my mother is far, far greater than is your god. She has more eternal love than your god has, and she is only human."

The monk had no answer ready for the moment, so he tried to lead the discussion away from this dangerous point of comparisons and change it to a certain dogma which, as he knew by long experience, never failed to make a deep impression on simple-minded natives.

"Your mother will die some day, and you and I will have to die some day, too. Yet My God has never died. Perhaps you haven't heard clearly the story that tells how He goes on living for ever and ever. In appearance only did He die. But three days after He had died He came to life again and with great pomp He rose up to heaven."

"How often?" the chief asked in a dry tone.

Astonished at this unexpected question, the monk answered, "Why . . . why . . . eh . . . once only, quite naturally once only."

"Once only? And has he, your great god, ever returned to earth?"

"No, of course not," Padre Balmojado answered, his voice burdened with irritation. "He has not returned yet, but He has promised mankind that He will return to earth in His own good time, so as to judge and to . . ."

". . . and to condemn poor mankind," the chief finished the sentence.

"Yes, and to condemn!" the monk said in a loud and threatening tone. Confronted with such inhuman stubbornness he lost control of himself. Louder still he continued: "Yes, to judge and to condemn all those who deny Him and refuse to believe in Him, and who criticize His sacred words, and who ignore Him, and who maliciously refuse to accept the true and only God even if He is brought to them with brotherly love and a heart overflowing with compassion for the poor ignorant brethren living in sin and utter darkness, and who can obtain salvation for nothing more than having belief in Him and having the true faith."

Not in the least was the chieftain affected by this sudden outburst of the monk, who had been thrown off routine by these true sons of America who had learned to think long and carefully before speaking.

The chieftain remained very calm and serene. With a quiet, soft voice he said: "Here, my holy white father, is what our god had put into our hearts and souls, and it will be the last word I have to say to you before we return to our beautiful and tranquil tierra: Our god dies every evening for us who are his children. He dies every evening to bring us cool winds and freshness of nature, to bring us peace and quiet for the night so that we may rest well, man and animal. Our god dies every evening in a deep golden glory, not insulted, not spat upon, not spattered with stinking mud. He dies beautifully and gloriously, as every real god will die. Yet he does not die forever. In the morning he returns to life, refreshed and more beautiful than ever, his body still trailing the veils and wrappings of the dead. But soon his golden spears dart across the blue firmament as a sign that he is ready to fight the gods of darkness who threaten the peoples on earth. And before you have time to realize what happens, there he stands before wondering human eyes, and there he stays, great, mighty, powerful, golden, and in ever-growing beauty, dominating the universe.

"He, our god, is a spendthrift in light, warmth, beauty, and fertility, enriching the flowers with perfumes and colors, teaching the birds to sing, filling the corn with strength and health, playing with the clouds in an ocean of gold and blue. As my beloved mother does, so does he give and give and never cease giving; never does he ask for prayers, not expecting adoration or worship, not commanding obedience or faith, and never, never condemning anybody or thing on earth. And when evening comes, again he passes away in beauty and glory, a smile all over his face, and with his last glimmer blesses his Indian children. Again the next morning he is the eternal giver; he is the eternally young, the eternally beautiful, the eternally new-born, the ever and ever returning great and golden god of the Indians.

"And this is what our god has put into our hearts and souls and what I am bound to tell you, holy white father: 'Do not, not ever, beloved Indian sons of these your beautiful lands, give away your own great god for any other god.' "

Having said this, the chieftain thanked the monk for all the kindness and attention which he and his men had received during their visit. Then they rolled up their serapes and petates, packed up their gear for the long trip home, and returned to their people to tell them not to trade a basket full of corn for a covered basket whose contents cannot be seen.

It remains to be told that today these Indians are as far removed from the true faith which alone can save men as they were when first they went to visit Padre Balmojado. And therefore we will not have the divine pleasure of finding them in heaven playing their harps for us.

Macario

Macario, the village woodchopper, had one over-whelming desire which he had nourished for fifteen years.

It was not riches he wanted, nor a well-built house instead of that ramshackle old hut in which he lived with his wife and his eleven children who wore rags and were always hungry. What he craved more than anything in this world—what he might have traded his very soul for—was to have a roast turkey all for himself combined with the opportunity to eat it in peace, deep in the woods unseen by his ever-hungry children, and entirely alone.

His stomach never fully satisfied, he would leave home before sunrise every morning in the year, weekday and Sunday alike, rain or shine. He would disappear into the woods and by nightfall bring back a load of chopped wood carried on his back.

That load, meaning a full day's job, would sell for one bit, sometimes even less than that. During the rainy season, though, when competition was slow, he would get as much as two bits now and then for his load of fuel.

Two bits meant a fortune to his wife, who looked even more starved than her husband, and who was known in the village as the Woman with the Sad Eyes.

Arriving home after sunset, Macario would throw off his pack with a heavy groan, stagger into his hut and drop with an audible bump upon a low crudely made chair brought to the equally crude table by one of the children.

There he would spread both his arms upon the table and say with a tired voice: "Oh, Mother, I am tired and hungry, what have we for supper?"

"Black beans, green chili, tortillas, salt and lemon tea," his wife would answer.

It was always the same menu with no variation whatever. Knowing the answer long before he was home, he merely asked so as to say something and, by so doing, prevent his children from believing him merely a dumb animal.

When supper was set before him in earthen vessels, he would be profoundly asleep. His wife would shake him: "Father, supper's on the table."

"We thank our good Lord for what he allows us poor sinners," he would pray, and immediately start eating.

Yet hardly would he swallow a few mouthfuls of beans when he would note the eyes of his children resting on his face and hands, watching him that he might not eat too much so that they might get a little second helping since the first had been so very small. He would cease eating and drink only the tea, brewed of *zacate de limon*, sweetened with a little chunk of *piloncillo*.

Having emptied the earthen pot he would, with the back of his hand, wipe his mouth, moan pitifully, and in a prayerful voice say: "Oh, dear Lord in heaven, if only once in all my dreary life I could have a roast turkey all for myself, I would then die happily and rest in peace until called for the final reckoning. Amen."

Frequently he would not say that much, yet he would never fail to say at least: "Oh, good Lord, if only once I could have a roast turkey all for myself."

His children had heard that lamentation so often that none of them paid attention to it any longer, considering it their father's particular way of saying grace after supper.

He might just as well have prayed that he would like to be given one thousand doubloons, for there was not the faintest likelihood that he would ever come into the possession of roast chicken, let alone a heavy roast turkey whose meat no child of his had ever tasted.

His wife, the most faithful and the most abnegating companion a man would wish for, had every reason to consider him a very good man. He never beat her; he worked as hard as any man could. On Saturday nights only he would take a three-centavo's worth nip of mezcal, and no matter how little money she had, she would never fail to buy him that squeeze of a drink. She would buy it at the general store because he would get less than half the size for the same money if he bought the drink in the village tavern.

Realizing how good a husband he was, how hard he worked to keep the family going, how much he, in his own way, loved her and the children, the wife began saving up any penny she could spare of the little money she earned doing odd jobs for other villagers who were slightly better off than she was.

Having thus saved penny by penny for three long years, which had seemed to her an eternity, she at last could lay her hands on the heaviest turkey brought to the market.

Almost exploding with joy and happiness, she took it home while the children were not in. She hid the fowl so that none would see it. Not a word she said when her husband came home that night, tired, worn out and hungry as always, and as usual praying to heaven for his roast turkey.

The children were sent to bed early. She feared not that her husband might see what she was about, for he had already fallen asleep at the table and, as always, half an hour later he would drowsily rise and drag himself to his cot upon which he would drop as if clubbed down.

If there ever was prepared a carefully selected turkey with a true feeling of happiness and profound joy guiding the hands and the taste of a cook, this one certainly was. The wife worked all through the night to get the turkey ready before sunrise.

Macario got up for his day's work and sat down at the table for his lean breakfast. He never bothered saying good morning and was not used to hearing it said by his wife or anybody in the house.

If something was amiss on the table or if he could not find his machete or the ropes which he needed for tying up the chopped wood, he would just mumble something, hardly opening his lips. As his utterings were few and these few always limited to what was absolutely necessary, his wife would understand him without ever making a mistake.

Now he rose, ready to leave.

He came out, and while standing for a few seconds by the door of his shack looking at the misty gray of the coming day, his wife placed herself before him as though in his way. For a brief moment he gazed at her, slightly bewildered because of that strange attitude of hers. And there she handed him an old basket in which was the roast turkey, trimmed, stuffed and garnished, all prettily wrapped up in fresh green banana leaves.

"There now, there, dear husband, there's the roast turkey you've been praying for during so many long years. Take it along with you to the deepest and densest part of the woods where nobody will disturb you and where you can eat it all alone. Hurry now before the children smell it and get aware of that precious meal, for then you could not resist giving it to them. Hurry along."

He looked at her with his tired eyes and nodded. *Please* and *thanks* were words he never used. It did not even occur to him to let his wife have just one little bite of that turkey because his mind, not fit to handle more than one thought at a time, was at this instant exclusively occupied with his wife's urging to hurry and run away with his turkey lest the children get up before he could leave.

He took his time finding himself a well-hidden place deep in the woods and as he, because of so much wandering about, had become sufficiently hungry by now, he was ready to eat his turkey with genuine gusto. He made his seat on the ground very comfortable, washed his hands in a brook near-by, and everything was as perfect as it should be at such a solemn occasion—that is, the fulfillment of a man's prayer said daily for an almost uncountable number of years.

With a sigh of utter happiness, he leaned his back against the hollow trunk of a heavy tree, took the turkey out of the basket, spread the huge banana leaves before him on the ground and laid the bird upon them with a gesture as if he were offering it to the gods. He had in mind to lie down after the meal and sleep the whole day through and so turn this day, his saint's day, into a real holiday—the first in his life since he could think for himself.

On looking at the turkey so well prepared and taking in that sweet aroma of a carefully and skillfully roasted turkey, he muttered in sheer admiration: "I must say this much of her, she's a great and wonderful cook. It is sad that she never has the chance to show her skill."

That was the most profound praise and the highest expression of thanks he could think of. His wife would have burst with pride and she would have been happy beyond words had he only once in his life said that in her presence. This, though, he would never have been able to do, for in her presence such words would simply refuse to pass his lips.

Holding the bird's breast down with his left hand, he firmly grabbed with his right one of the turkey's thick legs to tear it off.

And while he was trying to do so, he suddenly noted two feet standing right before him, hardly two yards away.

He raised his eyes up along the black, tightly fitting pants which covered low riding boots as far down as the ankles and found, to his surprise, a Charro in full dress, watching him tear off the turkey's leg.

The Charro wore a sombrero of immense size, richly trimmed with gold laces. His short leather coat was adorned with the richest gold, silver and multicolored silk embroidery one could imagine. To the outside seams of the Charro's black trousers, and reaching from the belt down to where they came to rest upon the heavy spurs of pure silver, a row of gold coins was sewn. A slight move the Charro would make now and then while he was speaking to Macario caused these gold coins to send forth a low, sweet-sounding tinkle. He had a black moustachio, the Charro had, and a beard like a goat's. His eyes were pitch black, very narrow and piercing, so that one might virtually believe them needles.

When Macario's eyes reached his face, the stranger smiled, thin-lipped and somewhat malicious. He evidently thought his smile a most charming one, by which any human, man or woman, would be enticed beyond help.

"What do you say, friend, about a fair bite of your tasty turkey for a hungry horseman," he said in a metallic voice. "See, friend, I've had a long ride all through the night and now I'm nearly starved and so, please, for hell's sake, invite me to partake of your lunch."

"It's not lunch in the first place," Macario corrected, holding onto his turkey as if he thought that bird might fly away at any moment. "And in the second place, it's my holiday dinner and I won't part with it for anybody, whoever he may be. Do you understand?"

"No, I don't. Look here, friend, I'll give you my heavy silver spurs just for that thick leg you've grabbed," the Charro bargained, moistening his lips with a thin dark red tongue which, had it been forked, might have been that of a snake.

"I have no use for spurs whether they are of iron, brass, silver or gold trimmed with diamonds all over, because I have no horse to ride on." Macario judged the value of his roast turkey as only a man would who had waited for that meal for many years.

"Well then, friend, if it is worth that much to you, I'll cut off all these gold coins which you see dangling from my trousers and I'll give them to you for a half breast of that turkey of yours. What about that?"

"That money would do me no good. If I spent only one single coin they'd clap me in jail right away and there torture me until I'd tell them where I stole it, and after that they'd chop off one hand of mine for being a thief. What could I, a woodchopper, do with one hand less when, in fact, I could use four if only the Lord had been kind enough to let me have that many."

Macario, utterly unconcerned over the Charro's insistence, once more tried to tear off the leg and start eating when the visitor interrupted him again: "See here, friend, I own these woods, the whole woods, and all the woods around here, and I'll give you these woods in exchange for just one wing of your turkey and a fistful of the fillings. All these woods, think of it."

"Now you're lying, stranger. These woods are not yours, they're the Lord's, or I couldn't chop in here and provide the villagers with fuel. And if they were your woods and you'd give them to me for a gift or in payment for a part of my turkey, I wouldn't be any richer anyhow because I'd have to chop them just as I do now."

Said the Charro: "Now listen, my good friend——"

"Now you listen," Macario broke in impatiently. "You aren't my good friend and I'm not your good friend and I hope I never will be your good friend as long as God saves my soul. Understand that. And now go back to hell where you came from and let me eat my holiday dinner in peace."

The Charro made a horribly obscene grimace, swore at Macario and limped off, cursing the world and all mankind.

Macario looked after him, shook his head and said to himself: "Who'd expect to meet such funny jesters in these woods? Well, I suppose it takes all kinds of people and creatures to make it truly our Lord's world."

He sighed and laid his left hand on the turkey's breast as he had done before and with his right grasped one of the fowl's legs.

And again he noted two feet standing right before him at the same spot where, only a half minute earlier, the Charro had been standing.

Ordinary huaraches, well-worn as though by a man who has wandered a long and difficult road, covered these two feet. Their owner was quite obviously very tired and weary, for his feet seemed to sag at the arches.

Macario looked up and met a very kind face, thinly bearded. The wanderer was dressed in very old, but well-washed, white cotton pants and a shirt of the same stuff, and he looked not very different from the ordinary Indian peasant of the country.

The wanderer's eyes held Macario's as though by a charm and Macario became aware that in this pilgrim's heart were combined all the goodnesses and kindnesses of earth and heaven, and in each of the wanderer's eyes he saw a little golden sun, and each little golden sun seemed to be but a little golden hole through which one might crawl right into heaven and see Godfather Himself in all His glory.

With a voice that sounded like a huge organ playing from a distance far away, the wanderer said: "Give unto me, my good neighbor, as I shall give unto you. I am hungry, very hungry indeed. For see, my beloved brother, I have come a long way. Pray, let me have that leg which you are holding and I shall truly and verily bless you for it. Just that leg, nothing else. It will satisfy my hunger and it will give me new strength, for very long still is my way before reaching my father's house."

"You're a very kind man, wanderer, the kindest of men that ever were, that are today, and that are to come," Macario said, as though he was praying before the image of the Holy Virgin.

"So I beg of you, my good neighbor, give me just one half of the bird's breast, you certainly will not miss it much."

"Oh, my beloved pilgrim," Macario explained as if he were speaking to the archbishop whom he had never seen and did not know but whom he believed the highest of the highest on earth. "If you, my Lord, really mean to say that I won't miss it much, I shall answer that I feel terribly hurt in my soul because I can't say anything better to you, kind man, but that you are very much mistaken. I know I should never say such a thing to you for it comes close to blasphemy, yet I can't help it, I must say it even should that cost me my right to enter heaven, because your eyes and your voice make me tell the truth.

"For you see, your Lordship, I must not miss even the tiniest little morsel of this turkey. This turkey, please, oh please, do understand, my Lord, was given me as a whole and was meant to be eaten as a whole. It would no longer be a whole turkey were I to give away just a little bit not even the size of a fingernail. A whole turkey—it was what I have yearned for all my life, and not to have it now after a lifetime of praying for it would destroy all the happiness of my good and faithful wife who has sacrificed herself beyond words to make me that great gift. So, please, my Lord and Master, understand a poor sinner's mind. Please, I pray you, understand."

And the wanderer looked at Macario and said unto him: "I do understand you, Macario, my noble brother and good neighbor, I verily do understand you. Be blessed for ever and ever and eat your turkey in peace. I shall go now, and on passing through your village I shall go near your hut where I shall bless your good wife and all your children. Be with the Lord. Good-bye."

Not once while he had made these speeches to the Charro and to the wanderer had it occurred to Macario, who rarely spoke more than fifty words a day, to stop to think what had made him so eloquent—why it was that he, in the depths of the woods, could speak as freely and easily as the minister in church and use words and expressions which he had never known before. It all came to him without his realizing what was happening.

He followed the pilgrim with his eyes until he could see him no longer.

He shook his head sadly.

"I most surely feel sorry about him. He was so very tired and hungry. But I simply could do nothing else. I would have insulted my dear wife. Besides, I cannot spare a leg or part of the breast, come what may, for it would no longer be a whole turkey then."

And again he seized the turkey's leg to tear it off and start his dinner when, again, he noted two feet standing before him and at the same spot the others had stood a while ago.

These two feet were standing in old-fashioned sandals, and Macario thought that the man must be a foreigner from far-off lands, for he had never seen sandals like these before.

He looked up and stared at the hungriest face he had ever believed possible. That face had no flesh. It was all bone. And all bone were the hands and the legs of the visitor. His eyes seemed to be but two very black holes hidden deep in the fleshless face. The mouth consisted of two rows of strong teeth, bared of lips.

He was dressed in a faded bluish-white flowing mantle which, as Macario noted, was neither cotton nor silk nor wool nor any fabric he knew. He held a long staff in one hand for support.

From the stranger's belt, which was rather carelessly wound around his waist, a mahogany box, scratched all over, with a clock ticking audibly inside, was dangling on a bit of a string.

It was that box hanging there instead of the hourglass which Macario had expected that confused him at first as to what the new visitor's social standing in the world might be.

The newcomer now spoke. He spoke with a voice that sounded like two sticks clattering one against the other.

"I am very hungry, compadre, very, very hungry."

"You don't need to tell me. I can see that, compadre," Macario asserted, not in the least afraid of the stranger's horrible appearance.

"Since you can see that and since you have no doubt that I need something substantial in my stomach, would you mind giving me that leg of the turkey you are holding?"

Macario gave forth a desperate groan, shrugged and lifted up his arms in utter helplessness.

"Well," he said, with mourning in his voice, "what can a poor mortal do against fate? I've been caught at last. There's no way out any more. It would have been a great adventure, the good God in heaven knows it, but fate doesn't want it that way. I shall never have a whole turkey for myself, never, never and never, so what can I do? I must give in. All right, compadre, get your belly's fill; I know what hunger is like. Sit down, hungry man, sit down. Half the turkey's yours and be welcome to it."

"Oh, compadre, that is fine, very fine," said the hungry man, sitting down on the ground opposite Macario and widening his row of teeth as if he were trying to grin.

Macario could not make out for sure what the stranger meant by that grin, whether it was an expression of thanks or a gesture of joy at having been saved from a sure death by starvation.

"I'll cut the bird in two," Macario said, in a great hurry now lest another visitor might come up and make his own part a third only. "Once I've cut the bird in two, you just look the other way and I'll lay my machete flat between the two halves and you tell which half you want, that next to the edge or that next to the back. Fair enough, Bone Man?"

"Fair enough, compadre."

So they had dinner together. And a mighty jolly dinner it was, with much clever talking on the part of the guest and much laughter on the side of the host.

"You know, compadre," Macario presently said, "at first I was slightly upset because you didn't fit into the picture of you I had in my mind. That box of mahogany with the clock in it which you carry hanging from your belt confused me quite a bit and made it hard for me to recognize you promptly. What has become of your hourglass, if it isn't a secret to know?"

"No secret at all, no secret at all. You may tell the world if it itches you to do so. You see, it was like this. There was a big battle in full swing somewhere around Europe, which is the fattest spot on earth for me next to China. And I tell you,

compadre, that battle kept me on the run as if I were still a
youngster. Hither and thither I had to dart until I went nearly
mad and was exhausted entirely. So, naturally, I could not take
proper care of myself as I usually do to keep me fit. Well, it
seems a British cannon ball fired in the wrong direction by a
half-drunken limey smashed my cherished hourglass so completely that it could not be mended again by old smith Pluto
who likes doing such odd jobs. I looked around and around
everywhere, but I could not buy a satisfactory new one since
they are made no longer, save for decorations on mantel pieces
which, like all such silly knickknacks, are useless. I tried to
swipe one in museums, but to my horror I discovered that
they were all fakes, not a genuine instrument among them."

A chunk of tender white meat which he chewed at this
instant let him forget his story for a while. Remembering that
he had started to tell something without finishing it, he now
asked: "Oh, well, where was I with my tale, compadre?"

"The hourglasses in all the museums were all fakes wherever
you went to try one out."

"Right. Yes, now isn't it a pity that they build such wonderful great museums around things which are only fakes? Coming back to the point: there I was without a correctly adjusted
hourglass, and many mistakes were bound to happen. Then it
came to pass not long afterwards that I visited a captain sitting
in his cabin of a ship that was rapidly sinking away under him
and with the crew all off in boats. He, the captain I mean,
having refused to leave his ship, had hoisted the Union Jack
and was stubbornly sticking by his ship whatever might
happen to her, as would become a loyal British captain. There
he now sat in his cabin, writing up his log-book.

"When he saw me right before him, he smiled at me and
said: 'Well, Mr. Bone Man—Sir, I mean, seems my time is up.'
'It is, skipper,' I confirmed, also smiling to make it easier for
him and make him forget the dear ones he would leave behind.

He looked at his chronometer and said: 'Please, sir, just allow me fifteen seconds more to jot down the actual time in my log-book.' 'Granted,' I answered. And he was all happiness that he could write in the correct time. Seeing him so very happy, I said: 'What about it, Cap'n, would you mind giving me your chronometer? I reckon you can spare it now since you won't have any use for it any longer, because aboard the ship you will sail from now on you won't have to worry about time at all. You see, Cap'n, as a matter of fact my hourglass was smashed by a British cannon ball fired by a drunken British gunner in the wrong direction, and so I think it only fair and just that I should have in exchange for my hourglass a British-made chronometer.'"

"Oh, so that's what you call that funny-looking little clock —a chronometer. I didn't know that," Macario broke in.

"Yes, that's what it is called," the hungry man admitted with a grin of his bared teeth. "The only difference is that a chronometer is a hundred times more exact in telling the correct time than an ordinary watch or a clock. Well, compadre, where was I?"

"You asked the ship's master for the chro . . ."

". . . nometer. Exactly. So when I asked him to let me have that pretty timepiece he said: 'Now, you are asking for just the very thing, for it happens that this chronometer is my personal property and I can dispose of it any way it damn pleases me. If it were the company's I would have to deny you that beautiful companion of mine. It was perfectly adjusted a few days before we went on this rather eventful voyage and I can assure you, Mr. Bone Man, that you can rely on this instrument a hundred times better than on any of your old-fashioned glasses.' So I took it with me on leaving the rapidly sinking ship. And that's how I came to carry this chronometer instead of that shabby outdated hourglass I used to have in bygone days.

"And I can tell you one thing, compadre, this British-made gadget works so perfectly that, since I got hold of it, I have never yet missed a single date, whereas before that many a man for whom the coffin or the basket or an old sack had already been brought into the house escaped me. And I tell you, compadre, escaping me is bad business for everybody concerned, and I lose a good lot of my reputation whenever something of this sort happens. But it won't happen anymore now."

So they talked, told one another jokes, dry ones and juicy ones, laughed a great deal together, and felt as jolly as old friends meeting each other after a long separation.

The Bone Man certainly liked the turkey, and he said a huge amount of good words in praise of the wife who had cooked the bird so tastily.

Entirely taken in by that excellent meal he, now and then, would become absent-minded and forget himself, and try to lick his lips which were not there with a tongue which he did not have.

But Macario understood that gesture and regarded it as a sure and unmistakable sign that his guest was satisfied and happy in his own unearthly way.

"You have had two visitors before today, or have you?" the Bone Man asked in the course of their conversation.

"True. How did you know, compadre?"

"How did I know? I have to know what is going on around the world. You see, I am the chief of the secret police of—of—well, you know the Big Boss. I am not allowed to mention His name. Did you know them—those two visitors, I mean?"

"Sure I did. What do you think I am, a heathen?"

"The first one was what we call our main trouble."

"The Devil, I knew him all right," Macario said confidently. "That fellow can come to me in any disguise and I'd know him anywhere. This time he tried looking like a Charro, but

smart as he thinks he is, he had made a few mistakes in dressing
up, as foreigners are apt to do. So it wasn't hard for me to see
that he was a counterfeit Charro."

"Why didn't you give him a small piece of your turkey
then, since you knew who he was? That hop-about-the-world
can do you a great deal of harm, you know."

"Not to me, compadre. I know all his tricks and he won't
get me. Why should I give him part of my turkey? He had so
much money that he had not pockets enough to put it in and
so had to sew it outside on his pants. At the next inn he passes
he can buy if he wishes a half dozen roast turkeys and a couple
of young roast pigs besides. He didn't need a leg or a wing of
my turkey."

"But the second visitor was—well, you know Whom I refer
to. Did you recognize Him?"

"Who wouldn't? I am a Christian. I would know Him
anywhere. I felt awfully sorry that I had to deny Him a little
bite, for I could see that He was very hungry and terribly in
need of some food. But who am I, poor sinner, to give Our
Lord a little part of my turkey. His father owns the whole
world and all the birds because He made everything. He may
give His Son as many roast turkeys as the Son wants to eat.
What is more, Our Lord, Who can feed five thousand hungry
people with two fishes and five ordinary loaves of bread all
during the same afternoon, and satisfy their hunger and have
still a few dozens of sacks full of crumbs left over—well,
compadre, I thought that He Himself can feed well on just one
little leaf of grass if He is really hungry. I would have considered it a really grave sin giving Him a leg of my turkey.
And another thing, He Who can turn water into wine just by
saying so can just as well cause that little ant walking here
on the ground and picking up a tiny morsel to turn into a roast

turkey with all the fillings and trimmings and sauces known in heaven.

"Who am I, a poor woodchopper with eleven brats to feed, to humiliate Our Lord by making Him accept a leg of my roast turkey touched with my unclean hands? I am a faithful son of the Church, and as such I must respect the power and might and dignity of Our Lord."

"That's an interesting philosophy, compadre," the Bone Man said. "I can see that your mind is strong, and that your brain functions perfectly in the direction of that human virtue which is strongly concerned with safeguarding one's property."

"I've never heard of that, compadre." Macario's face was a blank.

"The only thing that baffles me now is your attitude toward me, compadre." The Bone Man was cleaning up a wing bone with his strong teeth as he spoke. "What I would like to hear is why did you give me half of your turkey when just a few minutes before you had denied as little as a leg or a wing to the Devil and also to Our Lord?"

"Ah," Macario exclaimed, throwing up both his hands to emphasize the exclamation. And "Ah," he said once more, "that's different; with you that's very different. For one thing, I'm a human being and I know what hunger is and how it feels to be starved. Besides, I've never heard as yet that you have any power to create or to perform miracles. You're just an obedient servant of the Supreme Judge. Nor have you any money to buy food with, for you have no pockets in your clothes. It's true I had the heart to deny my wife a bite of that turkey which she prepared for me with all her love put in for extra spices. I had the heart because, lean as she is, she doesn't look one-tenth as hungry as you do. I was able to put up enough will power to deny my poor children, always crying for food, a few morsels of my roast turkey. Yet, no matter how hungry my children are, none of them looks one-hundredth as hungry as you do."

"Now, compadre, come, come. Don't try to sell me that," the dinner guest clattered, making visible efforts to smile. "Out with the truth. I can bear it. You said 'For one thing' when you started explaining. Now tell me the other thing as well. I can stand the truth."

"All right then," Macario said quietly. "You see, compadre, I realized the very moment I saw you standing before me that I would not have any time left to eat as little as one leg, let alone the whole turkey. So I said to myself, as long as he eats too, I will be able to eat, and so I made it fifty-fifty."

The visitor turned his deep eyeholes in great surprise upon his host. Then he started grinning and soon he broke into a thundering laughter which sounded like heavy clubs drumming a huge empty barrel. "By the great Jupiter, compadre, you are a shrewd one, indeed you are. I cannot remember having met such a clever and quick-witted man for a long time. You deserve, you truly and verily deserve to be selected by me for a little service, a little service which will make my lonely existence now and then less boresome to me. You see, compadre, I like playing jokes on men now and then as my mood will have it. Jokes that don't hurt anybody, and they amuse me and help me to feel that my job is, somehow, less unproductive, if you know what I mean."

"I guess I know how you mean it."

"Do you know what I am going to do so as to pay honestly for the dinner you offered me?"

"What, compadre? Oh, please, sir, your lordship, don't make me your assistant. Not that, please, anything else you wish, but not your helper."

"I don't need an assistant and I have never had one. No, I have another idea. I shall make you a doctor, a great doctor

who will outwit all those haughty learned physicians and
superspecialists who are always playing their nasty little tricks
with the idea that they can put one over on me. That's what I
am going to do: make you a doctor. And I promise you that
your roast turkey shall be paid for a millionfold."

Speaking thus he rose, walked some twenty feet away,
looked searchingly at the ground, at that time of the year dry
and sandy, and called back: "Compadre, bring your *guaje*
bottle over here. Yes, I mean that bottle of yours which looks
as though it were of some strange variety of pumpkin. But first
pour out all the water which is still in it."

Macario obeyed and came close to where his guest waited
for him. The visitor spat seven times upon the dry ground,
remained quiet for a few minutes and then, all of a sudden,
crystal-clear water sputtered out of that sandy soil.

"Hand me your bottle," the Bone Man said.

He knelt down by the little pool just forming and with one
hand spooned up the water and poured it into Macario's *guaje*
bottle. This procedure took quite some time, for the mouth of
the bottle was extremely small.

When the bottle, which held about a quart, was full, the
Bone Man, still kneeling by the pool, tapped the soil with one
hand and the water immediately disappeared from view.

"Let's go back to our eating place, compadre," the visitor
suggested.

Once more they sat down together. The Bone Man handed
Macario the bottle. "This liquid in your bottle will make you
the greatest doctor known in the present century. One drop of
this fluid will cure any sickness, and I include any sickness
known as a fatal and as an incurable one. But mind, and mind
well, compadre, once the last drop is gone, there will be no
more of that medicine and your curing power will exist no
longer."

Macario was not at all excited over that great gift. "I don't know if I should take that present from you. You see, compadre, I've been happy in my own way. True it is that I've been hungry always all though my life; always I've been tired, always been struggling with no end in view. Yet that's the way with people in my position. We accept that life because it was given us. It's for that reason that we feel happy in our way—because we always try making the best of something very bad and apparently hopeless. This turkey we ate together today has been the very peak of my life's ambition. I never wanted to go up higher in all my desires than to have one roast turkey with all the trimmings and fillings all for myself, and be allowed to eat it in peace and all alone with no hungry children's eyes counting every little bite going into my hungry stomach."

"That's just why. You didn't have your roast turkey all by yourself. You gave me half of it, and so your life's ambition is still not accomplished."

"You know, compadre, that I had no choice in that matter."

"I suppose you are right. Anyway, whatever the reason, your one and only desire in this world has not yet been satisfied. You must admit that. So, if you wish to buy another turkey without waiting for it another fifteen or twenty years, you will have to cure somebody to get the money with which to buy that turkey."

"I never thought of that," Macario muttered, as if speaking to himself. "I surely must have a whole roast turkey all for myself, come what may, or I'll die a most unhappy man."

"Of course, compadre, there are a few more things which you ought to know before we part for a while."

"Yes, what is it, tell me."

"Wherever you are called to a patient you will see me there also."

On hearing that, unprepared as he was for the catch, Macario got the shivers.

"Don't get frightened, compadre, no one else will see me; and mind you well what I am going to tell you now. If you see me standing at your patient's feet, just put one drop of your medicine into a cup or glass of fresh water, make him drink it, and before two days are gone he will be all right again, sane and sound for a good long time to come."

"I understand," Macario nodded pensively.

"But if," the Bone Man continued, "you see me standing at your patient's head, do not use the medicine; for if you see me standing thus, he will die no matter what you do and regardless of how many brilliant doctors attempt to snatch him away from me. In that case do not use the medicine I gave you because it will be wasted and be only a loss to you. You must realize, compadre, that this divine power to select the one that has to leave the world—while some other, be he old or a scoundrel, shall continue on earth—this power of selection I cannot transfer to a human being who may err or become corrupt. That's why the final decision in each particular case must remain with me, and you must obey and respect my selection."

"I won't forget that, sir," Macario answered.

"You had better not. Well, now, compadre, let us say good-bye. The dinner was excellent, exquisite I should call it, if you understand that word. I must admit, and I admit it with great pleasure, that I have had an enjoyable time in your company. By all means, that dinner you gave me will restore my strength for another hundred years. Would that when my need for another meal is as urgent as it was today, I may find as generous a host as you have been. Much obliged, compadre. A thousand thanks. Good-bye."

"Good-bye, compadre."

Macario spoke as though he were waking from a heavy

dream, yet immediately he realized that he had not been dreaming.

Before him on the ground were the well-picked bones of that half turkey which his guest had eaten with so much delight.

Mechanically he cleaned up all the morsels which had dropped and stuffed them into his mouth, so that nothing should be wasted, all the while trying to find the meaning of the several adventures that were crammed into the limited space of his mind.

The thing most difficult for him to understand was how it had been possible for him to talk so much and talk what he believed was very clever as, in his opinion, only a learned man could do. But then he knew that when in the woods he always had very clever thoughts; only at home in the presence of his wife and children he had no thoughts whatever and his mouth was as if glued and it cost him much labor to get out of it one full sentence.

Soon he got tired and presently lay down under a tree to sleep the rest of the day, as he had promised himself that he would after his holiday dinner.

No fuel did he bring back that night.

His wife had not a red cent in the house with which to buy food the next day.

Yet she did not reproach him for having been lazy, as in fact she never criticized anything he did or did not. The truth was that she felt immensely happy to be alive. For, during the day, and about noon, when she was busy in the yard washing the children's rags, a strange golden ray which, so it appeared, came not from the sun, but from an unknown source, had touched her whole body, while at the same time she had heard inside her heart a sweet music as if played by a huge organ from far, far above the earth.

From that moment on and all the whole day she had felt as

though lifted from the ground, and her mind had been at peace as she could not remember having ever felt before. Nothing of this phenomenon did she tell her husband. She kept it to herself like a very sacred property all her own.

When she served supper there was still some reflection of that golden ray visible on her face.

Even her husband noted it on giving her a casual glance. But he said nothing, for he was still heavily occupied with his own fortunes of the day.

Before he went to sleep that night, later than usual, for he had slept well during the day out in the woods, his wife asked him timidly: "How was the turkey, dear husband?"

"What do you think was the matter with it since you ask me how it was? What do you mean? Was there something wrong with it? It was quite all right as far as I could judge, with the little experience I've had eating roast turkey."

With not a single word did he mention his visitors.

When he had turned about to go to his cot, she looked at him, watching his face sidewise and thoughtfully. Something was new in him, something had come over him. Never before had he talked that much to her at one breath.

Next day was a hungry one for the whole family. Their breakfast, including that of Macario's, was always lean. Yet this morning his wife had to make it smaller still, for it had to be stretched into two more meals.

Soon Marcario was through with the few mouthfuls of black beans seasoned with green chili and a pot of *atole* for a drink. Complain he did not because he realized that the blame was on him.

He took up his machete, his ax and his ropes and stepped out into the misty morning.

Considering the way he went about his usual hard task of

chopping wood, he might as well have forgotten about the precious medicine and all that went with it.

Only a few paces had he gone when his wife called after him: "Husband, your water bottle."

This reminded him like a flash that the whole adventure of the day before might after all not have been a dream but reality. Last night, on thinking of the happenings, he had reached the conclusion that it might have been but sort of an imagination caused by a stomach not used to being filled up with roast turkey.

"It's still full of water," the wife said, bringing the *guaje* bottle out and shaking it. "Shall I pour the old water out and put in fresh water?" she asked, while playing with the cork cut from a corn cob.

"Yes, I know, woman, it's still full," Macario answered, not a bit afraid that his wife might be too hasty and spill the miraculous liquid away. "Yesterday I drank from the little brook. Just give me the bottle full as it is. The water is good; I got it out there in the woods."

On his way to work and some fair distance away from his hut which was the last at this side of the village, he hid the bottle in dense bushes, partly covering it with soil.

That night he brought home one of the biggest loads of heavy fine dry fuel such as he had not delivered for many months. It was sold at three bits, a price unheard of, and was sold that same night on the first call the older boy made. So the family felt like having come into a million.

Next day Macario went about his job as usual.

On the night before he had told his wife casually that he had broken his *guaje* bottle because a heavy trunk had dropped upon it, and she had to give him another one of the several they kept in the house. These bottles cost them nothing, for the older boys discovered them growing wild in the bush somewhere.

Again he brought home that night a good load of chopped wood, yet this time he found his family in a pitiful distress.

His wife, her face swollen, her eyes red from long crying, rushed at him the moment he came in. "Reginito is dying, my poor little baby, Regino, will be gone in a halfhour," and she broke into heartbreaking lamentation, tears streaming down her face.

Helplessly and stupidly he looked at her the way he always looked if something in the house happened which was out of the gloomy routine by which this home of his was run. When his wife stepped aside, he noted that there were present several neighbors, all women, partly standing, partly squatting close to the cot on which the child had been bedded.

His was the poorest family in the village, yet they were among the best liked for their questions, their honesty, their modesty, and because of that unearned virtue that the poor are always liked better than the rich anywhere and by everybody.

Those women, in their neighborly zeal to help the so very poor Macario, and on hearing of the child's being sick, had brought with them all sorts of herbs, roots, bits of bark as used by the villagers in cases of sickness. The village had no doctor and no drug store and for that reason, perhaps, it also had no undertaker.

Every woman had brought a different kind of medicinal herb or remedy. And every one of the women made a different suggestion as to what should be done to save the child. For hours that little creature had been tortured with scores of different treatments and had been given teas brewed from roots, herbs and ground snake bones mixed with a powder obtained from charred toads.

"He ate too much," one woman said, seeing his father coming to the child's bed.

"His bowels are all twisted up, there's no help," another one corrected the first one.

"Wrong, compadre, it's an infection of the stomach, he is done for."

The one next to her observed: "We've done everything possible, he can't live another hour. One of our kids died the same way. I know it. I can see by his little shrunken face that he is winged already for his flight to heaven, little angel, poor little angel." She broke into a loud sob.

Not in the least minding the women's chatter, Macario looked at his little son whom he seemed to love best of all as he was the youngest of the bunch. He liked his innocent smile and felt happy in his way when the little tyke would now and then sit on his lap for a few minutes and play with his tiny fingers upon the man's face. Often it occurred to Macario that the only reason for being alive rested with the fact that there always would be a little baby around the house smiling at him innocently and beating his nose and cheeks with his little fists.

The child was dying; no doubt of that. The mirror held by a woman before the baby's mouth showed no mark of breath. His heartbeat could practically no longer be noted by one or the other woman who would press her ear upon the child's chest.

The father stood there and gazed at his baby without knowing whether he ought to step closer still and touch the little face or remain where he was, or say something to his wife or to one of the other women, or talk to the children who were timidly crowded into one corner of the room where they all sat as if they were guilty of the baby's misfortune. They had had no dinner and they felt sure there would be no supper tonight as their mother was in a horrible state of mind.

Macario turned slowly about, walked to the door and went
out into the darkness of the night.

Not knowing what to do or where to go since his home was
all in a turmoil, tired as he was from his very hard day's labor,
and feeling as though he were to sink down on his knees, he
took, as if automatically, the path which led to the woods—his
realm where he was sure to find the quiet of which he was so
badly in need.

Arriving at the spot where, in the early morning, he had
buried the *guaje* bottle, he stopped, searched for the exact
place, took out the bottle, and quicker than he had moved in
many years ran back to his hut.

"Give me a cup filled with fresh clean water," he ordered in
a loud and determined voice on opening the door.

His wife hurried as if given new hope, and in a few seconds
she brought an earthen cup of water.

"Now, folks, you leave the room. Get out of here, all of
you, and leave me alone with that son of mine. I'll see what I
can do about it."

"No use, Macario, can't you see he has only a few minutes
left? You'd better kneel down and say the prayers with us
while he is breathing his last, so that his soul may be saved,"
one of the women told him.

"You heard what I said and you do as you've been advised,"
he said, sharply cutting off any further protest.

Never before had his wife heard him speak in such a harsh,
commanding manner. Almost afraid of him, she urged the
women out of the hut.

They were all gone.

Macario closed the door behind them, turned to the cot, and
when he looked up he saw his bony dinner guest standing
opposite him, the cot with the child in it between the two.

The visitor stared at him out of his deep dark holes he had

for eyes, hesitated, shrugged, and slowly, as though still weighing his decision, moved toward the baby's feet, remaining there for the next few seconds while the father poured a generous dose of the medicine into the cup filled with water.

Seeing his partner shaking his head in disapproval, Macario remembered that only one drop would have sufficed for the cure. Yet, it was too late now, and the liquid could not be returned to the bottle, for it was already mixed with fresh water.

Macario lifted the baby's head, forced the little mouth open and let the drink trickle into it, taking care that nothing was spilled. To his great joy he noted that the baby, once his mouth had been moistened, started to swallow voluntarily. Soon he had taken the whole to its last drop.

Hardly could the medicine have reached his stomach when the child began to breathe freely. Color returned slowly but visibly to his pale face, and he moved his head in search of better comfort.

The father waited a few minutes longer, and seeing that the baby was recovering miraculously fast, he called in his wife.

Only one look did the mother give her baby when she fell to her knees by the cot and cried out loud: "Glory be to God and the Holy Virgin. I thank you, Lord in Heaven; my little baby will live."

Hearing the mother's excited outburst, all the women who had been waiting outdoors rushed in, and seeing what had happened while the father had been alone with his son they crossed themselves, gasped and stared at Macario as if noting his existence for the first time and as though he were a stranger in the house.

One hour later the whole village was assembled at Macario's to see with their own eyes whether it was true what the women, running about the village, were telling the people.

The baby, his cheeks rosy, his little fists pressed close to his chin, was profoundly asleep, and anybody could see that all danger was past.

Next morning Macario got up at his usual time, sat down at the table for his breakfast, looked for his machete, ax and ropes and, taciturn as always, left home to go out to the woods and there chop fuel for the villagers. The bottle with the medicine he took along with him and buried at the same spot from which he had taken it the night before.

So he went about his job for the next six weeks when one night, on returning home, he found Ramiro waiting for him. Ramiro asked him, please, to come around to his place and see what he might do about his wife who had been sick for several days and was now sinking fast.

Ramiro, the principal storekeeper and merchant of the whole community and the richest man in the municipality, explained that he had heard of Macario's curing powers and that he would like him to try his talents on his young wife.

"Fetch me a little bottle, a very little glass bottle from your store. I'll wait for you here and think over what I perhaps could do for your wife."

Ramiro brought the bottle, an empty medicine flask.

"What are you going to do with the bottle, Macario?"

"Leave that to me, Ramiro. You just go home and wait for me. I have to see your wife first before I can say whether or not I can save her. She'll hold on all right until I come, don't worry over that. In the meantime, I will go out in the fields and look for some herbs which I know to be good medicine."

He went into the night, searched for his bottle, filled the little crystal flask half full with the precious liquid, buried the bottle again and walked to Ramiro's who lived in one of the three one-story brick houses the village boasted.

He found the woman rapidly nearing her end, and she was
as close to it as had been his little son.

Ramiro looked at Macario's eyes. Macario shrugged for an
answer. After a while he said: "You'd better go out now and
leave me alone with your wife."

Ramiro obeyed. Yet, extremely jealous of his young and
very pretty wife, pretty even now when near her death, he
peeped through a hole in the door to watch Macario's doings.

Macario, already close to the door, turned abruptly with the
intention to ask for a glass of fresh water.

Ramiro, his eyes still pressed to the door, was not quick
enough in getting away and so, when Macario, by a resolute
pull, opened the door, Ramiro fell full length into the room.

"Not very decent of you, Ramiro," Macario said, compre-
hending what the jealous man had been about. "Just for that I
should decline giving your young wife back to you. You don't
deserve her, you know that, don't you?"

He stopped in great surprise.

He could not understand himself what had come over him
this very minute. Why he, the poorest and humblest man in
the village, a common woodchopper, had dared to speak to the
haughtiest and richest man, the millionaire of the village, in a
manner which the judge at the county court would hardly
have risked. But seeing Ramiro, that mighty and powerful
man, standing before him humiliated and with the gesture of a
beggar trembling with fear that Macario might refuse to heal
his wife, Macario had suddenly become aware that he had
become a great power himself, a great doctor of whom that
arrogant Ramiro expected miracles.

Very humble now, Ramiro begged Macario's forgiveness
for having spied upon him, and in the most pitiful way he
pleaded with him to save his wife, who was about to give him,
in less than four months, his first child.

"How much would you ask for giving her back to me sane and healthy like she was before?"

"I do not sell my medicine for prices, I do not set prices. It's you, Ramiro, who have to make the price. Only you can know what your wife is worth to you. So name the price yourself."

"Would ten doubloons do, my dear good Macario?"

"That's what your wife is worth to you? Only ten doubloons?"

"Don't take it that way, dear Macario. Of course she means far more to me than all my money. Money I can make again any day that God will allow me to live. But once my wife is gone, where would I find another one like her? Not in this world. I'll make it one hundred doubloons then, only, please, save her."

Macario knew Ramiro well, only too well did he know him. Both had been born and raised in that village. Ramiro was the son of the richest merchant of the village as he himself was the richest man today—whereas Macario was the son of the poorest day laborer in the community as he himself was now the poorest woodchopper with the biggest family of the whole village to support. And as he knew Ramiro so very well, nobody would have to tell him that, once the merchant's wife was cured, her husband would try to chisel down on the one hundred doubloons as much as he possibly could, and if Macario did not yield there would be a long and nasty fight between the two men for many years to come.

Realizing all that, Macario now said: "I'll take the ten doubloons which you offered me first."

"Oh, thank you, Macario, I thank you, indeed I do, and not for cutting down on the price but that you're willing to cure her. I shall never forget what you have done for us, I'm sure, I shall never forget it. I only hope that the unborn will be safe also."

"It surely will," Macario said, assured of his success since he had seen his bony dinner companion standing where he liked best to see him.

"Now, bring me a glass of fresh water," he told Ramiro.

The water was brought and Macario counselled the merchant: "Don't you dare peep in again for, mind you, if you do I might fail and it will be all your fault. So remember, no spying, no peeping. Now, leave me alone with the patient."

This time Macario was extremely careful in not spending more than exactly one drop of the valuable liquid. As hard as he could he even tried to cut that one drop into two halves. By his talk with Ramiro he had suddenly understood how much his medicine was really worth if such a proud and rich man as Ramiro would humble himself before the woodchopper for no other reason than that his wife might be cured by the poor woodman's medicine.

In realizing that, he visioned what his future might be like if he would forget about his woodchopping and stick by his medicine exclusively. Naturally enough, the quintessence of that future was an unlimited supply of roast turkeys any time he wanted them.

His one-time dinner guest, seeing him cutting the one drop in half, nodded approvingly when Macario looked at him for advice.

Two days after Ramiro's wife had recovered fully, she told her husband that she was positively sure that the baby had not been hurt in the least by her sickness, as she could feel him all right.

Ramiro in his great joy handed Macario the ten gold pieces, not only without prattling over that high price but with a hundred thanks thrown in. He invited the whole Macario family to his store where everyone, husband, wife, and all the children, was allowed to take as much home as everybody could carry in his arms. Then he threw a splendid dinner to which the Macarios were invited as his guests of honor.

Macario built a real house now for his family, bought some pieces of good land and began cultivating them, because Ramiro had loaned him one hundred doubloons at very low interest.

Ramiro had done so not solely out of gratitude. He was too shrewd a businessman to loan out money without thinking of fat gains. He realized that Macario had a great future ahead of him, and that it would be a very sound investment to keep Macario in the village and make people come here to see him, rather than have him take up his residence in a city. The more visitors the village would have on account of Macario's fame, the more important would grow Ramiro's business. In expectation of this development in the village's future, Ramiro added to his various lines in business that of banking.

He gambled fast on Macario and he won. He won far beyond his most fantastic dreams.

It was he who did all the advertising and all the propaganda to draw attention to Macario's great gift. Hardly had he sent out a few letters to business friends in the city, than sick people flocked to the village in the hope of being cured of their maladies, many having been declared uncurable by learned physicians.

Soon Macario could build himself a mansion. He bought up all the land around and converted it into gardens and parks. His children were sent to schools and universities as far as Paris and Salamanca.

As his one-time dinner guest had promised him, so it came to pass, Macario's half turkey was paid for a millionfold.

Regardless of his riches and his fame, Macario remained honest and uncorrupted. Anyone who wanted to be cured was asked how much his health was worth to him. And as Macario had done in his first case, so he did ever after in all other cases—that is, the patients or their relatives would decide the price.

A poor man or woman who had no more to offer than one silver peso or a pig or a rooster, he would heal just as well as the rich who, in many instances, had made prices as high as twenty thousand doubloons. He cured men and women of the highest nobility, many of whom had crossed the ocean and had come from Spain, Italy, Portugal, France and other countries and who had come for no other reason than to see him and consult him.

Whoever came to consult him would be told frankly that he could do nothing to save him, if Macario saw the Bone Man stand at the patient's head. Nothing did he charge for that consultation.

People, whoever they were, accepted his final verdict without discussion. No longer would they try arguing with him, once he had told them that they were beyond help.

More or less half the people consulting him were saved; the other half were claimed by his partner. It happened often for weeks at a time that he would not meet one patient whom he could cure, because his dinner guest would decide differently. Such weeks the people in the land called "his low-power periods."

While at the beginning of his practice he was able to cut a drop of his precious medicine into two, he soon learned to cut each drop into eight. He acquired all devices known then by which a drop might be divided up into practically an infinite number of mites. Yet, no matter how much he cut and divided, regardless of how cleverly he administered each dose to make it as small as possible and yet retain its effectiveness, the medicine had frightfully fast become scarcer and scarcer.

He had drained the *guaje* bottle during the first month of his practice, once he had observed the true value of the liquid. He

knew that a *guaje* bottle will not only soak into its walls a
certain amount of any fluid it may hold, but worse, the liquid
will evaporate, and rather fast, through the bottle's walls. It is
for that reason that water kept in a *guaje* bottle of the kind
natives use will stay always cool even should the day be very
hot.

So he had taken out the medicine and poured it into bottles
of dark glass, tightly sealed.

The last little bottle had been opened months ago, and one
day Macario noted to his horror that there were only about
two drops left. Consequently, he decided to make it known
that he would retire from practice and cure nobody any
longer.

By now he had become really old and felt that he had a right
to spend the last few years of his life in peace.

These last two drops he meant to keep for members of his
family exclusively, and especially for his beloved wife, whom
he had had to cure already two times during the last ten years
and whom he was afraid he might lose—a loss which would be
very difficult for him to bear.

Just about that same time it so happened that the eight-year-
old son of the viceroy, don Juan Marquez de Casafuerte, the
highest personage of New Spain, fell sick.

The best doctors were called for help. None could do
anything for the boy. The doctors admitted frankly that this
boy had been stricken by a sickness not known to medical
science.

The viceroy had heard of Macario. Who hadn't? But he
owed it to his dignity, education and high social and political
position to consider Macario a quack, the more so since he was
called thus by every doctor who had a title from an accredited
university.

The child's mother, however, less given to dignity when the

life of her son was at stake, made life for the viceroy so miserable that finally he saw no other way out of his dilemma than to send for Macario.

Macario disliked traveling and rarely left his village, and then only for short trips. Yet, an order given by the viceroy himself had to be obeyed under penalty of death.

So he had to go.

Brought before the viceroy he was told what was expected of him.

The viceroy, still not believing in the so-called miracles which Macario was said to have performed, spoke to him in the same way as he would have spoken to any native wood-chopper.

"It was not I who called you, understand that, my good man. Her Highness, la Marquesa, insisted on bringing you here to save our son whom, so it appears, no learned medico can cure. I make it quite clear to you that in case you actually save our child, one-fourth of the fortune which I hold here in New Spain shall be yours. Besides, you may ask anything you see here in my palace, whatever it is that catches your fancy and whatever its value. That shall be yours also. Apart from all that, I personally shall hand you a license which will entitle you to practice medicine anywhere in New Spain with the same rights and privileges as any learned medico, and you shall be given a special letter with my seal on it which will give you immunity for life against any arrest by police or soldiers, and which will safeguard you against any unjustified court action. I believe, my good man, that this is a royal payment for your service."

Macario nodded, yet said nothing.

The viceroy went on: "What I promised you in the case that you save our son follows exactly the suggestion made by

Her Highness, la Marquesa, my wife, and what I promise I always keep."

The Marquez stopped for a few seconds, as if waiting for Macario to say something.

Macario, however, said nothing and made no gesture.

"But now, listen to my own suggestions," the viceroy continued. "If you should fail to save our son, I shall hand you over to the High Court of the Inquisition, charging you with the practice of witchcraft under pact with the Devil, and you shall be burned alive at the stake on the Alameda and in public."

Again the viceroy stopped to see what expression his threat had made upon Macario.

Macario paled, but still said nothing.

"Have you understood in full what I have said?"

"I have, Your Highness," Macario said briefly, trembling slightly as he attempted to make an awkward bow.

"Now, I personally shall show you to our sick child. Follow me."

They entered the boy's room where two nurses were in attendance, merely watching the child's slow decline, unable to do anything save keep him comfortable. His mother was not present. She had, by the doctor's order, been confined to her room as she was close to a complete breakdown.

The boy was resting in a bed becoming his age, a light bed made of fine wood, though not rich looking.

Macario went close and looked around for a sign of his dinner guest.

Slightly, so as not to make his gesture seem suspicious, he touched a special little pocket in his trousers to be sure he had the crystal flask with the last two drops of medicine about him.

Now he said: "Will you, Your Highness, I pray, leave this

room for one hour, and will Your Highness, please, give orders that everybody else will leave, too, so that I may remain alone with the young patient?"

The Marquez hesitated, evidently being afraid that this ignorant peasant might do his son some harm if left alone with him.

Macario, noting that expression of uneasiness shown by the viceroy, recalled, at this very instant, his first cure of a patient not of his own family, that is, Ramiro's young wife in his native village. Ramiro had hesitated in a similar way when told to leave the room and let Macario alone with the young woman in bed.

These two cases of hesitation had been the only ones he had ever experienced during his long practice. And Macario wondered whether that might carry some significance in his destiny, that perhaps today, with only two little drops of his medicine left, he beheld the same expression of hesitancy in a person who wanted a great service done but did not trust the man who was the only one who could render that service.

He was now alone with the boy.

And suddenly there appeared his partner, taking his stand at the boy's head.

The two, Macario and the Bone Man, had never again spoken one to the other since they had had a turkey dinner together. Whenever they would meet in a sickroom, they would only look at each other, yet not speak.

Macario had never asked of his partner any special favor. Never had he claimed from him any individual whom the Bone Man had decided to take. He even had let go two grandchildren of his without arguing his dinner guest's first claim.

This time everything was different. He would be burned

alive at the stake as a witch doctor convicted of having signed
a pact with the Devil. His children, now all of them in highly
honored positions, would fall into disgrace, because their
father had been condemned by the Holy Inquisition to suffer
the most infamous death a Christian could die. All his fortune
and all his landed property, which he had meant to leave to his
children and grandchildren, would be confiscated and given to
the Church. He did not mind losing his fortune. It had never
meant much to him personally anyhow.

What he did mind above all was the happiness of his
children. But more still than his children he was, in this most
terrible moment of his whole life, thinking of his beloved wife.

She would go crazy with grief on learning what had happened to him in that strange, vast city so far away from home,
and she would be unable to come to his aid or even comfort
him during his last hours on earth. It was for her sake, not for
his own, that this time he decided to fight it out with the Bone
Man.

"Give me that child," he pleaded, "give him to me for old
friendship's sake. I've never asked any favor of you, not one
little favor for the half turkey you ate with so much gusto
when you needed a good dinner more than anything else. You
gave me voluntarily what I had not asked you for. Give me that
boy, and I'll pour out the last drop of your medicine and break
the bottle, so that not even one little wet spot be left inside to
be used for another cure. Please, oh please, give me that boy. It
isn't for my sake that I ask you this. It is for my dear, faithful,
loyal and beloved wife's. You know, or at least you can
imagine, what it means for a Christian family if one of its
members is burned at the stake alive and in public. Please, let
me have the boy. I shall not take or touch the riches offered
me for curing him. You found me a poor man and I was happy

then in my own way. I don't mind being poor again, as I used to be. I'm willing to chop wood again for the villagers as I did when we met for the first time. Only, please, I pray, give me that boy."

The Bone Man looked at him with his deep black holes for a long time. If he had a heart he was questioning it at this moment. Now he looked down before him as though he were deliberating this case from every angle to find the most perfect solution. Obviously, his orders were to take the child away. He could not express his thoughts by his eyes or his face, yet his gestures clearly showed his willingness to help a friend in dire need, for by his attitude he tried to explain that, in this particular case, he was powerless to discover a way out which would meet halfway the problems of both.

Again, for a very long while, his look rested upon the boy as though judging more carefully still Macario's plea against the child's fate, destined before he was born.

And again he looked at Macario as if pitying him and as though he felt deeply distressed.

Presently he shook his head slowly as might someone in great sadness who finds himself utterly helpless in a desperate situation.

He opened his fleshless jaws, and with a voice that sounded like heavy wooden sticks clubbed on a board he said: "I am sorry, compadre, very sorry, but in this case I can do nothing to help you out of that uncomfortable pool you have been put into. All I can say is that in few of my cases I have felt sadder than in this, believe me, compadre. I can't help it, I must take that boy."

"No, you mustn't. You mustn't. Do you hear me, you must not take that child," Macario yelled in great despair. "You must not, you cannot take him. I won't let you."

The Bone Man shook his head again, but said nothing.

And now, with a resolute jerk, Macario grabbed the boy's bed and quickly turned it round so that his partner found himself standing at the boy's feet.

Immediately the Bone Man vanished from sight for two short seconds and, like a flash, appeared at the boy's head once more.

Quickly Macario again turned the bed so that the Bone Man would stand at the feet, and again the Bone Man disappeared from the child's feet and stood at the boy's head.

Macario, wild with madness, turned the bed round and round as if it were a wheel. Yet, whenever he stopped, for taking a breath, he would see his dinner guest standing at the boy's head, and Macario would start his crazy game again by which he thought that he might cheat the claimant out of his chosen subject.

It was too much for the old man, turning that bed round and round without gaining more than two seconds from eternity.

If, so he thought, he could stretch these two seconds into twenty hours only and leave the city under the viceroy's impression that the boy was cured, he might escape that horrible punishment which he had been condemned to suffer.

He was so tired now that he could not turn the bed once more. Touching, as if by a certain impulse, the little pocket in his trousers, he discovered that the crystal flask with the last two drops of the precious medicine in it had been smashed during his wild play with the bed.

Fully realizing that loss and its significance, he felt as if he had been drained of the last spark of his life's energy and that his whole life had become empty.

Vaguely, he gazed about the room as though coming out of a trance in which he had been held for an uncountable number of years, centuries perhaps. He recognized that his fate was upon him and that it would be useless to fight against it any longer.

So, letting his eyes wander around the whole room, he came to look at the boy's face and he found the boy gone.

As if felled he dropped to the floor, entirely exhausted.

Lying there motionless, he heard his one-time dinner guest speaking to him, softly this time.

He heard him say: "Once more, compadre, I thank you for the half turkey which you so generously gave me and which restored my strength, then waning, for another hundred years of tedious labor. It certainly was exquisite, if you understand that word. But now, coming to where we are at this hour, see, compadre, I have no power to save you from being burned at the stake on the Alameda and in public, because that is beyond my jurisdiction. Yet, I can save you from being burned alive and from being publicly defamed. And this, compadre, I shall do for old friendship's sake, and because you have always played fair and never tried to cheat me. A royal payment you received and you honored it like a royal payment. You have lived a very great man. Good-bye, compadre."

Macario opened his eyes and, on looking backwards, he saw his one-time dinner guest standing at his head.

Macario's wife, greatly worried over her husband's not coming home, called all the men of the village next morning to help her find Macario, who might be hurt somewhere deep in the woods and unable to return without help.

After several hours of searching, he was discovered at the densest part of the woods in a section far away from the village, so far that nobody would ever dare go there alone.

He was sitting on the ground, his body comfortably snuggled in the hollow of a huge tree trunk, dead, a big beautiful smile all over his face.

Before him on the ground banana leaves were spread out, serving as a tablecloth, and on them were lying the carefully cleaned bones of a half turkey.

Directly opposite, separated by a space of about three feet, there also were, in a like manner, banana leaves spread, on which was the other half of the turkey, but untouched.

"How strange!" said his wife, thick tears welling out of her sad eyes. "I wonder why he cut the turkey in two? It was his dream all during his life to eat it all himself! I just wonder who he had invited to eat the other half of his turkey. Whoever he was, he must have been a fine and noble and very gentle person, or Macario wouldn't have died so very, very happy."

Bibliography

A chronology of B. Traven's books, as first published in English and German.

The Death Ship (New York, 1934). Published in German as *Das Totenschiff* (Berlin, 1926).

The Cotton-Pickers (London, 1956). Published in German as *Der Wobbly* (Berlin, 1926).

The Treasure of the Sierra Madre (New York, 1935). Published in German as *Der Schatz der Sierra Madre* (Berlin, 1927).

Land des Frühlings (Berlin, 1927), a Mexican travel book not yet published in English.

The Bush, stories, some of which appear in this volume; published in German as *Der Busch* (Berlin, 1928).

The Bridge in the Jungle (New York, 1938). Published in German as *Die Brücke im Dschungel* (Berlin, 1929).

The White Rose (London, 1965). Published in German as *Die Weisse Rose* (Berlin, 1929).

The Carreta (London, 1935). Published in German as *Der Karren* (Berlin, 1930).

Government (London, 1935). Published in German as *Regierung* (Berlin, 1931).

The March to Caobaland (London, 1960). Published in German as *Der Marsch ins Reich der Caoba* (Zurich-Wein, 1933).

The Rebellion of the Hanged (New York, 1952). Published in German as *Die Rebellion der Gehenkten* (Berlin, 1936).

Die Troza (Zurich, 1936), not yet published in English.

Sun-Creation, "a legend," published incomplete in small magazines in the United States, but not yet in book form. Published in German as *Sonnenschöpfung* (Zurich, 1936).

The General from the Jungle (London, 1954). Published in German as *Ein General kommt aus dem Dschungel* (Amsterdam, 1939).

Macario, a Mexican folk tale; published incomplete in various magazines in the United States; this volume of stories publishes the first complete authorized text in English (New York, 1966). Published in German as *Macario* (Zurich, 1949).

Aslan Norval (Vienna, 1960), not yet published in English.

FOR thirty-five years, from 1876 to 1911, power in Mexico was in the hands of one man, Porfirio Díaz. Mexico's constitution had been altered to sanction his reelections, which were assured by his appointment of state governors and other officials. Opposition was controlled by a ruthless federal police called the *rurales*. It was a reign of peace and prosperity for the few and dire poverty for the many—half the entire rural population of Mexico was bound to debt slavery. Big landowners and foreign capital were favored as more and more Indians lost their communal lands.

In the final decade of Díaz's rule, however, opposition strengthened, and before his last engineered reelection he promised a return to democratic forms—which after the election he gave no signs of honoring. In 1910 revolution broke out; independent rebel armies under the leadership of Pancho Villa, Emiliano Zapata, Francisco Madero, and others upset the power of the landlords and eventually overthrew the Díaz regime.

In what have become known as the "Jungle Novels," B. Traven wrote during the 1930s an epic of the birth of the Mexican revolution. The six novels—*Government, The Carreta, March to the Monteria, Trozas, The Rebellion of the Hanged,* and *The General from the Jungle*—describe the conditions of peonage and debt slavery under which the Indians suffered in Díaz's time. The novels follow the spirit of rebellion that slowly spread through the labor camps and haciendas, culminating in the bloody revolt that ended Porfirio Díaz's rule.

In the 1920s, when B. Traven arrived in the country, peonage, although officially abolished by the new constitution of 1917, was still a general practice in many parts of Mexico. The author observed the system firsthand in Chiapas, the southernmost province, a mountainous and heavily forested region where the Jungle Novels, as well as many other of his stories, are set.

The mysterious B. Traven (1890–1969) was born in Chicago, spent his youth in Germany as an itinerant actor and revolutionary journalist, became a seaman on tramp steamers, settled in Mexico in the early 1920s, and began recording his experiences in novels and stories.

Ivan R. Dee is republishing eight novels and books of short stories by B. Traven, and is publishing the first translation into English of *Trozas*, the fourth of the Jungle Novels.

ELEPHANT PAPERBACKS

Literature and Letters
Stephen Vincent Benét, *John Brown's Body*, EL10
Isaiah Berlin, *The Hedgehog and the Fox*, EL21
Robert Brustein, *Dumbocracy in America*, EL421
Anthony Burgess, *Shakespeare*, EL27
Philip Callow, *From Noon to Starry Night*, EL37
Philip Callow, *Son and Lover: The Young D. H. Lawrence*, EL14
Philip Callow, *Vincent Van Gogh*, EL38
James Gould Cozzens, *Castaway*, EL6
James Gould Cozzens, *Men and Brethren*, EL3
Clarence Darrow, *Verdicts Out of Court*, EL2
Floyd Dell, *Intellectual Vagabondage*, EL13
Theodore Dreiser, *Best Short Stories*, EL1
Joseph Epstein, *Ambition*, EL7
André Gide, *Madeleine*, EL8
Gerald Graff, *Literature Against Itself*, EL35
John Gross, *The Rise and Fall of the Man of Letters*, EL18
Irving Howe, *William Faulkner*, EL15
Aldous Huxley, *After Many a Summer Dies the Swan*, EL20
Aldous Huxley, *Ape and Essence*, EL19
Aldous Huxley, *Collected Short Stories*, EL17
F. R. Leavis, *Revaluation*, EL39
F. R. Leavis, *The Living Principle*, EL40
F. R. Leavis, *The Critic as Anti-Philosopher*, EL41
Sinclair Lewis, *Selected Short Stories*, EL9
William L. O'Neill, ed., *Echoes of Revolt: The Masses, 1911–1917*, EL5
Budd Schulberg, *The Harder They Fall*, EL36
Ramón J. Sender, *Seven Red Sundays*, EL11
Peter Shaw, *Recovering American Literature*, EL34
Tess Slesinger, *On Being Told That Her Second Husband Has Taken His First Lover, and Other Stories*, EL12
B. Traven, *The Bridge in the Jungle*, EL28
B. Traven, *The Carreta*, EL25
B. Traven, *The Cotton-Pickers*, EL32
B. Traven, *General from the Jungle*, EL33
B. Traven, *Government*, EL23
B. Traven, *March to the Montería*, EL26
B. Traven, *The Night Visitor and Other Stories*, EL24
B. Traven, *The Rebellion of the Hanged*, EL29
Anthony Trollope, *Trollope the Traveller*, EL31
Rex Warner, *The Aerodrome*, EL22
Thomas Wolfe, *The Hills Beyond*, EL16
Wilhelm Worringer, *Abstraction and Empathy*, EL42

ELEPHANT PAPERBACKS

American History and American Studies

Stephen Vincent Benét, *John Brown's Body*, EL10
Henry W. Berger, ed., *A William Appleman Williams Reader*, EL126
Andrew Bergman, *We're in the Money*, EL124
Paul Boyer, ed., *Reagan as President*, EL117
Robert V. Bruce, *1877: Year of Violence*, EL102
Philip Callow, *From Noon to Starry Night*, EL37
George Dangerfield, *The Era of Good Feelings*, EL110
Clarence Darrow, *Verdicts Out of Court*, EL2
Floyd Dell, *Intellectual Vagabondage*, EL13
Elisha P. Douglass, *Rebels and Democrats*, EL108
Theodore Draper, *The Roots of American Communism*, EL105
Joseph Epstein, *Ambition*, EL7
Lloyd C. Gardner, *Pay Any Price*, EL136
Lloyd C. Gardner, *Spheres of Influence*, EL131
Paul W. Glad, *McKinley, Bryan, and the People*, EL119
Daniel Horowitz, *The Morality of Spending*, EL122
Kenneth T. Jackson, *The Ku Klux Klan in the City, 1915–1930*, EL123
Edward Chase Kirkland, *Dream and Thought in the Business Community, 1860–1900*, EL114
Herbert S Klein, *Slavery in the Americas*, EL103
Aileen S. Kraditor, *Means and Ends in American Abolitionism*, EL111
Leonard W. Levy, *Jefferson and Civil Liberties: The Darker Side*, EL107
Thomas J. McCormick, *China Market*, EL115
Walter Millis, *The Martial Spirit*, EL104
Nicolaus Mills, ed., *Culture in an Age of Money*, EL302
Nicolaus Mills, *Like a Holy Crusade*, EL129
Roderick Nash, *The Nervous Generation*, EL113
William L. O'Neill, ed., *Echoes of Revolt: The Masses, 1911–1917*, EL5
Gilbert Osofsky, *Harlem: The Making of a Ghetto*, EL133
Edward Pessen, *Losing Our Souls*, EL132
Glenn Porter and Harold C. Livesay, *Merchants and Manufacturers*, EL106
John Prados, *Presidents' Secret Wars*, EL134
Edward Reynolds, *Stand the Storm*, EL128
Richard Schickel, *The Disney Version*, EL135
Edward A. Shils, *The Torment of Secrecy*, EL303
Geoffrey S. Smith, *To Save a Nation*, EL125
Bernard Sternsher, ed., *Hitting Home: The Great Depression in Town and Country*, EL109
Athan Theoharis, *From the Secret Files of J. Edgar Hoover*, EL127
Nicholas von Hoffman, *We Are the People Our Parents Warned Us Against*, EL301
Norman Ware, *The Industrial Worker, 1840–1860*, EL116
Tom Wicker, *JFK and LBJ: The Influence of Personality upon Politics*, EL120
Robert H. Wiebe, *Businessmen and Reform*, EL101
T. Harry Williams, *McClellan, Sherman and Grant*, EL121
Miles Wolff, *Lunch at the 5 & 10*, EL118
Randall B. Woods and Howard Jones, *Dawning of the Cold War*, EL130

ELEPHANT PAPERBACKS

European and World History
Mark Frankland, *The Patriots' Revolution*, EL201
Lloyd C. Gardner, *Spheres of Influence*, EL131
Gertrude Himmelfarb, *Darwin and the Darwinian Revolution*, EL207
Gertrude Himmelfarb, *Victorian Minds*, EL205
Thomas A. Idinopulos, *Jerusalem*, EL204
Allan Janik and Stephen Toulmin, *Wittgenstein's Vienna*, EL208
Ronnie S. Landau, *The Nazi Holocaust*, EL203
Clive Ponting, *1940: Myth and Reality*, EL202
Scott Shane, *Dismantling Utopia*, EL206
Alexis de Tocqueville, *Memoir on Pauperism*, EL209
John Weiss, *Ideology of Death*, EL210

Theatre and Drama
Robert Brustein, *Dumbocracy in America*, EL421
Robert Brustein, *Reimagining American Theatre*, EL410
Robert Brustein, *The Theatre of Revolt*, EL407
Stephen Citron, *The Musical from the Inside Out*, EL427
Irina and Igor Levin, *Working on the Play and the Role*, EL411
Plays for Performance:
    Aristophanes, *Lysistrata*, EL405
    Pierre Augustin de Beaumarchais, *The Marriage of Figaro*, EL418
    Anton Chekhov, *The Cherry Orchard*, EL420
    Anton Chekhov, *The Seagull*, EL407
    Euripides, *The Bacchae*, EL419
    Euripides, *Iphigenia in Aulis*, EL423
    Euripides, *Iphigenia Among the Taurians*, EL424
    Georges Feydeau, *Paradise Hotel*, EL403
    Henrik Ibsen, *Ghosts*, EL401
    Henrik Ibsen, *Hedda Gabler*, EL413
    Henrik Ibsen, *The Master Builder*, EL417
    Henrik Ibsen, *When We Dead Awaken*, EL408
    Henrik Ibsen, *The Wild Duck*, EL425
    Heinrich von Kleist, *The Prince of Homburg*, EL402
    Christopher Marlowe, *Doctor Faustus*, EL404
    The Mysteries: Creation, EL412
    The Mysteries: The Passion, EL414
    Luigi Pirandello, *Six Characters in Search of an Author*, EL426
    Sophocles, *Electra*, EL415
    August Strindberg, *The Father*, EL406
    August Strindberg, *Miss Julie*, EL422